DRAGON LORDS: BOOK ONE

THE
BARBARIAN
PRINCE

Michelle M. Pillow

Futuristic Romance

New Concepts

Georgia

Dragon Lords: The Barbarian Prince is an original publication of NCP. This work has never before appeared in book form. This work is a novel. Any similarity to actual persons or events is purely coincidental.

New Concepts Publishing
5202 Humphreys Rd.
Lake Park, GA 31636

ISBN 1-58608-673-1
© copyright Michelle M. Pillow

Cover art (c) copyright 2004 Eliza Black

NCP books are available at special quantity discounts for bulk purchases for sales promotions, premiums, fund raising, or educational use. For details, write, email, or phone New Concepts Publishing, 5202Humphreys Rd., Lake Park, GA 31636,   ncp@newconceptspublishing.com,   Ph. 229-257-0367, Fax 229-219-1097.

First NCP Paperback Printing: 2004

Printed in the United States of America

Dedication:
To my mother.

Chapter One

Wanted: Galaxy Brides Corporation seeking 46 fertile, able-bodied Earth females of early childbearing years and A5+ health status for marriage to strong, healthy Qurilixian males at their annual Breeding Festival. Possibility of royal attendance. Must be eager bed-partners, hard workers. Virginity a plus. Apply with A5 health documents, travel papers, and IQ screen to: Galaxy Brides, Phantom Level 6, X Quadrant, Earthbase 5792461.

The idea had been simple. Uncover illegal virgin trading practices by Galaxy Brides. For years it had been rumored that Galaxy Brides used outlawed medic units to restore women's virginity. Virgins meant more trade with the numerous barbaric, male-populated, humanoid planets eager for fresh, young Earth brides. If the story broke, it would be huge. It was just the sort of thing to make a star reporter's career. It was just the thing to bring down evil breeding corporations that sold women to the highest bidder.

Morrigan Blake was just such a reporter--or so she thought. However, the medic units where such procedures took place were nearly impossible to find since they looked like any other medic unit. It would take a series of diagnostic tests to reveal the chip sequencing necessary for virginity replacement. She would just have to get the women to talk to her, which hadn't been easy either. The brides were being compensated well for their participation.

All right, thought Morrigan wryly, as she stared absently at her bare feet in the pedicure basin. Breeding corporations aren't exactly evil and virginity replacement isn't illegal in all quadrants.

The small metallic hands of the beauty droid worked frantically at her toes, as another pulled her dark hair into a traditional Qurilixian upsweep. Curls were left to hang down her back in long, thick waves. The droid had used a hair extender to get her normally short locks to grow. The weight was heavy on her neck and hard to get used to.

Morrigan was in the spaceship's expansive beauty parlor with the rest of the prospective brides getting ready for the official docking later that evening. They had spent the last month being pampered and primped for tonight. Looking down at her legs, Morrigan gave a half smile. If nothing else, the trip had given her a lot of free benefits--permanent hair removal, a body enhancing lift, and time to contemplate the perfect color for her toenails.

Galaxy Red number one or Galaxy Red number two? Okay, she was definitely getting bored.

According to her editor, she was to do a soft, romantic piece on the four Qurilixian Princes and their possible attendance at the festival. It had been sixty years since royalty attended a festival in search of a bride, and women on earth were always eager to devour details of far off royal romances and intrigue.

The last piece she did on the Lophibian royal wedding had boosted newspaper chip sales nearly forty percent and the Lophibian were a slime-dwelling species covered in scales. She had spent four months in the swamplands covered in bluish-green goo. Though the tinting effect it had on her hair had been lovely, Morrigan would not relive that trip for the world.

This was definitely a better assignment. If she could uncover a scandal and interview at least one of the four Princes, she could get two stories from one trip. Not to mention, she would be in for a huge promotion and pay raise. Plus, it did help that the men were rumored to be healthy, virile specimens and would photograph particularly well. Cute men sold chips.

It wouldn't be easy. There were no known pictures of the men on file and they were notorious for not giving interviews, especially about their private festivals. Oh, if she could pull this off! Maybe then she could get that vacation back to her own apartment she so badly deserved. She wondered if she remembered where exactly her apartment was.

"What about you, Rigan? Have you finished your Qurilixian etiquette uploads?" a nearby woman asked from her beauty seat. Her voice was soft and polite, matching her kind blue eyes. Her light brown hair whirled around her head in a frenzy caused by six robot hands. She was very careful not to move.

Morrigan turned at the sound of her name and gave Nadja a light smile. No one on the ship knew who she really was. They all thought her to be another excited bride in search of virile, warrior males Qurilixen was rumored to produce. To be chosen was an honor, or so the other women claimed. Morrigan's thoughts, on the other hand, went to a meat market, and they were the prime cut.

"Didn't you know?" Gena laughed next to Nadja. Her red hair was finished and her beauty droid was placing the customary short veil over the curly auburn locks. "Rigan finished her Qurilixian uploads first. It would seem she is most eager to please her new husband."

"Or to be pleased by him," someone added from across the circular room.

Morrigan closed her eyes, ignoring the abrasive women. Honestly, she didn't understand them. Sure, some of them were nice enough and even seemed intelligent and from a well educated background--like the softly spoken Nadja. But why in the galaxy someone would subject themselves to this trade was beyond her.

Being alone wasn't so bad. She had no one to answer to, except her boss, Gus. He never bothered her unless she was late with a story. She called her own shots, made her own deals. She never had to bother with a guy looking over her shoulder asking when she would be back from her assignment. Or deal with the jealousy that would inevitably come from a mission like this.

Though, Morrigan mused, forever trying to see all sides of a story though she wasn't always successful in doing so, it would be nice to have someone to talk to on late nights. Someone to rub my feet when they are sore. Someone to…. She smiled. Hey, I'll just take this beauty droid home with me.

"I wish I could be so ambitious. I'm afraid I didn't watch a single one of those boring uploads."

Morrigan couldn't tell who was talking since her eyes were closed. She hoped the others would think she napped so she didn't have to join in the nervous banter. She was afraid her excitement would be transparent. She was, after all, close to a big paycheck.

Morrigan had spent most of the first week on the ship's computer uploading Qurilixen facts into her brain. The rush of information had given her a wicked migraine, but it was well worth it since it freed up the rest of the trip for work. Already she had written and transmitted the beginning of her soft romance piece.

For weeks, her head had swum with too many of the planet's facts. It was on the outer edge of the Y quadrant, inhabited by primitive males similar to Viking clans of Medieval Earth. The Qurilixian worshipped many Gods, favored natural comforts to modern technical conveniences, and actually preferred to cook their own food without the aid of a simulator. They were classified as a warrior class, though they had been peaceful for nearly a century--aside from petty territorial skirmishes that broke out every fifteen or so years between a few of the rival houses.

The information she hadn't uploaded was mostly concerned with the wedding ceremony itself and a bit about the culture and law. She doubted the wedding was any different from the other formal ceremonies on the planet. Morrigan didn't plan on getting married while she was there, but hopefully she could see a ceremony and get some pictures. Whatever tidbits she couldn't pick up along the way, she could upload into her brain on the trip home.

Morrigan smiled wryly to herself. She was definitely going to be one of the 'unlucky' losers who got a free trip back. Hadn't the corporation already warned that not all the brides would be chosen?

"I tried on my gown this afternoon," said Gena, unintentionally breaking into Morrigan's thoughts. She pushed up her generous chest beneath the robe. "They are gorgeous, but I think I am going to go get my breasts enhanced again--just a little bigger--and I'm going to have my nipples enlarged. Those Princes won't be able to resist me. Maybe I'll marry all four of them, just for fun."

"How will you know who the Princes are?" a blonde asked from across the room. Morrigan buried her laugh behind her folded hand at the cynical words, recognizing Pia. Now, strangely, this seemed to be a woman who shared her uninterested views on marriage. "I've heard that all the men wear disguises. You could end up with a royal guard."

"Or a gardener," a brunette offered with a laugh.

"I hear they wear practically nothing at all," a woman with flaming red hair added. She had sparkling green eyes the color of emeralds. "Except the mask and some fur."

"You can't miss royalty," Gena said boldly with a kittenish smile of excitement. "You'll see it in the way they move."

Morrigan stood as her droid finished. She looked down at her own enhanced breasts showing from the gap in her white robe. They were a size larger than she was used to. It had been part of the company's complimentary beauty enhancement services for their part in the trip. They were real, just genetically altered for perfection. At first, she didn't like them. But, as she got used to the weight, she found they actually filled in her clothing quite nicely. She just hoped none of the men back at the office took too much notice.

Their spacecraft was outfitted with the best accommodations and services the star system had to offer. Personal droids were assigned to each passenger, and cooking units in each of their quarters could materialize almost any culinary delight, without straying from the strict mineral diets the corporation had them on. Even the doctor was mechanical.

The only company the women had been allowed the last month of travel had been each other. They were quarantined, to insure nothing unseemly happened, in what was affectionately referred to as the harem. The only communication with the ship's crew was by video relay. The brides were valuable merchandise. The quarantine had provided for a very anxious, catlike atmosphere between the competing women. Morrigan frowned. She was in apparent need of some company with testosterone.

As the other droids finished, the prospective brides began to slowly make their way back to their personal quarters to dress. Nervous excitement infectiously buzzed through the air as they tried their best to look unconcerned. Ignoring them all, Morrigan slipped her ID card from her pocket and slid it past the laser sensor to open her door.

Once alone, she sighed as she made her way past the array of machines and blinking sensors that illuminated different parts of the room as her presence registered. With a small, absentminded command from Morrigan, music played softly in the background. She retrieved a glass of scotch from the simulator, her customary drink before landing on a new planet. It helped to steady her nerves and to keep her wits about her.

Slowly, she went to an oval window full of sparkling stars. In the distance she could see the reddish-brown surface of the small planet of Qurilixen. Lifting the glass to the orb, she grumbled, "Cheers."

She sighed at the burn as the drink slid down her throat. Then, reaching behind the curl of the window's metal ledge, Morrigan pulled out a hidden container. She pushed the oval button on top, causing the lid to slide open.

Glancing around to make sure her droid was not in the room, she slid a clear recording disc onto her finger and stuck it into her eye. She blinked several times to get it into place before slipping a ring onto her pinkie finger. The sparkling emerald stone glittered in the mock firelight coming from the ship's fake fireplace.

The journey was nearly over and no one had said anything about the virginity conspiracy. She hated to admit it, but there just might not be a story at all. The rumors were vague at best. But Morrigan knew from living with the other women for a month, just which ones would be experienced in the way of men. She would just have to wait for the marriages to be complete before seeing who was proclaimed pure. Then she would have her story and, hopefully, she would be able to prove it.

* * * *

The docking door of the ship hid the Qurilixian men from view, but the woman could hear the music and laughter just beyond the hatch. Dusk was setting on the normally sunny planet, marking the beginning of the one dark night of festival. Normally, a soft green haze of light plagued the planet's surface.

Qurilixen had three suns--two yellow and one blue--and one moon, which made for a peculiarly bright planet. The green leaves of the planet's foliage were overlarge due to the excessive heat and moisture they received. The trees towered high above the planet's surface, like overgrown redwoods. Some of their trunks were as large around as the houses back on Earth.

The brides waited, single file, in the corridor leading out of the ship's port. Their bodies were covered in the fine gauze and silk of the traditional Qurilixian gowns. The slinky material stirred against the skin when they moved, hugging tight over the hips and flaring out around the legs in thin strips. Soft silk shoes encased their feet.

Morrigan looked down over her nearly exposed body and gave a wry smile. Since this was undoubtedly a male planet, men had assuredly designed these outfits. The gowns fell low over the breasts to reveal a generous cleavage. A belt of sorts went across their backs. But, instead of looping in the front, they continued to the sides, holding the wrists low like silken chains, and winding half way up the arm to lock over the elbows. The women couldn't lift their arms over their heads.

Qurilixian women were rare due to the blue radiation the planet suffered from. Over the generations it had altered the men's genetics to produce only strong, large male, warrior heirs. Maybe once in a thousand births was a Qurilixian female born. In the old days, they had used portals to snatch brides from their homes, bringing them back to their planet. There were even rumors that their species originated on Earth, but there was no proof.

The fact that they had no women of their own was why the services of corporations like Galaxy Brides were so invaluable to them. In return, the Qurilixian would mine valuable metal that was only found in their caves. The metal was a great power source for long-voyaging starships, all but useless to the Qurilixian who preferred living as simply as possible. They were not known as explorers.

Sensing the line was about to move, Morrigan looked forward and pressed the emerald on her finger two times to take a quick picture of the waiting women for her article. The recorder in her eye blinked black, signifying it was working. Later, she would be able to download the images.

Outside the ship, she could see the soft glow of crackling firelight from a giant bonfire pit. The smell of burning wood mingled with nature's exotic perfume. The Qurilixian moon overhead was large and bright, the biggest moon she had ever seen standing on a planet's surface. The bonfire flames lapped at the starry night, sending sparks into the cool air. She could not see into the distance, she noticed, and only got a vague impression of a mountain.

Morrigan stepped forward and the cheers of rowdy men on the festival ground washed over her. Morrigan blushed despite herself, feeling almost naked in her 'sacrificial' attire.

The grounds were set up with large pyramid tents. Torches lit dim earthen pathways. Ribbons and banners floated on the breeze in many brilliant colors. Near the back, the married men sat in throne-like chairs with their wives firmly upon their laps. Morrigan was happy to discover that her information so far seemed correct. By their long hair and tunic style clothing, they appeared very much like the Vikings. The married women could be heard laughing as they watched the spectacle of those barbarians too young to participate in this year's festival shout and pose for the prospective brides.

Morrigan swallowed nervously. Some of the women in front of her modeled before the watching crowd. She had the sudden urge to walk around them in an attempt to avoid the direct stage the docking platform had become. Dealing with slime-dwelling slugs was one thing--but humanoids? And not just any humanoids--strong, virile, women-starved, healthy, male humanoids. At the last minute, she remembered to snap a picture of the married couples and of the campgrounds.

"Oh, my!" Gena exclaimed in a breathless murmur, leaning forward to peer over Morrigan's shoulder. "Do you see them, Rigan? With men like that, who cares if you marry the gardener?"

Morrigan followed the woman's eyes, curiously looking down the docking plank to the ground. The bachelors, standing below them, were indeed handsome. Although those behind the men laughed and a few continued to pose their muscles, the true bachelors held perfectly still. Their bronzed bodies were like statues, with only their lungs expanding and contracting to show they lived.

Morrigan wanted to run back inside. Her feet refused to move. That was until Gena gave her an eager shove to get her descending down the plank.

The Qurilixian males were every inch the proud warrior class they were rumored to be, some even seemed to tower nearly seven feet tall in height. Fur loincloths wrapped around their fit waists to leave bare their muscular legs and chests. The fire glistened off their smooth, oiled skin. Golden bands of intricate design clasped around sinewy biceps. From their solid necks hung crystals bound with leather straps.

Morrigan's heart began to pound, partly in fear and partly in excitement. The sexual tension on the ship had been potent for the last month. Until that moment, Morrigan had been able to resist its lurid pull. But there was something to being at the campground--something erotic in its smell of burning wood and its rustic, yet colorful, sights. Music played, primal and earthy in the background, hypnotic, enticing, gyrating in its rhythms.

Black leather masks covered the men's faces, hiding them from forehead to upper lip. Their lustful eyes shone bright from the eye slits, like liquid metal, or was it her imagination? Morrigan didn't know.

Captured by a spell, she suddenly realized she was walking down an aisle made up of hot flesh on each side. They were so tall that the crowd behind them disappeared from view. She glanced to one side and then the other. Her heart continued to pound. Blood rushed inside her ears, deafening her.

Somehow, her feet managed to keep moving, propelling her forward in line. The watching crowd had gotten quiet as the bachelors studied the women, concentrating on them with their serious eyes and harshly pressed lips. Then her heart--and time--stopped. Her breath caught in her throat at meeting a solid blue gaze beneath a mask. The man's eyes narrowed and a slow, leisurely smile commanded her attention to his lips. The crystal about his neck began to pulse and glow with a white light.

Morrigan felt the cool night breeze caress the tops of her breasts, as real as a hand against her skin. Chills worked their way over her bare throat and face. Her short, blue veil fluttered over her dark locks. Her hand lifted without her commanding it to, as if to reach out. It was held back by the silk shackles of her belt.

Blinking slowly, the man nodded at her in greeting. She turned her head to watch as she passed by him. His smile dropped from his features, replaced by passionate intent and electrifying promises. Morrigan shivered as her heart began to race anew.

As she moved forward through the remaining line of men, she looked around. The others were handsome, but none caught her notice or returned her gaze for very long. And none were as spellbinding as the man with the radiant blue eyes had been. She wondered at the curious feeling in her veins each time she thought of it. She wanted to look back, but her neck refused to turn. He was so like all the others and yet somehow different.

Making her way to a raised platform laden with a gigantic feast, Morrigan forgot all about the emerald on her finger and her newspaper assignment.

What the little critters did to humans hadn't been pretty. Thinking of the popping stink pustules she had been forced to photograph, she gagged. It was enough to keep her stomach from rumbling.

In curiosity, her gaze roamed over the campground. The bachelors were missing. She had been in too much of a daze to see where they had headed. The dreamlike fog had astounded her at first, until she had determined it was just nerves. She was used to watching the spotlight from the sidelines, not being in the middle of it.

Servants carried pitchers full of a strange berry wine. Morrigan vaguely remembered its name roughly translating to mean 'Maiden's Last Breath'. Thinking that the liquor would definitely kill any adverse critters floating in the drink, she tried it. The sweet taste was intoxicatingly wonderful.

Most of the other women dined in jittery silence. Some flirted with the handsome servants who were too young to participate and who were more fully clothed than the bachelors had been. It was hard for the brides to lift their arms, so the attractive servants retrieved anything they desired for them. Some even went so far as to offer the women food by their own hand.

The sparkling emerald on her finger caught Morrigan's attention. She set down her goblet of the berry wine. She realized she spent most of the meal without taking a picture or video feed. How could she have forgotten her assignment? Shaking her head, she put her hand under the table and pressed the emerald once to begin recording.

Looking again for the men, she leaned to Nadja at her side and asked, "Where do you think they went off to?"

Nadja jolted, surprised to hear Morrigan speak. Lifting her glass, the woman began to answer but was cut off by the servant who rushed to fill her half-empty goblet. Nadja jumped in surprise, but let him.

"They go to make an offering to the Gods," the young man said. Nadja lowered her goblet to the table when he finished. The servant topped off Morrigan's goblet, urging her to drink with a wave of his hand. Morrigan smiled timidly at him, seeing that he had a thin scar across the tip of his nose. "They ask for blessing this night in finding a wife."

"Oh," Morrigan said. She smiled at the servant, thinking his superstitions adorable. He didn't move away. He looked

Chapter Two

Ualan of Draig smiled as the Earth woman walked past him. She was clad in his people's traditional garb. The material wrapped around her body, hugging her curves in a way that made a man ache to watch it. Whoever made up this tradition had been sadistic. Already he was tortured, tight with longing.

His bride had hair the color of midnight and wide eyes that he would gladly spend the rest of his life looking into. Slowly, he felt a change beginning in his limbs as the crystal glowed about his neck with untold promises. Ualan smiled. The Gods had indeed been kind to him.

As her hand lifted to him, he was surprised. The brides rarely moved, except to walk, while inside the procession of finding. If they did, it was ultimately considered a good omen, though some of the elders believed it meant for a hard beginning. Ualan was optimistic. His marriage would surely be blessed. His body had instantly felt the fiery connection between them when she looked at him.

When the last bride passed, the mighty Qurilixian bachelors turned to trail in the other direction. They were abnormally quiet, as was tradition. Those who had been blessed needed to go to the temple and give thanks. Those who hadn't needed to regroup. Besides, it was good to let the travel weary women rest. For those who were chosen by the crystal, it would be a long and pleasured night.

* * * *

The feast was laid out on large trenchers, set directly before the brides, and spread over long wooden tables like a buffet. The married couples dined on their own, around the campfire at a distance from the prospective brides. Morriga saw that the wives were feeding their husbands by hand.

She was hesitant to taste the roasted two-horned pigs a blocks of Qurilixian blue bread with whipped cheese laid on plates in front of her. Though it smelled wonderful, had never had a meal that wasn't first purified in a simulator. Thinking of all the alien parasites that might it, she held back. She had done a story on this issue down at her drink, again urging silently for her to drink it. Morrigan lifted it and took several obvious gulps. The servant grinned and walked away to attend some of the other ladies in need of more wine.

"Are you nervous?" Nadja asked in a hush when they were alone. She didn't wait for the woman to answer. She giggled apprehensively. "I can barely sit still. I think this drink has a lot of liquor or something in it."

Morrigan's head was becoming a bit light. She continued to drink anyway, knowing it would take more than a little wine to get her drunk. But, when her head spun lightly with a fog, she rethought her assumption about the drink and mustered up her courage to try the blue bread. She hoped it would soak up the liquor and keep her head level. She wouldn't be able to write her story if she were too drunk to remember what happened.

"Rigan," Nadja began in a hush. Morrigan looked over at the woman's pale face. Her blue eyes danced around in her porcelain skin. Leaning forward, she whispered, "I'm scared. I think I've made a mistake. Do you think they would let me go back to the ship?"

"What's wrong?" Morrigan asked. She had spoken to the woman a few times, but mostly Nadja had kept to herself.

"I...," Nadja paused and shook her head. Her eyes seemed close to tearing. "They're very big, aren't they?"

"Who, the men?" Morrigan asked needlessly. She thought of the magnetic blue eyes of the warrior, visualizing them as if he was before her. Oh, yes, they were very big.

"Yes," Nadja whispered. Her wide gaze looked down as she swallowed nervously. "Do you think they will … will hurt us? They seem bigger than most Earth men."

Morrigan looked at the woman in surprise. "Nadja, have you been with a man before?"

Nadja shook her head, embarrassed.

"Not even a droid?" Morrigan insisted. She herself wasn't exactly a virgin. She had been with a droid once and, though it was fine, it was nothing special. A quick mind sweep on her home computer could repeat similar sensations in less time and with much less energy.

Morrigan had known that she would have to get rid of her virginity in order to get her story. Though, to her disappointment, none of the technicians had said anything to her about it, except to clarify her status as they went through her records. However, she decided it was possible that they suspected who she was after the history scan.

"No," Nadja gulped. Her gaze roamed over the fluttering tents in the distance. Shivering, she admitted, "I was always too embarrassed to go to the clubs and try one. But, I've seen pictures. Do you think that these guys are ... shaped differently?"

"I haven't given it much thought. I think galaxy law requires the species to be, uh, physically compatible before they are matched up. Otherwise, the marriage would do no good. Besides, I hate to sound crass, but the whole point of this is so they can propagate their species."

"I suppose," Nadja said, not seeming to relax at Morrigan's cold examination of their situation. She drank more of her wine. Without having to be asked, a servant was right there to fill it for her. She drank that cup too.

"Did you ask any of the others?" Morrigan inquired, when the servant had retreated down the table. She tried to keep the hopeful note out of her tone. "Have any of them said anything about not being with a man before? Or maybe having been with a man?"

"We've never discussed it." Nadja shook her head in denial. Morrigan forced smile.

"It's really not that big of a deal. I hear several of the women have had their virginity replaced. So it can't be that bad, can it? It hurts for a second, but no more than the series of shots we got on the way here."

"I suppose you're right, though I hadn't heard that." Nadja seemed to calm down as she nodded her head. It didn't last long. Suddenly, she tensed, making Morrigan turn her eyes down the raised dining platform. Nadja's voice left her with a breathy, "Oh!"

Where there had been silence, music again filled the air. Its low rhythm was as sweet as a warm sun and as gentle as the wind's caressing kisses. One by one, the prospective brides fell silent. The handsome warriors made their way to stand below the tables under the wondrous gazes of the brides. Their gaze scanned and quickly fixed upon the women of their choice. Morrigan heard Nadja pant nervously, but she had no words to offer the woman. Her eyes had found those of haunting blue.

There were fewer men than before. Morrigan guessed it was because they had decided not to choose a mate. She blinked slowly, noticing again the strangely glowing crystal hanging on the man's neck. A spark of intensity coursed through her as she looked at it. It was electric fire in her veins, molten. Glancing about, she noticed that all the men had a glowing crystal. She had little time to wonder as her blue-eyed captor began to climb the platform steps to stand before her.

Her head rolled back on her shoulders as she tried to breathe. Why was this handsome stranger looking at her like that--like she was a meal about to be devoured? Why was she suddenly enjoying his perusal?

Morrigan swallowed nervously. Her mouth fell open to accommodate her hastened breath. She waited in eager anticipation, mind numbed to everything around her. The man came closer. Her gaze swept over his naked, glistening chest--so smooth, so strong, so tanned. They moved unabashedly over his thick arms encircled tightly by the band of gold--arms that could crush, arms that could touch and caress and take without having to ask permission.

Then he spoke, his accented voice soft and deep. It was like crushed velvet to the skin, as he said simply, "I am Ualan. Come."

Morrigan froze, licking her lips nervously. Her head swam with the potent berry wine. She never actually thought one of them would try to pick her for marriage. Men had never shown exceptional interest before, especially these types of men.

Come. The word held such command, such finality. She forgot her newspaper chip assignment, forgot her editor, her self-appointed mission to find a scandal.

Ualan's hand rose, as if to touch her. She waited, eager to feel him and yet confused by the urge. Her skin pulled in his direction, tingling with a strange current that seemed to flow from his body into hers. The wine swam violently in her veins like a mystical drug. Suddenly, Morrigan wondered if she shouldn't have tried a bigger sex droid. Maybe the results would have been different and she wouldn't be so incredibly drawn to this man before her.

Some of the women around her stood and were led off in various directions. Their movements were drifting and slow.

Morrigan felt Nadja get up. She glanced at her. The woman's blue eyes were glassy and dazed as she was led down the platform. All of a sudden, Morrigan realized she was the only woman left sitting with a man before her. The un-chosen ones glared at her in angry jealousy. Her heart leapt in panic, tempted to let one of them take her place.

Just as she was about to suggest he move to another, Ualan's head tilted in confusion when she did not immediately obey him. Placing his palms flat on the table, he leaned closer and glanced down at his glowing crystal before looking into Morrigan's stunned eyes.

Morrigan leaned back. Did he actually try to smell her?

"Come," he whispered again. Though the tone was still soft, it was edged with the hard insistence of a command. His eyes turned liquid, as if he might forcibly pull her at any moment. That was when she realized they were being watched. The music had faded. The married couples had stopped laughing, their frowning faces and serious, over-bright eyes focused curiously on her in expectation and incredulity.

All right, she thought. I'll bite. Take me to round two.

Unable to resist, and unwilling to stay the center of all that attention, Morrigan nodded weakly and stood to follow him. The man's full lips again tugged with a promising, yet hesitant smile. His eyes calmed in relief and he nodded to her before turning around.

Vaguely, she heard the return of laughter fall over the gathered Qurilixian. She was led down the dining platform steps. The music came back too and couples began to dance around the bonfire pit.

Ualan didn't touch her, but Morrigan could feel him directing her by an invisible thread. There was magic in the air, binding her to him, seemingly controlling her brain. Yet, she heard music, smelled the wood smoke on the night wind. Her limbs could move where she commanded them, if she commanded them hard enough. The stars glistened, seeming to swim around in her brain, and the moon was so big that it felt as if a spotlight were shining on them from above.

Ualan said nothing as he led her forward over the dirt worn pathways. Pyramid tents passed by her vision in a variety of colors. Her eye strayed along Ualan's backside, hesitating at the gray fur loincloth hiding his buttocks from view. She swallowed. Her hands began to reach, but were stopped by the silken ties. As she tried again to touch the fur Ualan turned to glance at her, a knowing smile on his firm lips and reflecting from his eyes. Morrigan jolted in embarrassment, shaking out of the spell he cast on her. With a blush, she turned her gaze away.

"Where are we going?" she asked, coming more to her senses.

Ualan stopped and turned around in surprise to hear her speak. Even under the leather mask, she could tell he was handsome. He again glanced down at his crystal, momentary confusion passing over his mesmerizing blue eyes. Moving near a tent, he tilted his head to the side, and said, "Come."

Morrigan hesitated and shook her head, not willing to follow his orders like an insipid female. An unfamiliar sensation pulled inside of her, warring within her limbs. Part of her wanted to obey him, but her logical mind did not let her move forward. This was not part of the plan. This wasn't part of her assignment. Oh, he was attractive in that accursed loincloth!

Around the campsite she could see the other women ducking into the various tents with hardly a protest. She heard shouts of merriment drifting about on the breeze from the married couples in their own celebration. The fire still burned bright, music still played, encouraging couples to dance in celebration. Morrigan had yet to see the musicians.

The curse of an inquisitive mind overcame her and she had the strangest urge to go exploring. When else would she get such a chance again? Beginning to take a step back from the tent, Morrigan said in growing distraction, "Go ahead and get started without me. I'll be there in a minute."

Ualan followed her eyes to the table where the married couples sat enjoying each other's company. His jaw tensed. His bride was beginning to move away from him.

"Come," he ordered, his tone growing harsh.

"Relax, buddy," Morrigan eased, with no intention of following him 'back to his room'. That scenario ended the same way on every planet. Give the girl some wine, say 'me Ualan, you pretty, come', and wouldn't you know it, you had yourself the makings of a private orgy and a killer hangover.

No, but thank you just the same, caveman, Morrigan thought with an amused laugh.

"Look, I'm sure you're a swell guy and all," she began, her tone patronizing as she refused to look back at him. She began to move away.

Morrigan, realizing that she had left her ring on and it was still recording, was about to touch the emerald when she felt a hand on the back of her neck. Closing her eyes at that first warm caress, she nearly collapsed. His callused hand dug into her long hair beneath the veil, pulling her forward. Her knees weakened and she fell into his palm, no longer interested in the campsite when she saw his face hovering close to hers.

It was insanity. He was a stranger. She was in outer space on a primitive planet to do a story. If she was smart she would run away from him. Her legs wouldn't move. She was stunned by him, captivated. All right, so suddenly she wasn't very smart.

Ualan held her back from his warrior-toned flesh, but she could feel its warm invitation. She could smell the exotically bestial scent of him--so primal and raw. She licked her lips. Seeing the response in her, Ualan smiled, although he still looked baffled by her hesitance. Or was it something else she saw in his eyes? Fear? No, this God-like creature was too much of a warrior to feel fear. Morrigan could be sure of that. Self-confidence radiated confidently off his very nature.

"Come," he whispered softly to her, pleading, urging her with that one simple word. Leaning forward, he nuzzled his smooth cheek tenderly to hers. The whispering caress sent her heart a-fluttering. With more authority straining his thick accent, he insisted again, "Come."

Morrigan's hands lifted, this time able to touch his waist. She wanted to go with him. Who would ever find out? What could be more perfect? Tomorrow she would be gone and he would stay here. There would be no complications, no heartbreak. Only, would he expect her to marry him? It wasn't as if he loved her. Surely, he wouldn't be too disappointed when he discovered she was gone. He could always find someone else at the next festival.

Ualan's skin was on fire, blazing with an animalistic heat. His finger rubbed over the pulse at the base of her neck.

Morrigan trembled at the warm stroke. She waited for his kiss--sure she would die if she didn't feel his mouth on hers. It didn't come.

The tall warrior pulled back, looking deeply into her eyes. Then, glancing around the campsite as if looking to see if anyone noticed them, he drew her forward, pulling gently at her neck to make her walk. Once her legs began to move, following him inside, she could not stop them.

* * * *

"My lord, the brides have all entered the tents."

King Llyr looked up from where he nuzzled his wife's throat. The royal couple shared a soft smile. His eyes glistened in pleasure. The night was warm, his wife's body soft and all of their sons had been blessed this glorious night with wives. They couldn't have been happier.

"Thank you, Mirox," Queen Mede answered for her husband. When they were alone, she whispered in parental concern, "It will be a long night for our sons, but an even longer night for us."

"They are good men, strong and true," the King said. Though he would never admit it, he too was both nervous and excited for his sons. This was a big night for them, perhaps one of the biggest. "I am sure they will all be blessed with good fortune and we, my Queen, will be blessed with many grandsons."

"I hope you're right, my love, I hope you're right," the Queen murmured, content to let her husband pull her back into his embrace. There was nothing they could do but wait until morning.

Chapter Three

Morrigan's fingers itched to pull the mask from Ualan's features, to better study his face. With a body like his, he could have been scarred ugly and the girls would still have come running. He walked backwards into the tent, taking her with him lest she try to pull away again.

Leaving her standing alone in the middle of the tent, Ualan went to draw the front flap closed. Morrigan shivered. She wasn't such a fool as to pretend she didn't know what he wanted from her, looking at her with his come-hither eyes and touching her with his caressing hand. She had never really gotten this far on a date before, and this had to be the shortest date in recorded history.

The tent was very large with fur rugs laid out to cushion the dirt floor. Torches were set near the walls. A large bed, covered in satin and silk, was in the direct middle. Silk hung from the top of the tent, hazy as a dream, to surround the corners of the bed.

Around the edges of the tent, at the three pyramid corners, were three very different arrangements, all blatantly erotic and hard to ignore. In the first corner sat a giant basin full of steaming water, surrounded by silk gauze curtains, and an array of bottles. The tub was large enough to fit both of them easily.

The second corner held a throne-like chair, leather binding straps, iron shackles, and an assortment of whips. Morrigan shivered afresh. She had to turn away quickly, too embarrassed to be caught showing too much interest in the set up.

In the last corner, there was a relatively safe table of food and wine.

"Choose," Ualan breathed near her ear. Goosebumps tickled her flesh. Morrigan jumped, not realizing he had come so close to where she stood. She blinked, her head whipping around to study his face. The mask hid him from view, but it could not hide the lust in his eyes or the command in his words as he waited for her to act. Ualan reeked of potent sexuality.

"Ah, yeah," Morrigan began, biting her lip. Thinking that the last table was the least threatening, she began to move towards the food. A tray of chocolates, with nut toppings, was delicately arranged into a pyramid of temptation. There was fresh fruit, looking like strawberries, but deeper in color and much larger, with a brown cream sauce.

Morrigan ignored the sweets, grabbing a goblet of wine instead. She drank it in two gulps, sputtering it out in a mighty blast when she felt a hand graze lightly over her bare shoulder.

Ualan slowly picked up a chocolate and held it out for her to taste. She tried to take it with her fingers, but he gracefully eased past her hand and stuck it in her mouth. He watched in puzzlement, as she jerked away from him and shuffled nervously around the table out of his reach.

"Thanks, I can get it from here," she mumbled. Chewing the delicious morsel, she swallowed it and licked her lips, before wiping her mouth on her hand.

Ualan was puzzled.

"Listen," Morrigan began. "I--"

"Shh," Ualan whispered, shaking his head. His eyes closed briefly, and when he again looked at her it was with a puzzled expression. Morrigan thought that for a man of many actions, he wasn't a man of many words. Softly, he said, "Your name."

"This isn--" Morrigan began anew, frustrated when he cut her off.

"Name," he stated louder, turning more serious. His arms stiffened in warning.

"Rigan," Morrigan answered at his hard tone, only to correct, "I mean Morrigan Blake. But, you can call me Rigan, everyone does."

Pleased by her answer, he nodded in approval and began to reach for her again. Morrigan continued to ease out of his range as he rounded the table for her. He stalked her like a beast, his eyes intent and focused on her every movement.

"Now, if you please, I'll just be going," Morrigan said, easing her way to the tent flap. She did her best to smile as she waved tentatively at him. The gesture was more one of protection than of departure. Ualan looked like a wild creature perusing her, with his molten gaze and physical prowess. "Thank you for everything and good luck with that wife finding thing. I hope it goes well for you."

"It would not please me," he said darkly. He dropped his hand and sighed in growing frustration. Looking down at his crystal that burned brightly, he appeared bewildered by her rejection. There was a long silence, his stance challenging her to try and escape him. Morrigan knew that he would easily overtake her if she were to run.

"Listen," Morrigan reasoned. She tried to keep the condescending tilt from her tone, but it was hard. "I know you must be disappointed to have your little plans here spoiled." She waved her hand over the erotically charged tent as she spoke. "But, no means no. So, better luck next time. There are plenty of other women out there who weren't chosen by your fellow warriors. They would be most willing to come here with you, I just don't happen to be one of them. All of the other girls are most eager to get hitched up--"

Ualan took a threatening step forward at her words. Morrigan flinched.

"Back off, caveman!" she warned, going rigid and giving him her most menacing glare. The withering look didn't have the desired effect, because he smirked in arrogance. Still, it wasn't amusement she saw in those deep blue eyes of liquid fire. He was livid.

Ualan watched the Earth woman before him. His whole body tensed in aggravation. This is not how the elders foretold the bridal night. He wanted to yell at her, but honor forbid it. He could only say as few of words as possible when interacting with her. It was tradition. Maybe he wasn't as blessed by the Gods as he had been wont to think. This wench was proving to be the most aggravating of....

Urgh! Blast it all, anyway.

"Now, let's just calm down a little, okay sparky," Morrigan said, forcing her shoulders to relax. She eyed him warily, wondering if his English was bad. That could explain the confusion. Slowly, she began to enunciate her words. "I do not wish to get married."

He frowned.

"Now you," she said pointed at him with her hand before walking her fingers in the air, "walk out there and find another woman from the ship. Grab her." She shook her fist. "And lead her back to your bed."

By the time she had finished illustrating her words, she was pointing at the bed.

"Do you understand?" she continued slowly, perhaps a bit too slowly in her ire.

His frown deepened.

"Great," she said to herself. "Out of all the warriors out there, I have to get the gardener who can't speak my language." Looking at him, she fumed, stating louder, "It's called research, barbarian. You know, studying up before you take on a new task so you know what you are getting yourself into."

His frown turned into a full-blown scowl.

"I can't talk to you, caveman. I'm leaving."

Spinning on her heels, she almost made it to the tent opening. Almost.

Ualan darted forward, stalking his prey with deathlike speed. Taking her firmly by the shoulder, he stepped around her and blocked the exit. His eyes burned as he stared her down. It was either try to mow him over bravely or slowly retreat like a coward. Morrigan frowned warily. She was definitely a coward.

Ualan watched the timid creature nearly jump out of her skin as he again touched her. He forced himself to calm down. Perhaps she was just nervous. Her wide gaze kept looking over his body in a half-fascinated, half-wary sort of way. He knew she desired him. The crystal proved as much. Besides, even without the crystal, he could smell the potent flavor of her sex.

He knew that the tents were rumored to intimidate some Earth women with delicate sensibilities, unused to a man's attentions. Seeming to have an idea, he asked bluntly, but quietly, "Have you been with a man?"

Morrigan blushed in horror. Her mouth worked, as she said, "I ... I...."

His jaw lifted, waiting.

"That is none of your business!"

"Answer," he urged patiently, heartened by her discomfort. Being a male dominated race, his people were not so shy when it came to discussing such things. But he had been told that women were different. When he instructed her to her new role, she would not be so shy--not that his vanity minded the way she would blush when catching herself looking at him like a starving mirascat.

"Answer," she mocked, with a snarl. "Me Ualan, you woman--uh, uh."

He cocked his head. His stiff mouth saying he was unamused by her humor.

Morrigan sighed. Out of the blue, an idea struck her. Her eyes were shadowed over her lids, as she said, "Yes, yes I have."

Ualan managed to glide forward before she knew what he was doing. When Morrigan blinked, he was standing directly before her. All right, maybe it had been the wrong thing to say. It didn't seem he was dissuaded from his task--so much for the theory that the Qurilixian preferred virgins.

Bending over, his hand caught her arm in its callused grasp. Murmuring against her throat, he groaned, "Then you have no reason to deny me. Choose."

Morrigan shivered at his nearness. Seeing his lips bending so close, she was tempted to give up the battle. Why was she fighting him so hard? It wasn't as if she had a lot of male suitors back home vying for mattress time.

Then, she saw his arrogant smirk when she hesitated answering. Oh, the battle was on. This barbarian was not going to get the best of her. It was a matter of principle now. She didn't care who this caveman thought he was. He could be the King of the Seven Galaxies for all she cared. You just didn't treat women like a piece of steak to be pushed around and chewed on at will.

"You don't understand," Morrigan whispered, blinking her wide eyes in a way that seemed so innocent and disarming. Ualan's nostrils flared. "I've been with several men. In fact, that is what my job is back on Earth. I'm a prostitute."

There! Morrigan thought, hard-pressed not to laugh when her words sunk in. The mean old barbarian didn't like that one, did he?

"So, you see, you won't want me." Morrigan's will was weakening against the teasing promise of his lips as he moved closer to study her. She was scared of him, but thrilled by the assurance of his body. He sniffed her like a dog in heat. Morrigan tried to lean away. Her words not as confident as she caught the virile scent of his exotically oiled body, she weakly questioned, "Why don't you just wait another year for a virgin if you don't like the other women here tonight? Surely you'll have first pick since you struck out this year."

Morrigan knew she needed to get out of the tent and work, but her eyes begged her to stay for just a moment longer so they could look more fully at him. In light of his touch, work didn't seem so important at the moment. However, since work was her life, Morrigan was puzzled by the revelation. Maybe it was the wine. That was it--she was just a little drunk.

"The crystal does not lie," he whispered throatily and with confidence. "The Gods have spoken."

"What--?" Morrigan began, glancing around his neck at the glowing pulse of the crystal. Instantly, she could feel its power over her--tempting, inviting, demanding--just like its wearer. Her blood sang with the powers of the Qurilixian wine. But, in contrast to the wine on Earth, the Qurilixian blend did not exactly encourage sleep. "I don't believe in your Go--"

"Silence!" He began to slide his hands more insistently over her, pushing down the silken strands woven around her arms. His tilting, thick accent rolled over her in waves. "You question too much. You want this. Make your choice."

Morrigan gulped. He appeared very sure of himself and that fact.

Her mouth opened as if to protest. It would seem she would need more convincing. Ualan immediately pressed his lips to hers in a bold kiss. His tongue parted her mouth, drawing in her bottom lip to suck gently.

Her plea turned into a moan of surprise. Ualan growled, pulling her fiercely to his chest. Every hot, oiled inch of him molded to her skin. Her desire flowed into his nostrils, strong and potent.

The silk and gauze of her dress was no match against his fire. It was insanity and Morrigan knew it. She tried to fight his touch, tried to pull back, but her brain kept insisting, just one more feel, just a little longer, just let him touch you a little longer, longer....

Breaking free of her mouth, Ualan stared boldly at her chest. It heaved with deep pants. He smiled, tasting victory.

With a purposeful finger, he flicked at the strap holding her gown up.

"Choose," he commanded her.

Morrigan looked around the tent, intrigued by the hot water, drawn to the bed, shamefully curious of the throne. She couldn't utter the words. She couldn't decide. She couldn't ask for it. She was too overwhelmed. Her body sung in ways she had never known possible. Between the wine and the power of the crystal and man, she couldn't think straight.

"Wine," Morrigan answered weak of breath and limb. Her hands trembled where they lay pinned against him, against the strong beating of his heart. She tried to push. It was a sorry effort. He was too strong, too tall, too overwhelming. "Please, can you go get me a different wine?"

His mouth opened as if to protest. Morrigan felt his fingernails clawing lightly at her back. She put her hand to his firm lips to stop him from speaking. Her wide eyes took him in with their desperation. Lying, she promised, "Go, I bid you. Then, then when you get back, we will finish this--all right?"

Ualan glanced over her body with a brutal growl of barely contained passion. His stomach tensed. Slowly, he nodded and took his hands from her skin.

Morrigan's flesh jumped in instant protest. Her body ached. Her thighs and stomach quivered with stinging need. Her breasts were swollen with the anticipation of his touch. Morrigan watched him stride from the tent, taking her at her word.

"Oh," she breathed, too stunned for a moment to move. "The corporation said nothing about meeting you."

Morrigan was slow coming to her senses. When she was sure Ualan was away from the front of the tent, she poked her head out of the flap. With him gone, her body shivered as if chilled to the bone.

He was a strange man to be sure, acting on tradition and primal instinct. But what had she expected? He was a Qurilixian, not an Earthling. He grew up around men, probably used to spouting orders and having those orders followed. Although they were almost the same genetically, their customs were completely different.

Well, thought Morrigan, with a wry twist of her mouth. Not completely different. Had it been the Middle Ages on Earth, we would understand each other fairly well.

Though, Morrigan imagined a medieval Earthling would have spoken more, especially while trying to seduce someone. However, there was something dangerous and alluring about Ualan's silent perusal. It was almost animalistic, the way he looked at her. It was as if he was unashamed of his desires and expected her to be unashamed of hers. What he didn't say with words, she could read in his eyes and feel on her skin, as if he put the thoughts into her flesh with his will.

Morrigan frowned, vowing that, as soon as she got home, she was going to purchase the biggest damned sex droid her savings could buy. Robo-man would put this barbarian to shame--she'd make sure of it.

Seeing no one was outside the tent, Morrigan snuck out into the night. Dipping behind a blue tent and a red, she stopped to get her bearings.

"Do not fight it, Olena," she heard from within the red tent. "I can feel that you want me. You chose me."

A woman's throaty moan followed the confident decree. Morrigan shivered, half tempted to go back to Ualan's tent and see what else his firm body had to offer her. It wasn't like she had to stay married to him or anything if they just had sex. And, who would know? Not her editor. Not anyone who mattered.

"Focus, girl," she whispered to herself. "He's the big lug who thinks dragging a woman off into the sunset by her hair is romance."

Morrigan heard the woman Olena moan again, this time louder. Her body shivered. She wasn't sure what she was doing outside of the tent. She had really thought there would be more talking before everyone got to know each other so intimately. If this was dating, she really had been off the scene a little too long.

Crossing quickly over to a green tent, Morrigan stopped near the flap opening. Seeing a crack, she couldn't help but peek inside.

"Choose," a man said.

Morrigan leaned closer, trying to see who he was with. What was with all this choosing? Did the Qurilixian English teacher have a serious vocabulary problem? Suddenly, she felt as if they were abducted by aliens--handsome, virile aliens, but strange ones nonetheless.

"I ... I can't choose, Olek," she heard Nadja answer. "Not yet."

Morrigan saw a flash of skin as the woman moved past the opening. Soon, the man was behind her, his naked buttock flexing as he walked.

A dangerous jolt overcame Morrigan. She knew she should turn away. But these men were just too delicious for the eyes. Licking her lips, she tried to get another peek. It wasn't as if she was a peeping-tom. She was an investigative reporter. Then, to her horror, she heard a low voice behind her.

"You cannot run. The crystal will always find you."

* * * *

Ualan's hand began to tremble as he tried to contain himself. He clenched it into a fist. His mouth tightened into a harsh line. By all that was sacred, what had he done to the Gods to deserve this aggravation?

Ualan knew she was fighting what he stirred in her. He was a warrior, up to the challenge of a good fight. Although, he did growl in frustration to find his bride had escaped his tent. He suspected she would try, though he was still disappointed. He forced himself to relax. She was a mystery, one he would have to figure out. He didn't have a choice.

Truthfully, he was unnerved by her admission of many men. He would just have to watch her very carefully. It would not do to have her play him false. It was rare that it should happen, but it had happened.

Ualan remembered how she melted to his kiss. It seemed there was a way to quiet her spirited tongue after all. She might fight him, but she was not immune. Seeing her nearby, crouched by his brother's tent, he smiled. It had not been hard for him to track her. Silently, he came up behind her. Forcing his face to be stern, he stated, "You cannot run. The crystal will always find you."

Chapter Four

Morrigan jolted in alarm at the bold words. Spinning on her heels, she saw Ualan standing, wine goblet in hand. The crystal at his neck pulsed. At the same moment a heat spread between her thighs and her nipples hardened. Her face drained of color, horrified at being caught watching the other couple.

"You don't understand," Morrigan began, with a feeble lift of her hand to stop his progress.

Ualan glanced at the tent opening and grinned, holding out the goblet for her to take. Morrigan's cheeks stained a bright, flaming pink that even the darkness couldn't hide. She knew he understood all too well what she had been doing.

Morrigan balked. Refusing to take the goblet he offered because it would take her closer to his delectable body, she shook her head. Distracted, she tried to ignore the powerful draw of his chest. "It's not what you think. My friend is in there and I wanted to make sure she was all right. I don't want you barbarians hurting her or anything."

Again, his head moved but he said nothing. When Morrigan did not reach for the goblet, Ualan let it slide from his hand. It landed with a soft thud on the ground, spilling the wine into the dirt.

"Come," Ualan said with a curl of his fingers. Intent now burned hotly in his gaze and flooded into his face. If she wasn't mistaken, she thought she detected some anger in his word, or was it exasperation?

The crystal pulsed in his frustration. Morrigan's blood roared in her veins. The sound of moans came from within the field of tents. Sexual energy rose in the air. All the talk on the ship of sex with able-bodied men, combined with the largeness of Ualan's form, filled her head. A chant was struck up in her brain, singing sweetly, what harm is there in one night?

Treacherous brain.

Ugh, most treacherous body.

Absently pushing the emerald on her finger to make sure the camera was off, Morrigan stepped forward. Laying her hand over Ualan's heart, next to the crystal, she felt him tense beneath her palm. He eyed her warily, as if he expected her to try something deceitful. Her eyes dipped down to look at the glowing stone. She didn't dare touch it.

"Come," he spoke tenderly, when she didn't move.

Morrigan nodded her head. He wove a spell around her senses. It was a deliciously wicked curse she could not be free of.

One night, she promised herself. No one will ever find out.

Ualan's eyes closed briefly and he seemed to sigh in relief that she was finally willing. Some of the tension he carried all night eased out of him. Taking her by the hand so she could not change her mind, he quickly led her through the pyramid-studded maze back to his tent.

Once inside, he did not let go. He took her hand and pulled her forward to him. His eyes shone from the slits of the mask, probing her. Pressing her fingers once more above his heart, he breathed, "Choose."

Morrigan quivered. His heart beat beneath her fingers in strong, barbaric thuds.

When she didn't readily answer, Ualan groaned and took her free hand in his. Pulling it to the fur loincloth about his waist, he showed her how much he desired her by pressing her fingers boldly onto his potent erection. Almost like a plea, he said again, "Choose."

"I don't know," she whispered, thinking how strange these silent warrior men were. She didn't move her hand from the hard press of his desire, nor did she leave the excited beat of his heart. She flexed her fingers, easing slightly forward to feel him, but not too much as to be brazen or inviting. Frankly, the enormous size of his member terrified her. She looked over his mask with the sudden urge to rip it from his features, but part of the thrill was in not seeing.

Ualan grunted, rotating his hips against her hesitant fingers. His breath came deep. Closing his eyes, he saw she needed more persuasion. He nodded, before urging hoarsely, "Undress."

He did not wait for her to comply. He met the flesh of her shoulders and with an urgent push he worked the material off her arms. With a quick jerk, her breasts were freed for his viewing.

Morrigan gasped, drawing her hands away from him. Like a man possessed, he touched her chest, cupping the tender globes into his eager palms. His heated fingers melted around her, massaging her nipples as if they were the finest things he had ever held. Ualan licked his lips. His eyes stayed focused, almost possessively, on what he did.

Morrigan tried to back away. He pursued her. She tried to bat his hands with hers. He ignored her attempt.

"Stop," she whimpered. But, as her head rolled back on her shoulders and her mouth gasped for air, her body urged otherwise. She gulped.

Ualan held back, not giving her body what it begged for. Finally, after thorough torture, his fingers moved over her soft skin to her hips. Freeing her completely of the Qurilixian gown, he pulled back to stare.

Morrigan blushed, but did not back away. One did not back away in a dream. The fog was all around her, encircling them. She didn't want to wake up just yet. Emboldened by the isolation of the planet and knowing that after tomorrow she would never see Ualan again, she stepped forward.

Devouring his chest with her eyes, she hesitantly ran her finger down the center of his throat, over his nipples and down his flat, tensing ribcage. Her nails tripped over the fur along his waist in an agonizingly slow journey across his stomach. Watching his mask, she saw his nostrils flare. His chest rose evenly and his eyes bore forward into hers. He didn't stop her. In fact, it seemed he was silently urging her in approval. Turning her hand, she began the journey back up.

With a grunt, Ualan expressed his displeasure in her change of route. Unflinchingly, his eyes gazed forward into her as he pulled the side of the fur loincloth, instantly freeing himself when she would not. Morrigan gasped, stumbling back. Wide-eyed, she stared at his member. It looked nothing like the small protrusion on the droid. Her mouth went dry. Realizing she stared, her eyes pulled away, frightened. She quickly turned from him.

Ualan confidently looked his fill of her naked form. His gaze took in her brightly painted toenails, her smooth legs, her athletic thighs, and the divot of her navel, her strong hips, her lovely breasts, and slender arms. The soft dark hair of her nether region was cropped short and shaved into a narrow line that guarded her opening.

Ualan smiled in amusement, thankful for the view her embarrassment gave him of her backside. For a woman who claimed to have had many men, she wasn't acting like it. Later, when the ceremony was over and they could speak more freely, he would have to teach her the dangers of lying to her husband. But for now....

"Turn," he commanded, his need for her hot. He was not finished inspecting his new bride.

Morrigan had been just about to reach for her discarded clothing when the word hit her like a blast. His accent was hoarse, thick, tortured. How could she not obey it? Her eyes met his, not daring to venture downward. He came to her, glorious and proud.

"Hold still," he ordered. She didn't dare move. She whimpered when his finger touched her cheek. Lightly, it trailed her features, between her eyes, down the slope of her nose, into the indention above her lips. Her mouth parted. He traced her lips in a feathery caress.

Soon, the veil fluttered from her heavy locks. Her hair tumbled in dark silk waves over her shoulders. Ualan watched in obvious pleasure as her eyes dreamily closed.

Keeping his touch light, he drew his hand over her throat. He moved in aimless circles, taking his time with her flesh--purposefully tormenting it, as he made her more fevered parts wait.

Morrigan was in heaven, every nerve inside her radiated around his touch. Her mind followed its every whispering move. Her back arched, trying to push fully at his teasing hand when he discovered the valley between her breasts. Her mind relented, the fog deepened.

Her eyes fluttered open, almost frightened to see the look on his face. He was concentrating on his fingers, watching them figure skate over her heating flesh as if this was the most important thing he'd ever done. His touch danced figure-eights around her breasts, coming closer to the center with each sweeping pass.

Morrigan moaned, overwhelmed by her passion for him. It was like nothing she had ever experienced. He was like nothing she had ever seen before, and being a star-traveling reporter she had seen a lot.

She began to disobey his order, and lifted her hands to touch him. As her fingers met his heated flesh, his hand stopped and he looked up with a challenging fight in his eyes. Morrigan quickly lowered her hands back to her sides. He moved his fingers again.

The glowing crystal pulsed between them, giving off a heat that joined them even as it bit into their flesh. Just as his pass would have taken him directly over the peaked buds awaiting him, his hand changed course, dipping over her stomach.

Morrigan tried to fight it, but the whimper wouldn't stop as it snuck past her throat. The soft, feminine sound of confusion and surrender was more than even the war-hardened Qurilixian could resist. Her fingers twitched nervously. Her breath came in pants.

For Ualan, what had started as a show of power quickly turned into a lesson in self-deprivation. He had to concentrate to keep from consuming her. Gripping her hair, he forced her head back, thrusting her breasts up for the delight of his lips. His mouth came down to lightly lick the tip of a nipple. He thought to only get a hint of what would come with marriage. But, as he soon discovered, one taste was never enough. Like a drunkard craving ale, he tasted her again. His mouth opened, taking a nipple into its depths, swirling it with the rough texture of his tongue, nipping it deliciously with his teeth.

Morrigan bucked. She felt as if she was drowning in a pool of turbulent sensations. He was dragging her under the tide of his passion, but she couldn't escape. She didn't want to. She was his prisoner and, for the moment, nothing else mattered.

Ualan kept distance between their bodies, but all the while his mouth trailed kisses, now over the valley of her breasts to give ample attention to the other side. When she spasmed against him, he grinned against the creamy globe and pulled her closer.

Morrigan trembled, uncertain of what to expect. She only knew she didn't want him to stop.

Ualan groaned, a low animalistic sound, against her heated flesh. His hands discovered the firm pleasure of her derrière. The heat of his erection pressed dangerously close to her tender stomach, searing her skin. Morrigan froze, suddenly afraid of his demands. The fire was too much for her innocent mind to process. She needed to step back and think. She needed to ... oh!

Ualan's strong arms gripped tighter, refusing to let her pull away. Releasing her breast, he claimed her mouth in a swift, passionate embrace. Kissing her with the same fervor he had shown her chest, he tasted her lips before delving beneath the surface to suck her tongue into her mouth.

As abruptly as his assault on her body began, it ended. Quickly pulling away, he grabbed his loincloth and wrapped it around his waist before she could even think to protest it. Morrigan blinked in confusion. A cold chill swept her body as she watched him. His breath was calm and he didn't look at all affected by what had transpired.

"Dress," he commanded softly.

Morrigan's body stung, unfulfilled and burning with an ache she couldn't possibly begin to explore with him staring at her dispassionately like that. With a long, irritated growl, she began gathering the Qurilixian gown from the floor. Slipping it over her body, she left the belt ties off her arms so she could move more freely.

Combing her fingers through her hair, Morrigan searched for a hair tie. Not finding anything of use, she tied the locks into a giant knot at the nape of her neck to hold it from her face. She refused to look at him until she had finished. When she turned around, he was gone.

* * * *

Ualan stormed through the encampment, too irritated to remain in his tent. His arms tingled with the desire to find a sword and lop off his bride's frustrating, yet beautiful head. His lesson was finished. Anymore and he wouldn't be able to stop himself. The smell of her passion filled his head. But the law was strict. Until the women chose, the men could not push it further than he already had. Surely, once he explained her refusal to choose, he would be pardoned for it.

In fact, if she wanted, she could demand justice for his actions and put him on guard duty for a month in the lowest level of dungeons. It was a dreaded task, often used as a punishment for small offenders. Spending such a long time in the dark was hard on those used to this bright planet--not because they were afraid, for they could see very well in the dark, but because the blue sun nourished them and gave them life.

"This is no place to be on the bridal night," came an amused chuckle. "How do you expect to woo her if you aren't near her?"

Ualan stopped. His solid blue eyes turned to study a pair of beast-like green. Agro was dressed in the traditional tunic and breeches of their people. It was an old style, one the men felt no reason to change. It worked well in combat and in practice.

Ualan's jaw tightened in irritation, as he looked over his good friend. The man's eyes dipped down over Ualan's oiled skin and loincloth in amusement. Ualan stepped forward, his eyes daring the man to laugh.

"I take it she hasn't chosen," the man said with a curl of knowing humor to his beard-covered lips.

Ualan's fist tightened in response. He was not allowed to speak.

Agro was already married and seemed to be enjoying the pleasures of the feast, as was evident by the drunken glaze in his eyes. But Ualan wasn't fooled. He knew well that Agro's senses were sharp.

"She will never choose with you out here," the man, sounding wise, as he began to move past. Then he stopped to speak. Ualan knew that Agro couldn't help himself. "By all that's sacred, you're an ugly man, Ualan. Get back to the tents before you scare off our women, too."

Ualan grinned wickedly at the taunt. A fight would do much to restore his good humor. He might not be able to speak, but he could act. Balling his hand into a fist, he rewarded Agro with a swift punch to the face.

* * * *

Morrigan was furious. How dare he touch her like that and then leave as if it were no big deal? But, more than her fury, she was humiliated by the treacherousness of her body. One look and she had crumpled to his demands, following his order like a harem slave.

Dress, she fumed. I'll show you dressed, you big, overbearing caveman!

Satisfied that Ualan would not be coming for her again anytime soon, Morrigan crept to the tent's opening. It was still dark out, but she knew that this night would last longer than the nights on Earth. That was why the Qurilixian had chosen it for their Breeding Festival. She remembered it vaguely from her uploads--something about the moonlight making them aroused or some such nonsense.

So much for accurate uploads from Galaxy Brides, she mused bitterly. Ualan had hardly looked aroused by her, at least not like she'd been by him. It shamed her to remember it. *I should write a piece on inaccurate uploads and expose the cretin who made them as a fraud who knows nothing about planetary or cultural facts.*

To Morrigan's surprise, she heard moans of pleasure still coming from various tents around the encampment. It would seem Qurilixian men were certainly insatiable, when they chose to be. She felt an unwanted stirring and an urge to turn around for just one more taste of Ualan's passions.

"What is the matter with me?" Morrigan hissed to herself, comforted by the sound of her own voice. She would not put herself through that humiliation again. A loud scream of ecstasy pierced the air and she grimaced. "Galaxy Brides, my ass. More like Galaxy Sluts. All right, focus Morrigan, you have got to gather information."

But saying it was harder than actually doing it. Unlike her other assignments, there was no clear person to interview. She had no idea who the royalty were or if they had even attended. The Qurilixian didn't believe in crowns or purple flowing robes to mark their aristocrats, so there was no pointed sign reading, 'here, look here, this is a Prince'. For all she knew, the Princes were amongst the ones who hadn't taken a bride back to their tents. They could all be at home getting drunk and watching each other grow old. Not that she could blame them. None of the women on the spaceship seemed like royalty material to her.

Moving through the pyramids, Morrigan tried to make her way around to the married couples. But, when the tall throne chairs came into view, she was met with disappointment. No one was left at the thrones. Sighing in frustration, she crept closer.

"Ah! Ah!"

Morrigan jolted in alarm at the high-pitched screech, her heart squeezing in her throat, only to relax as she realized the sound came from inside a nearby tent. In frustration, she shook her head.

Concentrate! she scolded herself.

Near the bonfire, Morrigan heard a sultry woman's laugh followed by the growl of a man. She crept in the shadows, careful to stay hidden from view.

A healthy specimen of female beauty came rushing forward, taunting her naked lover with her bared charms. Laughing, she threw back her head and made her way to one of the throne chairs before the fire. The man growled again, swiftly stalking her with unrefined, animalistic stealth.

Morrigan gasped. Her breath deepened as she watched the couple begin to make love before the flames. She couldn't take her eyes away, though she knew she should. It was forbidden, what she was doing. But it was also erotic and dangerous and thrilling. Her blood began to stir and rush. Her flesh began to tingle and heat. Her lips went dry, eager for Ualan's kisses to wet them once more.

The man caressed the woman's skin in long strokes. He tested her wetness with is fingers. His lips savored her small breasts, worshiping. Then, turning, the woman braced her hand on the throne so her lover could enter her from behind. The man held back, biting and licking the flesh of her backside.

"Oh," another moan from a tent.

"Argh," this time it was a man from across the encampment.

"Mm," Morrigan bit her lips. Her body flamed. Her head spun in circles until she couldn't concentrate, couldn't think beyond her passionate flesh and churning desires, dizzy--so dizzy. It was as if a spell had been cast and she was the sorry recipient of it. What was happening to her? Her body was going crazy with passion and fire. The sexual tension was so thick that she imagined she could smell it.

True, before tonight, she had been on assignment in some of the most dismal of places with creatures no human could be attracted to. Her work kept her from her own kind, making relationships impossible, except with other journalists who she had vowed never to become involved with.

When she was on Earth, it was always researching or uploading planetary facts into her brain, readying herself for her next assignment. But, it didn't mean she was ignorant. It didn't mean she didn't know. Out of all she had borne

witness to, Ualan was the first man she had met that had ever
stirred her senses to wakefulness, had brought her from one
dream into another. And he did it all with very few,
low-toned, blood-stirringly erotic words. Come. Choose.

As she spied, the man stood behind the woman. He
grabbed her hips. Morrigan unconsciously touched her
breast. Her heart pounded beneath her fingers. Inching with
aggravating slowness, the man entered his lover. She threw
glorious waves of red-brown hair over her shoulder at him.
The man grabbed the locks, using them to control her to his
passion.

Unexpectedly, Morrigan felt a caress on her arm. She
shivered, instinctively knowing it was Ualan come to fetch
her back to his tent. She didn't move, dazed as her eyes
strayed to the thrusting man's buttocks, her ears jealous of
the woman's cries of passion.

Ualan pulled on her arm, forcing her to stand. She kept her
back to him as his lips found her earlobe. The leather mask
brushed her neck. The soft breeze swept over her heating
skin. The thrusting man's passions became louder and more
claiming as he moved forcefully behind his screaming lover.

Ualan did not pull her back, allowing her to watch, not
judging her for it. His people were not inhibited when it
came to such things. He continued to kiss her skin, nip at her
earlobe, to lick at her rapid pulse. His own eyes strayed to
the couple. His hand fell from Morrigan's arm, not
restraining her to him, but for the tantalizing motion of his
lips on her skin.

"How?" Morrigan began, breathless. She couldn't finish as
her hips began to mimic the light thrusting of their own
accord. But they were frustrated for they thrust at air, not
solid, scorching man flesh. *How are you doing this? How
are you controlling me?*

Ualan misunderstood the weak question, and answered,
"My crystal will always find you."

Morrigan pressed her buttocks against Ualan's erection.
She felt the fur covering him and hated it for keeping him
from her. The night was filled with passion, with unforeseen
magic. It pulsed through the long night of the festival. It was
in the air. It was in every fiber of Morrigan's body, until she
thought, *it doesn't matter. Tonight it doesn't matter. Take*

whatever Ualan offers. Take it, live it, and then keep it secret. No one will ever know. Take it. Take.

As the couple climaxed, Morrigan closed her eyes, forgetting what she had sworn to moments before. She wanted Ualan to finish what he started. Maybe then she could think clearly. Hushing a desperate entreaty, she said, "Take me back to the tent, Ualan. Please, take me ... back."

Ualan growled, turning her tenderly about so he could lift her into his arms. He did it easily, his arms folding protectively around her. The crystal still glowed, but she ignored it. She didn't care if all they felt was its magical effects. Tonight, she would forget her scientific approach to everything and believe in magic.

He did not kiss her as he walked, instead choosing to study her intently. Morrigan read a myriad of emotions on his face--the most predominant was passion. But, beyond that, hidden behind his eyes was a searching, a longing, and an ache she could feel inside her breasts as if it was her own.

Chapter Five

Once back in the tent, Ualan set her before him. He lifted his hands to Morrigan's face, sweeping across the soft features. His eyes dipped to her breasts, heaving delightedly with her breath. A wicked smile came to his lips. It sent chills over her. Instinctively, she knew he was contemplating punishing her for trying to escape him yet again.

Slowly, he stalked her, forcing her to back away. Morrigan glanced at the bed, ready for him to take her. He forced her past the silken paradise it offered. She touched him, but he pushed her fingers away. Keeping his eyes fixed steadily on her, he continued to move her back until Morrigan's legs bumped into the edge of the bondage throne.

Ualan's wicked smile broadened. He moved his fingers from her cheek, down her neck and the beating pulse beneath her flushed skin. With a rip, he pulled her gown from her body, exposing her to his whim. Morrigan's nipples peaked, excited by his power. He didn't touch them, refusing to answer their beckoning call.

With a firm shove, he pushed her naked body on the throne. Morrigan gasped, unable to stand once he towered so commandingly over her. This was his game and he was in control. Part of her wanted to fight him, to resist. But she was weak. She was slave to his whims.

Ualan leaned into her face, his hot breath caressing her skin as he moved his lips just beyond her flesh's arching reach. The strangely erotic feel of smoothed wood, carved to mold into her buttocks, caught her by surprise and she gasped as it teasingly spread her cheeks.

Ualan's whispering breath continued lower, over her chin. It found a place to gush between her breasts. His lips drifted over a ripe nipple, teasing it with a feathery kiss that sent a shockwave of passion through Morrigan's limbs. She bucked off the throne, only to settle once more out of fear that she would anger him and he would stop his excruciating torment of her flesh.

His breath continued across her. Her neglected breast arched as he neared it, ready and waiting for its reward like the other had received. It was left wanting. Morrigan groaned, her hips pressing down on the throne. Her eyes sought his. Her fingers rose to grab his hair and force him forward.

Ualan held back. With the swiftness of a striking snake, his fingers curled around her wrists and brought them hard to the arms of the chair. He held them there as she struggled. All the time he breathed on her, the hot, feathery fanning of torment.

When she understood him enough to stop struggling, Ualan forced the heat of his breath lower, over her ribs, across her flat stomach, around her contracting navel. Her legs spread, wanting him lower. He held her wrists hard to the throne, making it impossible to fight. Not that she could. Morrigan tensed, her legs waiting for him to get just low enough that she could wrap him to her and force him to touch her.

To her agony, he did touch her. But it was not as she would have him. His tongue edged out from his firm lips--so slow, so distressing, so very painful to watch. Morrigan couldn't look away. Her mouth opened wanting the feel of his lips for itself.

With a tender lick that she felt in every concentrated nerve, he slid his tongue into her navel. Morrigan screamed, her body alighting with fierce excitement. Her legs worked, trying to find hold over his shoulder, only to be blocked by his arms holding her down.

Ualan's lick moved down in a direct path to her seeking womanhood. His tongue met the top arch only to circle around to the side. Morrigan protested, thinking she was about to die from the torment. His tongue darted away only to come back freshly wetted. It traced the indent of her leg. Morrigan tried to squeeze his head, trying to control the controller. Ualan growled, pulling back from her. Morrigan was instantly sorry for her actions and she tried to repent by letting her legs fall back to the sides where he'd put them.

Morrigan's eyes rolled back in her head. Ualan's hands left her. She didn't dare move. Keeping herself as he wanted her, she peeked from lowered lashes. Ualan stood proudly before her. The fur was pooled on the floor. The height of his naked member towered for her to see. He was shameless, waiting patiently for her gaze to make the journey back up his body.

"Are you ready to choose?" he questioned when she finally met his eyes.

Morrigan took in his athletic form with the expression of a hunting lioness. She didn't answer with words, hoping he would accept her stillness as a response.

His was a body formed of hard work and exercise, not enhanced by machines. There was vitality to him, a power and control unknown to other men. He was the proud warrior, the conqueror. And by the look in his eyes, he would soon be her conqueror.

There was tenderness in his expression and an aching she didn't understand. Gently, he leaned and kissed her mouth, rubbing his lips over hers in a soft hold. Morrigan couldn't help herself. She moaned lightly against him. Her body sang with the fire of his touch--so sweet.

Ualan pulled back and continued to study her for a long moment, his eyes taking in her every breath. There was so much inside his gaze that Morrigan had to look away. She couldn't understand the questions or the tormented emotions she found there. Her body was too weak to try.

Leaning over, Ualan picked her gown from the ground, stroking it several times in a way that made her wish it was her body he held. He then ripped the material apart, tearing it beyond use. Morrigan shivered. Without her clothes, she would not be able to leave him again. She was his prisoner.

Still caressing the material in his large hands, he came forward. His eyes stayed steady on his captive as he laid the material on her lap. Morrigan gasped as it brushed her heated skin. Then, taking a fine strip from the top of the pile, Ualan brought it to her prone wrist. With a few deft movements, he tied her arm to the chair.

When he had tied her other wrist in the same manner, he stood. His naughty smile of pleasure sent chills over her. Morrigan tried to lift her hands to stand, but the bonds were too tight. When she remained where he wished her to be, he nodded in approval of his work.

Morrigan watched, silent as he began to circle around her. Her head strained as she tried to turn, but he disappeared behind the chair.

"Where are you going?" she asked, breathless. "What are you doing?"

Suddenly, a blindfold was placed over her head from behind. Darkness surrounded her as he tied it over her eyes. She listened for him, trying to see where he was, trying to sense if he looked at her. Then, a soft crack of a whip resounded behind her head. Morrigan jumped, thrilled, frightened. Her heart beat in erratic waves. Her mind swam with raw emotions. The whips cracked again, to her side, smacking loud against the wood like a hand to the flesh.

Morrigan tensed waiting for the feel of a strap to her helpless skin. Her eyes closed beneath the blindfold. The whip snapped again and again. Each time she jumped, sure that it drew closer to her anticipating flesh.

Crack!

The loud snap came next to her arm, not touching her. She jumped, straining her arms against her binds.

Whoosh--crack!

It sung through the air to land behind her head. She jolted.

With each hit, her body grew more intense. The wood pressed into her backside--hard and unforgiving. Her body arched, dying from anticipation and fear. Then, gradually she felt a brush against her flesh. It wasn't the beating she had expected. Her mouth shot open in surprise. She could not see Ualan but she could feel the tickle of his whip as he dangled it over her flesh.

Achingly slow, it was dragged over a nipple. Morrigan whimpered, panted, cried out softly. The fight left her until she was completely under his spell. Nothing else matted but his will for her. She was tired of being in control, wanted to be free from decisions so she let him decide for her. Who wanted to think with the fog that was in her head? From beyond her touch-focused brain she thought to have heard him chuckle--a dark sound, dominating and demanding.

The whip tapped and stroked her flesh. It brushed her thighs, kissed her feet. Then, as he drew it away another smack sounded. A gush of wind blew around her thighs as the whip crashed between them on the wood. Morrigan moaned, liking the vibration this action caused between her legs. She stiffened, too scared to move lest she get in the whip's way, but eager for him to do it again.

Very pleased with her response, Ualan hit again. Morrigan moaned louder. He watched her body strain and tense and his eyes turned a subtle shade of gold.

When she did not protest, Ualan's actions became bolder in his game. With a light slap, he hit the whip to her calf. It stung the flesh but did not hurt. Leisurely, he slapped her other leg, moving to hit upon her thighs. The whip's hard touch brought the blood to her flesh, making it tingle and burn with excitement. Next, the whip snapped her stomach. Morrigan arched her breasts, wanting them to be next. She was not disappointed. The whip snapped her nipples, both at the same time. Its stringy tip was like the slap of countless fingers.

"Yes," Morrigan groaned, past embarrassment, urging him onward.

The whip snapped her breasts again, this time more firmly.

"Ah, yes," she said, no longer caring who heard her. Let the others hear her cries for once.

The whip struck her stomach, followed by quick successions to her parted thighs. The tips wrapped around her hips to her sides. Her hips jerked with each commanding blow.

"Ualan," she said.

Hearing his name on her lips, pleading for him to come to her, Ualan paused. It was almost more than he could bear. Unable to resist, he struck her heated center with his torturous pleasure. The blood rushed to the nub swollen with desire. Her hips bucked hard, spasming with the intense scream of a quickly approaching orgasm. Her body trembled. If he struck her again, she would continue up the rocky path of her climax.

But he did not strike. She was denied release. She waited, tense. Her body was poised. Her mouth was open waiting for that climaxing scream. Sweat beaded her flesh the longer she waited.

Ualan sat back to watch her. All Qurilixian knew this was to be a hard night, perhaps one of the hardest in their lives. Self-denial wasn't something that came easy to a conquering race. He wasn't finished disciplining her yet. Before he gave her the gift of release, his little bride would know who controlled her.

Sweat beaded Morrigan's body. Images and bright colors swam in her brain, carrying thoughts of forbidden passion, of thrusting men atop their women, of women riding hard atop their men, of nails scratching into flesh, of Ualan's fingers curling around her skin. Moisture pooled within her, wet and hot as her body begged for his touch.

Ualan tossed the whip aside. Kneeling before Morrigan, he lifted her weakened foot into his hand. Her body worked absently, trying to get the will to move but unable to. Ualan's hands found the flesh of her leg, caressing in long strokes. She shivered. His mouth lowered to her foot, kissing her toes before sucking one into his mouth.

His hands didn't stop. His mouth was insistently tender, soothing the ache he had whipped into her skin. Morrigan writhed, panted, sighed. She was beyond anything but the feelings he gave to her.

Ualan's lips trailed her flesh, both her legs, her hips, stomach, and breasts, denying their sweet centers. His hands followed--rubbing and stroking. His teeth bit lightly on her nipples, only to soothe them with his lapping tongue. Morrigan strained against her binds. Her head fell back, her mouth gasping for breath. She was speechless.

"Choose," he whispered as he made way to her neck. He paused in his task, his breath hard and heavy, giving away his matching torment. "Choose."

Morrigan struggled for breath. All she managed was a whimper. Ualan's hands continued a wayward path over her arms and then disappeared altogether. She waited, gasping for air. He did not return. Hearing movement, Morrigan discovered that he had freed her. She wound her hands up into her hair, pulling the blindfold from her features with an exhausted tug. Hungrily, her eyes searched for him.

He was not as she suspected. Sitting back on his heels, again dressed, he studied her, watching with his cool blue eyes through the slit in his mask.

"Ualan," she began in a whisper. Vulnerably, she closed her eyes, reminded that he was a stranger. She didn't even know his face. The words died on her lips unspoken.

Ualan left her there, waiting for her body to calm from its disappointment. It had been cruel to bring her so far and not give her the release she sought. He was willing to risk a thousand years in the dark dungeon for the memory of her passion laden skin, but he would not risk dishonoring his family name to claim her like he wanted without her permission and the blessing of the council of elders.

Ualan reached to smooth back a tear, curiosity shining in his confused eyes. Without speaking, he stood, motioning his hand for her to do the same. Grabbing a large sheet from the side of the tub, he wrapped her up in its warm depths. Next, he led her to the bed.

Morrigan was too weak to think. Her body could not take another of his punishments. She was tired. Lying next to him, she hugged the sheet to her chest. She lifted herself up on her arm to study his hidden face. He stiffened at her look. Lightly, she stroked the mask, wondering what mysteries it hid from her and almost too scared to find out.

But, she was a journalist and curiosity was her curse. She wished he would reveal himself, wondering why he held back from her, wondering why he denied them both what he had wanted too. Suddenly, she cursed, wishing she had finished her uploads like a good reporter. She honestly thought she'd have time to fill in the blanks on the way back. She hadn't expected Ualan.

He stiffened in question at the sound of her soft whispering of anger, but did not stop her gentle hand as she fingered the ties by the side of his head. His liquid gaze bore into her. She trembled and hesitated.

Looking him full into the face, she said, "You understand that I can't stay here with you. All the torturing in the world won't change my mind."

Ualan sighed in aggravation. He had not moved from his place on the bed. His chest rose in even breath. Neither of them noticed that the crystal still glowed, though not as brightly.

He studied her face, before tilting his jaw to her. Whispering, he insisted, "Choose."

"I have a life away from here," she continued, not knowing if he understood her. "Please, don't touch me anymore tonight. I can't take your punishments. I need you to leave me alone."

Ualan didn't move. His eyes grew sad, his breath shallow. Morrigan swallowed. Her life might not be perfect, but it was hers. Falling in love with a man like Ualan was insane, but it was an insanity she was feeling the pinching affliction of. It was hard to explain and rationalize, but she felt as if they understood each other on a basic level. He knew what she needed and had almost given it to her. When she needed to relinquish control to finally feel the depths of her pleasure, he had controlled her.

Better to be trapped away from this planet, than to be trapped next to him as a reminder of this night and these feelings, thought Morrigan.

Maybe she was still drunk from the wine. Maybe she was just too spent to think straight. She hadn't slept well the last several nights and it was pretty late. Aloud, she said, "You understand, don't you. Tell me you understand."

Ualan said nothing. Morrigan's fingers trembled. She pulled the mask slowly over his features. She was not disappointed. He was beautiful. His face matched his body. His nose was straight and strong. His cheekbones high like his people. Morrigan brushed a strand of hair from his enigmatic eyes, pleased that he did not stop her.

Touching his cheek with her palm, she whispered, "Do you understand?"

Slowly, a smile found his lips. It was a pleasant smile, not mocking or demanding, not passionate or harsh. Brushing the back of his knuckles over her cheek, he returned her gentle caress.

"Yes, Morrigan," he whispered, his voice soft. She could detect the slight tilting of his Qurilixian accent. His words were not stilted as before, but flowing with soft ease from his lips. Her eyes took in his face, devouring it to memory as she had his body. He closed his eyes, forcing her to relax next to him. An unexplainable sadness came over her, as she heard him whisper in acceptance, "You chose."

When her body began to settle and her heart to slow, she opened her eyes. Glancing at the stranger at her side, she saw his eyes were closed. He respected her wishes and didn't touch her. She was glad for it. Her body couldn't take those emotions again even if it wanted to and, right now, her aching limbs definitely didn't want to.

Ualan's chest rose in even breath. His body nestled beneath sheets, which molded to every naked inch of him. The light from the torches had dimmed by small degrees to a softened hue, but still gave off plenty of light to see by. Ualan was a handsome man, breathtakingly so.

Lightly, she moved her hand to hover over his unmasked features. They dipped to touch him, but hesitated as she drew them back. She could not risk waking him. It was already clear that she had no power to fight him off and, if she looked into his penetrating eyes, she might be tempted to stay for another round. Instantly, she looked to the bondage throne and shivered.

Ualan was glorious in his nakedness. He was carved firmly in all the right ways--from the intimate curve of his leg and buttocks to the strong man-arms and chest. Morrigan took a deep breath and held it. Everything around her was so surreal, like a dream. Any moment she expected to wake up in her own small cubical apartment on Earth, or in any of the various company space pods she used for travel. The space pod was more of a home to her than her own apartment was.

Looking around, she wondered what it would be like to live in such a place, with such a man. She doubted she could last on one planet, knowing that soon the wanderlust that had obsessed her since girlhood would eventually set in. And what would she do? Lay around waiting for Ualan to come have sex with her--or almost sex?

Though, in the short term the idea had merit, in the long run she would go crazy. She was a writer, a journalist. Her mind craved knowledge and excitement. Her intellect itched for facts, no matter how mundane they seemed to others. Her very nature yearned for more, always more. No, Ualan and this simple tent-sleeping life he led were not for her. She would just have to keep the sensations he caused inside of her as a memory reserved for lonely, deep space nights, when only the stars and endless distance were hers for company.

Sleep was too tempting to her troubled thoughts. Yawning, Morrigan closed her eyes and willingly let rest overtake her.

* * * *

Morrigan awoke alone to the soft humming of a bird. It was an odd sound, soft and long, and very out of place in her dreams. Before opening her eyes, she yawned, stretching her tired limbs over her head. She felt dead, as if she had slept for an eternity. Though her muscles were tight and pulled angrily as she moved, she was more rested than she had ever remembered being. There was a haze to her dreams, a haze to....

"Ualan," Morrigan whispered in surprise. Yawning, she opened her eyes, seeing that he hadn't been a dream. He was gone, but she was left in his tent. The torn strands of her dress were lying on the ground as proof of the night she barely remembered. The memories were muddled by a cloud in her brain. It was as if she were drunk, without the side effects of a morning hangover.

She rubbed her temple. The recorder stuck irritatingly to her dry eye. She tried to poke it free, loosening it with several blinks until it slid. Morrigan yawned again.

"Ualan?" she asked louder, her voice hoarse. She guessed he was gone. Morrigan sighed in heavy relief. She was glad he understood she was not staying. She had been worried he would make more out of their night together than he should.

Rolling her neck, she noticed a pile of fresh clothing laid out for her on the end of the bed. They were more concealing than her outfit of the night before. It was a two-layered dress, but looked more comfortable than the harem gown. The under tunic was tighter fitting and light gray. It was the softest undergarment she had ever had against her skin. Sighing, she looked around for her underwear. She found them ripped, so had to go without.

The over tunic's sleeves were long, belling around the elbows. The dark blue-gray material was magnificent, fitted at the waist and flowing out in the fashion of a medieval tunic gown. Silver embroidery edged the gown in an intricate Qurilixian pattern and on the bodice, in the center of the chest, was the emblem of the dragon.

Morrigan could understand how the rumors that the Qurilixian race was once from Earth started. There seemed to be much medieval influence in their lives--from their dress to their penchant for long hair. She vaguely remembered some of the married men having Viking-like beards and braids

Smiling, she slid the gown over her head. It was kind of Ualan to leave it for her. She made a mental note to thank him. If she was lucky, he would let her take it with her back home. She would like to have a keepsake to remember him by. Squinting, she fingered her emerald, and wondered if she had taken a picture of him. If not, she would have to--just for later.

Chapter Six

The three suns were shining brightly on the red Qurilixian soil and the council that had gathered in the morning hours to observe some of the newly married men. Now, fully dressed in their customary clothes, the new husbands stood proudly. It was a good day for them.

The brides were still abed. It was expected they would be absent this morning if the men had done their duty by them. The wine would have helped them into a deep, relaxed sleep--once sleep was what they chose.

The King and Queen frowned to see that only one of their sons had made it to the preliminary showing. But it was not unusual. Some of the other men were missing as well. Though this part of the ceremony was tradition, the elders let the absences slide.

Agro scowled through his darkened eyes. Ualan grinned at him. He'd have to remember to thank the man later for the fight, though he doubted his black-eyed comrade would think of it as a favor.

Besides, how could he not smile? He had spent the entire night with a woman who would share his passions and his bed. It was more than he could have hoped the Gods to bless him with. Since boyhood they were taught to give offering for a steady and beautiful wife. Not all men would find such a thing. He was truly blessed. In light of his pride, he could even forgive her hesitance in choosing.

"Lord Ualan?" called the council, waiting for his verbal confirmation.

Ualan stepped forward without his mask. His father, a large man of matching girth and coloring, was one of the center figures at the council's table. The man nodded at him to speak. Even though he did not smile, Ualan saw the matching pride in his eyes. He was very pleased.

"It's done," he stated loudly. A smile broke out on his father's face. The wind whipped Ualan's hair about under the gaze of the council. Raising his hand high to the council, he showed the glowing crystal and arrogantly bowed his head. Turning about, he showed the crystal to all. They acknowledged in silent approval of him and waited for the next man to step forward.

* * * *

"Rigan, it is time," Ualan called from where he raised the tent flap. Dipping his head beneath the opening, he went inside. He expected to see Morrigan still abed. She wasn't. Looking around, he realized she had disappeared again. The smile that had graced his features all morning melted with a wave of fury.

"God's Bones!" he thundered, storming out of his tent. His face took on look of a beast and his eyes transformed from blue to gold. His teeth grew slightly in his mouth, sharp and pointed. His head snapped harshly, his senses enhanced as he shifted dangerously in his anger. With a sound that was more of a growl, than actual words, he swore, "I will teach you, dear wife, once and for all that your place is by my side."

* * * *

The ship had left without her.

Morrigan cursed, staring up at the dimming twin lights of the Galaxy Brides spacecraft as it faded into oblivion. Glancing around the spot the ship had been, she frowned, seeing the imprints of its landing. She couldn't believe it. It had actually taken off without her.

"A true lady doesn't use such words."

Ualan stood silently watching her. Relief flowed through him when he discovered she hadn't run off like he first feared she might. She had chosen, but would she try to change her mind?

She had been easy for him to track in his Draig form. It wasn't commonly known that Qurilixian men possessed the gift of shifting. He'd changed back, as he did not want to scare her. It was learned long ago that new brides needed time to adjust before being told of this little fact. Usually, they had no problem with the magic arts or the mystics who practiced them. But show them their lovers turning into a beast with fangs and they went running for the horizon. Go figure.

When Morrigan turned around, her face was tight with worry. She shaded her eyes to look at him. He was dressed in a tunic that matched hers in blue-gray color and basic design. They had the same silver embroidered edges, only his patch was larger on his chest and his tunic was more of a long shirt that split at the sides than an actual dress. It hung nearly to his knees. Morrigan gulped. He was handsome, but there was something to be said for the loincloth.

"Good thing I'm no lady," Morrigan quipped, again turning to the sky. She shook her head, giving another curse just for the benefit of her listener.

All around them the light of the three suns shone. Morrigan thought she saw the beginning of a village at the base of the nearby mountain peak. It was hard to see any of it in the depths of the big-leafed forest. What people she passed on the way to the ship had nodded politely to her, seeming to study the dragon emblem on her bodice as she moved.

Ualan frowned, but let the comment pass. Instead, he offered, "You have no need to worry. Your belongings have been moved to our quarters."

"Our quarters?" She snorted. "Listen, buddy, I don't know what you think you are doing. I already told you last night, I am not staying with you. I am on the first starship out of here."

Ualan's brow rose at the challenge. All right, so she was still a little sore about her discipline. Perhaps he had pushed a little too far. The thought did not bring remorse, but a small smile he didn't dare show her. Her angry body could account for her foul mood. He couldn't blame her. And, being that this was the first day of their married life, he decided to graciously forgive her. Besides, if she had pushed him to that point, he would have been thundering mad. Thinking of Agro's face, he smiled. He had been thundering mad.

"What are you smiling at, barbarian?"

His grin widened. His wife was gorgeous in her ire, with her flushed cheeks and spirited eyes. She would do his family name proud. The Qurilixian people appreciated strength in character. He would just have to teach her how to properly channel her strength. It wouldn't do for her to constantly be scowling at him.

"Come," he said.

It was too much of an order for Morrigan's liking. She almost refused, but then the crystal about his neck glowed. She forgot what she was about to say. Her eyes became transfixed on it.

"They are waiting," he murmured, seeing the haze fall over her eyes. He looked down, frowning. His crystal was getting impatient. They had to finish it before it enthralled them both and they acted like fools.

Stepping forward, she took his offered arm. He began leading her to where the main bonfire had burned so low that it was almost out. A crowd gathered to watch.

"Where are we going?" she asked, regaining herself. She looked more at him and the crystal than around the campground.

"To present ourselves to the council," he answered.

"I can't. I need to find someone with a transport before that ship gets too far away to catch. Who knows when I will be able to book another flight to Earth," Morrigan rushed. Even though it was a protest, the crystal kept it from coming out too harshly.

"You spent the night in my tent," Ualan said, as if that should explain everything. When she frowned, stating she didn't understand what that had to do with anything she had been saying, he explained, "If you do not come this morning, you will dishonor both of us. All know where you were last night, Morrigan. And they heard."

Morrigan balked, fighting the blush that tempted her cheeks at the shameless jibe. She almost hit him.

"Can the council get me up to that ship?" she insisted, glancing back. It was completely gone, replaced by the green, cloudless sky of the planet.

"If it were to be done, they would be the ones to do it," he returned, seeing that might be the only way to get her to come along with him. Already they were late and his people were beginning to stare at their hesitance.

This pacified her some and she let him lead her forward.

"So do I just ask them, then?"

"No," he answered. "This is not the place. I must introduce you first."

Morrigan lifted her eyes to the platform. In the center of the standing councilmen sat one very regal lady in purple, next to a man in the same shade. To Morrigan's amazement, she noticed they both wore crowns.

"Royalty," she whispered. Ualan glanced at her. "I thought royalty didn't wear crowns here."

"Only for special ceremonies."

"Oh." Morrigan sighed at the smile he bestowed upon her. She was led to stand before them. Oh, that upload programmer is dead meat!

"Queen Mede, King Llyr, may I present Lady Morrigan Blake of the Earthen people," Ualan introduced, giving a bow. Morrigan, a quick study, curtsied. The royal couple looked her over carefully, their eyes shining brightly. Morrigan wondered if it was the atmosphere that made everyone's eyes look so liquid.

"You're late," the King said, studying Ualan. A worried frown creased between his eyes. "Is all well?"

"That was my fault, majesty," Morrigan broke in. She gave another curtsy for good measure.

Ualan glanced at her, his eyebrow rising. This was a public ceremony. She had not been addressed.

The King looked confused. Glancing at his wife, he questioned, "What did she call me?"

Morrigan noticed everyone was staring at her in confusion. Weakly, she explained, "Majesty is what we call royalty on Earth."

"Ah," the Queen said. She began speaking in her Qurilixian tongue to her husband. It was a soft, smooth language. When she finished, the King smiled in understanding. Suddenly, Morrigan realized that Queen Mede was a rare Qurilixian woman. She had to get a picture of this. She pushed on her emerald finger. Finishing her discourse with the King, the woman turned back, and instructed, "Proceed."

Ualan bowed again, taking the crystal from his neck. He handed it to Morrigan, who took it in confusion. When she just looked at him, holding the hard stone in her fingers, he instructed, "Smash it."

"Then that's it?" she asked in a hush, thinking that a perfectly symbolic way to end their 'relationship'. Her serious dark brown eyes watched him warily. "We'll be done with this?"

Ualan smiled at her, a truly breathtaking smile and nodded in agreement. "Yes, smash it and it will all be over."

"All right then." Witnessing his handsome grin, Morrigan was almost sorry she was going to end it with him. Lifting up the crystal, she shrugged and dropped it to the red earth. It landed but did not break. Then, Morrigan stomped on it with her slippered foot. It broke with the ease of glass, much easier than it should have. The gathered cheered.

Morrigan jolted in surprise at the sound. Her head and eyes became clear as a mist left her mind. Staring at Ualan, it was like watching a man emerge from a dream. Her body became sore, throbbing all over as if she had run a mile full-out. Her head buzzed as if she did indeed have a hangover that she could now begin to feel the effects of. She blinked heavily and began to look around, as if seeing everything for the first time.

Before she could ask Ualan what was happening, the Queen said, "Welcome to the family of Draig, Lady Morrigan. I hope you will enjoy your new home."

"Oh, I'm not staying," Morrigan said, in blinking distraction. Even her voice sounded more real to her ears. She blinked several more times, trying to get her bearings. "I have a flight to catch."

Ualan turned red. He could see the crystal haze had left her eyes. Now the real work of a marriage was to begin. The crowd began to titter with laughter at her words. The councilmen's eyes narrowed. The Queen and King shared puzzled looks.

Standing, the King strode over to Ualan. Looking down at the woman, he motioned, saying in his native tongue, "What is this talk of leaving?"

"It's nothing," Ualan said in the same language. His fists gripped in his embarrassment. "I'll straighten it out."

"See that you do, son," the King said, placing his hand on his oldest boy's arm. "I won't have our family name soiled by an unhappy marriage. There are those who wish to see our line ended and I will not grant them the contentment of seeing my house divided, even in my son's marriage to an Earth woman."

Morrigan understood the world 'Earth' and nothing more. It gave her hope. But seeing Ualan's angry face, took that hope away.

Taking his wife's hand, Ualan grabbed her up into his arms, scorching her senses in an all-claiming kiss that left no doubt to the crowd that he had indeed found a bride.

Morrigan was stunned by the public onslaught. Her hands beat weakly at the attack. Her heart raced to feel his lips move so savagely, tearing at her sensitive mouth. It wasn't the dreamy kisses of last night. Those kisses had been a sweet hazy paradise. This kiss conquered her from her curling toes to her dizzying head. When he let her go, she looked dazedly on the crowd, their shouting ringing in her brain.

Ualan bowed to the King, before dragging his dazed wife from the stage like an insolent child. Morrigan stumbled behind him, her lips tingling full of sensations. Without the haze of the crystal, she was confused. Her logic told her to yell, her body told her to leap and demand he do it again. Thankfully for Morrigan's self-respect, logic won.

Morrigan was led into the shelter of the nearby forest, glad to be away from the crowd. Led, was maybe too light a word. Ualan was practically dragging her stumbling feet behind him.

Strange yellow ferns passed under her trampling feet as Ualan followed what could only roughly be referred to as a forest path. Various woodland critters shuffled away in fright, strange creatures that Morrigan ignored in their haste. Blinking as a purple bird flew past her head, she tried to pull back.

Ualan, misunderstanding her jerking movements, thought she tried to escape him. He gripped her tighter.

"Ow," she screeched at him. He only walked faster.

Coming to a clearing by a clear cool lake of crystal waters, he finally released her hand. Spinning on his heels, he glared down at her. "What do you think you were doing?"

"Me?" Morrigan gasped. She pulled her injured hand to her waist. The beauty of their surroundings was lost on her. She only saw red.

"If you ever try to humiliate me in public again, wife, I will break your neck, do you understand?" Ualan growled. Fury raged in his eyes, threatening his body with a shift. He resisted the urge to change, turning away from her in his effort for control.

"I am not your wife! You drugged me, you accursed gardener! With that wine and the crystal! Admit it!"

He spun on his heels to glare at her. Oh, he was livid.

Well, so was she.

"Don't you dare to deny it!" Morrigan hissed. With red cheeks she rushed at him with a torrent of anger. Poking him in his very unmoving chest, she shouted, "I felt it as soon as I broke that crystal. What kind of sick people are you, slipping drugs on unsuspecting women?" Lowering her tone like a simpleton, she said, "Oh, here, take this drink, you'll like it," before finishing in a furious rush, "You'll only wake up nine months pregnant, married to a serving boy. But hey, he needed a wife."

Ualan didn't move.

With growing heat, she slapped the dragon on his chest. "No thank you, cavemen. Not this girl. I am on the first flight back to Earth and you can't stop me. You tricked me and--"

"You chose," he growled angrily, grabbing her by the arm and shaking her. His eyes were lava. "Your will was free. I did not trick you. The crystal showed me to you and you chose to be my wife."

"I chose to go. I told you that. You said you understood!" Morrigan screamed, trying to tear away from him and failing. Her eyes were close to spilling over with angry tears. She did not want to be stuck here on this backwards planet, forced to live in a damned tent.

"You chose to be my wife," Ualan stated. A fear overcame him, but he didn't let her see it. His kind only had one chance at marriage. If she took it back ... He shook his head. That wasn't going to happen. "You cannot take it back."

"Wife?" Morrigan spat. Despite her anger, he was devilishly handsome. Her heart skipped when he looked at her. The whole planet must be insane. You didn't get married after one night and less than a hundred words.

"Yes, wife," he insisted. "We have been chosen--"

"If I hear one more time that I was chosen, so help me...." Morrigan's words cut into him like a knife to the chest. She shook her fist at him in warning. Taking a deep breath, she said, "We are not married. Stop saying that we are! We aren't going to live together. I am not going to bear you children. I am not going to cook for you or rub your feet nor do any other of the mundane housewife task, you overbearing--"

"What was last night, then, if we are not married?" he asked quietly, very aware of her rising voice. His words were soft, but the hard razor-edge was unmistakable. He jerked her further into the trees, heading away from the lake. When they were in the confines of the forest, he leaned over her and kissed her.

It was a searing, probing, claiming kiss that shot all the way to her toes. Morrigan struggled, not daring to let him end the fight like that. Not again. This Morrigan wasn't drunk or drugged. Just as abruptly as he took it he let her mouth go.

"Last night was," Morrigan hesitated, finally managing to rip free of his hands. His taste stung her lips. "It was ... nice. But it didn't mean I was signing on to be Mrs. Caveman. I have a job. I have a life. It's a good life and it doesn't include you. I'm sorry, Ualan, but your crystal was wrong. Go dig yourself up a new one and next year you'll have better luck."

"Nice?" Ualan questioned in disbelief. He rolled his eyes to the tree branches, spouting out a lot of words she couldn't understand. By his tone, Morrigan guessed it was better she didn't recognize them.

She watched his stalking movements, momentarily distracted. Suddenly he turned to her, pouncing forward to trap her against a tree. The bark poked her back sharply, but it was more forgiving than the hard man pressed to her delicate breasts.

"Tell me you didn't feel it. And be warned, Morrigan, I will know your lie." Ualan's hand became bold on the front of her gown, rubbing at her in indecent strokes. "Tell me you weren't begging my name with your lips."

"I was drug--"

"Tell me you don't want me inside of you even now. I can feel your heat burning into my hand." To prove his point, he stroked her between the legs and she shivered. "Tell me you don't want me to take you right here, to end the torment I put into you last night. I saw your passion, Rigan. I saw how you liked to watch. How you longed for me to take you the same way. I smelled you as you nearly came by my whip."

"This is not happening," Morrigan whined in exasperation. Trying to sound reasonable in an unreasonable situation, she laid a gentle hand on his arm and pushed. Breaking up had never been so hard. Ualan let her go. Through her gulping breaths, she said hoarsely, "I don't want to fight with you about this. You will find someone, Ualan. Someone perfect who can stay here with you and bear you children and cook and clean and do everything your little barbaric heart desires. Someone who will know how to be a wife to you. I am not that girl."

"You chose me. The Gods chose you for me."

"No, you came to me," she said with logic. How could she fight cultural superstition? It was so frustratingly unreasonable. "All the rest is superstition."

"It was willed by the Gods. The crystal found you for me. You belong here. I will hear no more of this. Come, we go home."

"Ualan, don't. I will not be forced."

"When you took off my mask and allowed me to speak freely, you chose," he said. "You chose to be my wife and you chose to come to my tent. You were not forced to be with me. Insult me again, and I will not be lenient with you, wife."

Now he was just calling her that to annoy her. Morrigan sighed heavily, her patience almost completely gone. He was forcing her to feel too much at once--anger, desire, frustration.

"Your mask?" she repeated, her voice growing weary.

He nodded once, hard.

His words from the night echoed in her brain. Quietly, she said in sudden understanding, "Choose. You meant choose you, not choose a...."

She turned red and couldn't finish. As she hit her fist absently along her thigh, her eye camera sent a spark through her and she saw the image of him standing gloriously naked in front of her. She hit the emerald on her hand several times to get the image out. It was too late. It was renewed in her mind. Blushing, without the aid of liquor to stem her inhibitions, she stepped away from him.

Ualan took up her scent, smelling her continued desire for him. He smiled, knowingly. She might be fighting him, but she wasn't immune.

"It's a mistake," Morrigan whispered, unable to look at him without picturing him naked. Her cheeks flamed. She hoped he thought it was her anger. "I didn't know what I was choosing. Surely there are grounds for divorce if I didn't know or maybe an annulment of some sort? We didn't do anything together--not really."

Morrigan's throat let loose a sound of torment.

"If you will not obey your new law, then obey your old one. You signed a contract. That is why your people left you here. Now speak no more of it, I will not start an intergalactic incident over your misunderstanding. We are married, resign yourself to it." Ualan's chin lifted proudly. Why did the Gods curse him so? What had he done?

"I am not going to be ordered about by you," she spat. Why was he being so pigheaded?

"I am your master," he growled. He stopped to sniff the air. They weren't alone in the forest. "You will obey me."

"I will never have you as my master. If you were my master, than I would be a servant and this girl doesn't do clean. Find yourself a new maid...."

Ualan leaned over, not listening to her continued tirade as he snatched a green plant with a yellow center from the ground. He was at her side in two seconds. Morrigan gasped, stuttering to a halt as he took her arm in his large hand and shook her. When her head snapped to him, a scream of fear and outrage forming readily on her lips, he rubbed his fingers beneath her nose, crushing the little plant. Instantly, she was out.

Chapter Seven

She was the new maid.

Morrigan flinched, not daring to wonder who had changed her into the plain gray tunic and white apron she wore. It felt like she was out for only a second. But, when she opened her eyes with a gasp of anger and ready to fight, she was lying on the couch in the middle of a large open suite--without Ualan.

At least it wasn't a tent.

The home had a gorgeous floor plan with a lot of space. Morrigan frowned, wishing the man lived in a hovel she could at least tear apart and ridicule him for. Maybe it wasn't his home. It would make sense. Ualan the caveman didn't seem like the cultured, refined type.

The walls were of red stone, which were covered with blue and silver tapestries. Shivering, she turned her head to look away from the gruesome battle scene depicted on the wall hanging. She recognized the Qurilixians by their bulging muscles on one side of the battle, but she didn't want to think about the scaly, upright beasts on the other side, running from them.

"Let's just hope those things are a myth," she murmured. They would have to be. The Qurilixian men wore no armor in the depiction.

"My lady?" a servant asked, his gaze following hers. He tried to hide his frown of disappointment, but she saw it.

Morrigan froze, almost having forgotten about Mirox. She recognized him from the feast the night before as the servant with the scar across his nose. He seemed younger than the rest of the men, but was still respectably large in size. Sheepishly, she said, "Nothing."

It was a large room with high vaulted ceiling like a cathedral. At the very top there was a domed glass window, with a switch that drew blinds over it to block out the light of the three suns. It was the only window and the main source of light. There were torches on the walls that would fire up with a push of a button if more light was needed. They were kind of like lamps. Mirox explained that they had no need for lighting, as all but one day a year was shrouded in sunlight.

On the first level, where she found herself sleeping, there were two circular gray couches surrounding a gigantic pit fireplace in the middle. The couches parted at each corner so one could pass through. Blue throw pillows with the embroidered insignia of a dragon lay neatly on the suede material. The black grates in the center surrounded a fire that was left burning. Morrigan looked, but she couldn't see any wood in the bottom of it.

In the corner was the longest row of curving stairs she had ever seen. Climbing their marble steps, she reached the top, only to discover a huge bed. It was rectangular in design, set atop a large fur rug on the marble floor. A gigantic mirror acted as a headboard. Morrigan gasped, turning a little red.

The upper level was much bigger than what she had seen from the first floor. It pushed way back with its own smaller globe ceiling to let in light. There was a barren fireplace in the wall. It too was oversized. Looking around, she suddenly realized how large Ualan actually was. It made her shiver.

A black dragon was again embroidered on the gray coverlet of the bed. A hall led through a walk-in closet, half full of Lord Ualan's belongings. He mostly had tunics, many pairs of leather boots, and some vicious weaponry. The other side was empty, except for her bags. She slipped the ring off her finger and took the opportunity to get the itchy eye camera out before moving on.

At the end of the hall was a viewing platform. When she pushed a button, wide curtains swept back to reveal the mountainous forests of Qurilixen. The platform was very high, above a steep cliff. If she leaned to the side, she could see the platform where she had been introduced to the royalty. Funny, she had not seen this balcony from the ground. Next to the platform, the rows of pyramid tents were being dismantled. She quickly turned, not wanting to remember the night spent in the campsite.

The main level had three doors. One led to a bathroom, whose shower looked more like a rocky waterfall than a shower. Set next to the waterfall was a natural hot-spring tub, which she was told bubbled constantly with hot water and automatically cleaned and renewed its water supply. It had something to do with the mineral from the mountain the home was built upon. Mirox was happy to inform her that the natural springs were all over the planet.

The toilet she didn't even want to think about. It actually required the flushing of water to remove 'undesired waste' from the marble bowl.

Morrigan shivered. That was so twentieth century Earth--yuck! She understood wanting to live simply, but there were definitely some things it would be wise for this backwards race to adopt.

The second door led to a large kitchen. It took on the look of the rest of the house and did not have a food simulator. The kitchen had a marble sink with running water, a matching marble countertop--both in creamy white--with the black insignia of the dragon inlaid on the top. There was a stove, an oven, and a variety of appliances she would never know how to open, let alone use.

Again Mirox was right behind her, happy to inform her that almost everyone took their main meals in the common hall. Well, at least she wouldn't be expected to cook. Thinking of food had made her stomach growl in vicious agony, but the only thing her new 'master' had in his alien refrigerator was health food.

"What happened to the plates of chocolate," she grumbled, vaguely remembering the way the chocolate had melted in her mouth. Choosing a handful of oranges the size of peanuts, she looked at Mirox. "Have you ever had a problem with space parasites?"

Mirox looked confused.

"Never mind." Morrigan was too hungry to debate for long. It took awhile to peel the little fruits, but they weren't so bad. She left the peels messily on the countertop and moved on.

The last door led outside the home. It was locked, though she tried gallantly to open the iron giants. Again, there was Mirox, telling her the doors only opened to voice activation and her voice had yet to be programmed into it.

"That's not fair," she said darkly.

"It is for security, my lady," supplied Mirox, "so that none can enter without being invited."

"So if I set this place on fire, I'd die before they let me out?"

"Yes, my lady, if there wasn't anyone to open them for you."

"Stop calling me that," she growled darkly, glaring at her new prison walls in growing abhorrence. "I'm the new maid."

At that Mirox laughed. "I don't know what it is like on Earth, my lady, but here the servant actually cleans."

He gave a meaningful look at the mess she had been systematically making of his lordship's rooms as she explored. Lord Ualan's clothes were all over the floor of the raised platform, crumpled into a pile and tumbling over the stairs. Throwing dirt from a potted plant over the nice, clean marble floor, Morrigan smiled in satisfaction.

"Then I guess his lordship can just go ahead and fire me," she returned, throwing more dirt with a look of mischievous pleasure.

"Why would you wish to be set afire, my lady?" the surprised servant asked, not lifting a hand to stop her tirade.

"Stop that! I am not a lady. I am a slave."

Mirox froze, his face turning pale. Bowing graciously, he turned away from her with as much dignity as he could muster. His movements were stiff and Morrigan wondered what it was she had said to make him in such a hurry to get away from her. He shouted a command at the front doors and rushed out.

"Hey," Morrigan hollered, running after him in chase. She tried to get through the heavy metal doors, but they slammed in her face before she saw anything but the red wall of the outside hallway.

Frowning at the doors, she said to them sarcastically, "Well, I guess now I can deduce I live in an apartment and not a house, 'cause that weren't no front yard."

Spinning on her heels, she looked at the home. There was no getting out unless Ualan let her out. She sure wasn't scaling the side of the cliff from his room.

Smiling, she inspected her dirty handiwork. If he didn't want to let her go now, then she would just have to make sure he wanted her out by tomorrow morning. Smiling wider, she bet she could get herself evicted from this nightmare life by that very night.

Laughing like a vixen, Morrigan's eyes lit with her scheming. "Welcome home, my lord, and welcome to your new living hell."

* * * *

Ualan felt as if he was tossed into the bowels of a torin beast. The large herds of the stupid animals were great for producing meat and fertilizer, but could be used for little else. And they smelled vile.

Today should have been a happy day of relaxation and celebration and, most importantly, the releasing of some very severe sexual tension. Instead, it was spent trying to calm his nerves enough to face his little irritation of a wife. Just when he thought it couldn't get any worse....

Ualan sighed, murmuring for his door to open. Stepping into his home, he froze. It had been destroyed.

Yep, unquestionably the bowels of a torin.

Slowly drawing out his sword, his eyes first went to his couch looking for his wife. She wasn't there and he couldn't smell her blood in the room. Deliberately, he relaxed and painstakingly placed his sword on a low table by the door. The metal entryway slid shut behind him, silent and smooth.

His home looked like it had been ransacked. The couch cushions were thrown all over the dirt-covered floor. His clothing was wrinkled and trampled, and if he wasn't mistaken that was the coverlet from his bed bunched up on the nook dining table in the far corner. Closing his eyes and taking a deep breath, he silently muttered every black curse he knew.

It didn't help.

He snarled as he darted forward to the plant Morrigan had tipped over. Cursing, he repotted it and set it aright. Not too much damage had been done to it, but he was forced to tear down a few of its broken leaves. It would be at least a year before they grew back.

Just then, he heard his darling housekeeper splashing in the bathroom. Even in his anger at her blatant disregard for his home and his property, his nostrils flared in anticipation. The noise that left his throat when he stalked across the floor sounded more like the beginning roar of a lion than the voice of a man.

Coming into the bathroom, Ualan paused, disappointed. She wasn't in the hot springs like he had expected, but sat on the stone edge dipping her feet into the bubbling water.

It looked as if she had been there for some time by the way the strands of her hair plastered to her forehead and neck in little trails. Her cheeks were flushed to a slight red. She still wore the outfit of the maid, which he had leisurely, and to his greatest masculine pleasure, dressed her in while she was out.

Kicking her feet in the water, she angled her head as if she hadn't a care in the world. Ualan put his hands on his hips, his eyebrows raised in displeasure. Clearing his throat, he startled her on purpose.

Morrigan jumped, spinning around to look at him. She smiled sheepishly, her gaze took in his hard expression. She would have had to be a fool to miss the anger seeping in his eyes. She trembled and was almost sorry she had destroyed his home. Almost.

"This is a pretty swank pad you got here, caveman," she smiled sweetly. Ualan's eyes narrowed in warning.

"It was," he growled with meaning. Morrigan took her time stepping out of the tub. She wanted to believe she acted like she wasn't bothered by him, but in truth her limbs couldn't work any faster. Her heart stuck in her throat. Man, but he was a fine barbaric specimen.

"So are you rich or what, caveman?" she asked, blinking with her wide innocent eyes.

"Why does this matter?" Ualan grumbled. She had looked at him like that once before. He would not be taken in by it again.

"I want to know what I'll be leaving behind when I go," Morrigan purred, stepping onto a towel she had placed on the cold marble floor to soak the water from her feet. Carefully, she began placing her feet into his slippers. They were overlarge but warm and made of fur on the top. She pushed a strand of sticky hair from her head and waved her fingers before her face. "Whew, that thing is better than a spa treatment on Quazer."

"You aren't going anywhere, wife. You're staying right here where you belong."

"All right, caveman, calm down," she soothed. Her eyes flashed anger, but she held back. "But you don't know what you are getting yourself into."

"Do you accept my authority?"

"No," Morrigan snorted, hands on hips. "So, how much money do you have? I have a shopping spree in mind. I want to buy every frivolous thing I can get my hands on. Starting with a food simulator."

"I will provide for you. That is what you need to know," he said in distaste over her rudeness. Money was not a woman's concern.

"Hmm, so that would be no on the money then. Too bad, I need a loan to get me back to Earth if you don't have access to a bank base. Besides, you're not much of a catch with no dowry, are you, caveman?" she smirked. She couldn't resist calling him that. It seemed to irritate him so much. "So, what do you do for a living anyway, oh mighty poor one?"

"Quiet," Ualan ordered. He was distracted. It seemed the steam had also moistened the front of her maid's uniform to her body and her nipples were beginning to bud. If he just reached out and....

"What? You don't have a job?" she inquired, mocking him. His eyes darted up from her chest to stare at her in warning. "Don't tell me we live with your parents, ugh. No wonder you don't want to let me leave. You're not much of a catch at all."

"Enough," Ualan commanded. He let her think what she wanted. "You make my head spin, woman."

She shrugged her wide eyes seeming to say, sorry.

He wasn't fooled.

"Did you tell Mirox you were a slave?" he asked with a frown. She tried to slide past him in his slippers, but he blocked her escape. Thinking better of trying to plow him over, she stepped back.

"Yeah. What of it? I am, aren't I? You're keeping me here, forcing me to wear this uniform."

Ualan let loose a long string of Qurilixian curses until he saw her studying him avidly trying to memorize them for herself. He flinched and took a deep breath. He looked as if he wanted to touch her, but he didn't dare with his shaking fists. He wasn't sure he would keep them from strangling the very life from her. "Very well, then. If that is your wish, so be it."

Morrigan instantly grew cold. She had expected a fight, not agreement. His eyes were almost sorrowful as he looked at her, but soon his jaw stiffened and he turned away.

"I will inform the Queen of your decision," he said loudly over his shoulder. "Go grab your bags--if you can find them under this mess."

"Wait," Morrigan demanded, growing truly worried. She began to chase after him. Grabbing his large arm, she stopped him. He stiffened, looking at her hand before staring boldly into her eyes. Weakly, she asked, "What did I just do?"

"You declared yourself a slave," he said, giving her a long drawn out sigh just to torture her. Morrigan's gaze was drawn to his lips. "So I go to give you to the Queen. She will be pleased, she needs someone to cook and clean the castle. Though, I must insist you don't do to her home what you have done to mine. Slaves who perform badly are thrown to the soldiers. It makes for good sport and it keeps the men's spirits up. Though, they would be most happy to receive you--you being used to such attentions. The other girl they have is getting pretty … how should I put it … worn in?"

Morrigan turned pale. She searched his face. He appeared very serious.

"Is that true? Are you lying to me?"

Ualan cocked his head. "Didn't Galaxy Brides give you the uploads on our ways? How else are all the men to find a woman if we don't share the unattached ones?"

"I didn't get to them all," she said, thinking of how she hated cleaning and cooking and how terrible she was at it. She shivered. She would be thrown to the soldiers, she had no doubt, and being repeatedly raped wasn't her idea of a good time.

"It's called research, slave. You know, studying up before you take on a new task so you know what you are getting yourself into," he said, throwing her words from the night before into her face. The jibe was not lost. She balked. "Now, release my arm. I go to do as you wish. The Queen will want you to start right away."

"Wait! I didn't mean it. I don't want to be a slave. Do you have to tell the Queen about it? I take it back."

Ualan's back was turned to her and he gave a devious smile. He hid it before turning around quizzically. Looking at her in dispassion, he said, "You seem to take back your word quite a bit, slave. That will not please the Queen."

"I meant it as an expression, like we use on Earth. I didn't mean it as a declaration of intent."

"Sorry, I can't help you," he said, solemnly shaking his head. "You declared it to Mirox and he was duty bound to report it to the royal family. I am sure they already know."

"Ualan," she began in a desperate pull to his sleeve. Her eyes pleaded with him for mercy.

He waited for her to speak.

"Can't you help me? Isn't there something you could do?"

"Why should I?" he shrugged a large warrior shoulder. "You have given me nothing but headaches. Look at what you did to my home. I should be so lucky to get rid of you."

Morrigan glanced around, sickened with her actions. This was backfiring. Ualan began to turn from her.

"What if I fix it?" she asked, heartened when he again paused to look at her. His arms crossed thoughtfully over his chest, covering the dragon she found there. "Isn't there anything you can do to get me out of being a royal slave?"

"You can petition the royal courts, but that could take months," he mused thoughtfully. "With your ignorance of our customs, a pardon might be given."

Months of cooking and cleaning an entire castle! Morrigan recoiled, missing the vast amusement in his blue gaze. I'll be sent to the soldiers within the hour! I can't cook. What if I poison the royal family? Oh, no. I'll be hung for sure.

Ualan watched her face growing paler with each moment. It brought his battered ego much satisfaction to see her distress.

"Ualan," she insisted. Her face scrunched up and he could tell her next confession was causing her great pain. He widened his stance and lifted his jaw, not giving her an inch. "When I said I don't do clean and that I don't cook. I wasn't making that up. I really can't clean or cook."

His eyebrow rose, doubtful.

"No, really," she insisted. His gaze was studying her so intensely, that she felt as if she was on fire. She didn't know when it had stared, but his intoxicating man-smell was beginning to get to her. She tried to take a delicate step back, putting distance between them so she could think straight. "I have three maid units and a back up in case one breaks. Every meal I've ever had was materialized in a food simulator."

Ualan smirked, he couldn't help himself.

"I don't even know what raw meat looks like, unless you count a cow grazing in the field. I've never prepared a dish in my life."

"A woman should know these things, Morrigan," he said seriously. His gaze dipped to the cords working nervously in her neck.

"I know," she breathed, seeing her chance and taking it. "That is what I have been trying to tell you, Ualan. A woman who stays with you should know those things. I don't. I haven't the faintest clue. You don't want me here. You can't. Can't you just do whatever it is you need to divorce me and let me go on my way?"

"You seem smart, slave," he murmured, nodding in thought. Lifting his hand, he brushed a piece of hair from her cheek. She jolted in surprise at the contact, her body remembering more than her head cared to about his touch. Her skin stung. He drew back.

"Thank you," she began at the compliment.

"Smart women can learn these things."

Morrigan gasped, her temper flaring, "You rotten--"

"Tsk, tsk, tsk," he scolded. "I have yet to give you your last option, slave. Be quiet or I will deliver you and your waspish tongue to the Queen straightway. Let her have you and your ill temper."

Morrigan scowled, but bit her tongue. Grumbling, she asked, "What is it?"

"You can be my slave until the royal family will hear you speak," he murmured. "You would be allowed to stay here … with me."

Morrigan began to deny him, but then thought better of it. She would have to hear him out.

"What would I have to do?" she asked. Her question and its implications were very clear. Unbidden, her eyes turned up to his bedroom. She shuddered.

"No, little rebel. You will not be permitted there. The bed is for a wife. Are you ready to be a wife?"

Morrigan shook her head furiously. This man wouldn't take no for an answer.

"Very well." Ualan didn't bother to hide his disappointment.

"Then you would have me where?" Morrigan said, gulping. Her mind reeled with all the things a big strong man like

Ualan could do to her, in all the ways he could bend and lift her.

"Slaves are too low to take to bed. I would not lower myself. Honor forbids it. Unless you agree that you are my wife and I your master husband, then there is nothing I can do ... to you."

His meaning was clear in the heat of his gaze as he looked her over. The maid uniform seemed a little too tight and Morrigan's cheeks instantly flushed.

"So if I agree...?" she asked.

"You will only have to clean my home and cook my meals, unless you choose to serve me in other ways. What was it you suggested, Rigan? Rubbing my feet?"

It was certainly a better offer than the whole castle. Still....

"I told you," she began carefully. "I don't know how. What happens if I make a mistake? What happens if I ... what will you do to me?"

"I will punish you."

"Oh." Maybe a mistake would not be so bad. Better this handsome warrior than the whole Draig guard. "All right, I will do that."

"What?" he prodded, torturing her with his smug look.

"I'll stay here and clean this up. How hard could this one room be?"

"There is only one problem," Ualan responded, stepping forward.

Morrigan's sucked in a deep breath. Her head was forced back to look at him. He was so tall, towering over her. The warm scent of him overcame her and she wanted to fall into his deep chest and enfold into his arms. When he spoke, his words were low and sultry, as if he knew exactly what he was doing to her senses.

"You haven't asked me if I wanted a slave," he murmured down to her, giving her spine-tingling chills. "Your list of skills is very lacking. You might be more trouble than you are worth."

"Do you...?" Morrigan breathed, looking at his firm mouth. She began to rise on her toes, but then thought better of it and held back.

"Why would I consider it?" Ualan's breath fanned hotly over her neck and she shivered in response. "What would be in it for me?"

"What do you want?" Morrigan closed her eyes, waiting for his kisses. Her hands trembled with the effort it took to hold back. Without the mist of the crystal, she had no excuse to feel such a way.

"No," he mused, pulling away. Though he didn't hold her, she felt as if she would fall at his departure. "I don't know that you have anything I want."

Morrigan felt as if he slapped her.

"I will give you a trial, slave, because I do not wish to embarrass my name with your mistakes before the Queen." Stepping away from her, he took up his sword and put it to his waist. "Have my home clean by the time I get back tonight. Then we will speak more on it."

Chapter Eight

"Well," the King asked of his son. They had been waiting anxiously for his return to the hall. Mirox still sat, pale and worried, on the lower seats, where he had been ever since he ran to inform the royal family of Ualan's wife's charge. "Did she indenture herself?"

The main hall had steep, arched ceilings with the center dome for light. It was larger than the one in his room. Banners of the family crest lined the walls, one for each color of the family lines--blue-gray for Ualan, purple for his parents, and green, black and red for each of his brothers. Each had the silver symbol of the dragon. Lines of tables reached across the floor for dining. The red stone floor was swept clean and the hall was all but empty.

"She did," Ualan said. He had been incensed the moment he'd found out. For someone who claimed to know nothing about their marriage customs, she appeared to know a lot about avoiding wifely duties. However, that was until he had seen her confusion. His heart had relaxed and he was again able to breathe.

"By all that is sacred," his mother said softly. Mede turned her sorrowful eyes away from her son. Directing her words to Mirox, she commanded, "Mention this to no one, loyal servant, and go."

Mirox bowed, quickly running from the hall.

The Queen turned back to her oldest son. She was satisfied nothing would be said by the servant. She did not wait for Prince Ualan to come forward, but stood and went down to him. Touching his cheek, there was great sorrow in her eyes. "I am sorry, my son. There is nothing I can do for you."

"Mother," he leaned and kissed her cheek. "It is not over yet, and you have raised a warrior. Warriors do not run from a fight."

The King, who did not show so much affection, nodded in agreement and with pride in his son.

"She has agreed to be my slave," Ualan said. "And I am a hard taskmaster."

"What?" the Queen asked. "Why would she try to deny you only to indenture herself to you? Is she mad?"

Ualan smiled, as did the King who seemed to understand his son's thinking better than his wife did.

"I don't think she knew she was denying me," Ualan said.

"Then, by all means, bring her forth and let her be pardoned from it, if she will give no protest," said Mede, her color returning. She was relieved that her son wasn't going to be cursed to a lifetime of loneliness, for he could never find another wife.

"No," he said.

"What, you wish to be alone?" asked his father.

"No, let her be my slave, father," Ualan said. "Do not pardon her yet. This bride of mine has too much spirit. I would see some of it broken before I pardon her. She will learn to obey her husband."

"Well considered," King Llyr agreed. "It would not do for the family to be embarrassed by this woman's defiance of you. Between you and your brothers, this morning was almost too much. If you hadn't claimed her like you did, the other houses would besiege our gates and our people might have opened the doors to let them in. For if the future King cannot control his wife…."

Mede frowned and waved away her husband's words with a grimace. It was well known in the family circle that appearances were deceiving. His Queen as much ruled him as he did her. She warned her son, "Ualan, it is a dangerous thing you play at."

"The best things always are," he answered, kissing her cheek. She rolled her eyes heavenward at his overconfident smirk.

"Just be careful, son. Be sure you don't break her heart in this quest," Mede said. "Once broken, that organ will not so readily beat again."

Ualan nodded stiffly, not liking the words for the truth they held.

"I go to train," Ualan said, intent on exercising with his brother Zoran. Anything would be better than watching Morrigan as she bent over cleaning his floor. The image brought to mind many sordid ideas.

When they were alone Llyr looked at his wife. Shaking his head, he said, "I fear for the kingdom."

"Our son is a good man," the Queen returned, moving to take his hand. She looked lovingly at him, an expression she saved for these private moments.

"It's not the future King I'm worried about," he answered, kissing her soundly. After nearly a hundred years of marriage, they were still madly in love.

"Oh, I wouldn't worry about Morrigan Blake." The Queen smiled, secretly. "Our new Princesses are strong, but I don't think they are strong enough to resist a Draig."

"No woman who ever lived has been strong enough to resist a Draig." The King grinned. His eyes flashed a daring green as he leaned forward to prove his point.

* * * *

Morrigan's cleaning was almost as bad as her mess. Righting the cushions and hanging the clothes had been easy enough, but crawling around on the floor to pick up crumbs of dirt was killing her back. Suddenly, she wished she had spent more time watching the maid units, instead of just turning them on as she walked out the door. She really had no idea what those little things did. She just came home and her place was sparkly.

If it killed her, she was never going to make another mess again. And she was buying all her maid units puny husband droids to boss around.

"Urgh," she groaned, crawling on her hands and knees across the floor. She was trying to use her gown to sweep the dirt towards the plant. The hard marble was bruising her knees and palms, but it was the only way she could think of.

The muscles of her arms kinked, her neck ached, and her temples throbbed. This was definitely hell. Standing, she stretched her back. The floor still looked dusty.

"Water," she mused, knowing that it worked for counters. Going to the kitchen, she noticed the countertop was still wet. She figured it would dry on its own. Finding a bowl from the cupboard and filling it with water, she then saw some soap sitting on the edge of the sink. Uncorking the lid, she smelled it. It was nice and lemony. She shrugged and poured the whole bottle into the bowl causing instant suds. What harm could it do? It smelled clean.

When the bowl was full, she looked at it and then at the floor. Perhaps it wasn't enough. Just to be sure, she filled another bowl of water and carried them out to the front hall.

Seeing that the worst trail of dirt was before the stairs, she dumped the first bowl of water with a swoosh. The liquid went everywhere. Then, turning, she dumped the other bowl of water in the other direction.

"There," she sighed, proud. The dust was already lifting off the floor and disappearing in the water. Plus, as a benefit, the room smelled lemony fresh. "We'll just let that dry and it will be good as new."

Picking up the bowls, with a sense of accomplishment, she didn't bother to rinse them as she stacked them back in the cupboard. She was finished.

* * * *

"God's Bones!"

Ualan stepped into the water pooled on his marble floor and slid across the soapy surface, nearly crashing into his couch trying to right himself. Water soaked into his muddy boots and he cursed.

"Rigan!"

Morrigan came running out of the kitchen. Seeing the dirt trail his sliding feet made, she cried out, "Oh, I just finished that! Look what you did!"

The look on her horrified face was priceless. Ualan carefully waded through the watery mess heading for drier ground. He was splattered with mud from head to foot. He and the soldiers had been practicing swordplay with his brother in the lower swamps. It had been great fun.

"Stop!" Morrigan yelled. "You're getting it dirty!"

Ualan looked around at the puddle. Wryly, he said, "It is hardly clean."

"You, jerk! I spent all day on that floor!"

"All day," he asked, doubtful. It looked as if she had spent nary a minute on it, but to dump water on the marble.

"Ah!" Morrigan held out her hands. "Look at my hands. I have been crawling around on them all day, trying to sweep that dirt with my apron. I swear someone should invent a tool to make it easier."

Ualan tried not to laugh. Her apron was filthy, attesting to her words.

Thinking he didn't believe her, she lifted her skirt past her bruised knees and said, "See my knees are even killing me."

This time he did laugh, though he took full advantage of the view.

"I can't see," Ualan grumbled with a dark, sensual dip to his words. "Lift it higher."

Morrigan paled, dropping the skirt. She was not impressed with him.

"Look what you did," she commanded with a point. "Take off your boots."

Ualan looked at her, his eyes shooting sparks of fire. His anger had completely faded. She was just too earnest. He began to chuckle.

"Oh," she mourned. Her body ached all over and she was lightheaded from lack of food. A handful of grape-oranges were all she'd had to eat in two days. Turning to him, she asked, "You're probably going to blame your mess on me, aren't you, caveman? And look at you. You're filthy."

"Spoken like a true wife," he murmured with a secretive smile. Her face dropped.

"I am not your wife. I'm your slave, caveman. There is a huge difference."

He stayed quiet.

"Well at least to me there is," she continued. "Here I bet you treat your wives like slaves."

"Only when they deserve it," he said. His body was stretched with a good hard day of mock battling. That, and her beautiful face flushed red with anger, put him in a delightful mood. "And usually they are only made to be bed slaves. If you are interested, declare yourself my wife and then we can take turns being the master. I have some rope--"

"Caveman," she grumbled, glad when the single word stopped him from finishing the thought. She began stomping away, completely affected by his words and hating herself for it. Her hands flopped as she walked. "I don't care what you do, I'm taking a shower. And I am not picking up after you so you can just forget it! I don't care if I have to sleep with a hundred soldiers!"

Ualan smiled. It was too much. For the moment, he didn't care that his home was wrecked or that water was matting his expensive fur rugs. He could afford to buy a hundred more of them. He followed her.

Ualan put one hand on the bathroom door when she would slam it shut. Morrigan glared at him. She tried in vain to push him out. He stood, waiting for her to expend her energies. His hand was enough to stop her progress.

"That wasn't an invitation, caveman," she said at last, giving up on trying to force him out of the room.

"A slave never bathes before her lord," Ualan said, stepping past her. Sitting on the edge of the natural hot spring, he tossed his dirty hair over his shoulder in challenge. "But, she does bathe her lord."

It took a moment for his words to sink in. Morrigan shook her head and tried to run out the door. "Oh, no--"

Ualan caught her by her long hair and she gasped in surprise. Her hair was still tied into a knot. Frowning, he pulled her back to him gently. Morrigan huffed and mumbled under her breath about barbarians and cavemen and beating them all over the heads with clubs.

Ualan moved her so she was standing in between his massive legs. Squeezing her into place with his thighs, he softly combed his fingers through her hair, unknotting it. Morrigan was afraid to move. She could feel him stroking the locks. Her scalp tingled. By the time he had finished, she was breathless.

"Turn," Ualan ordered, his voice low.

Cursing herself the entire time, she obeyed, coming around between his legs. His eyes were level with her chest. Reaching over, he pushed the door closed, trapping her in.

Her hair spilled in waves down her shoulders like dark silk, framing her wide eyes and pale features. Her lips parted, begging him unwittingly for his kisses. She had a mouth that deserved to be kissed and often. But she had started this game and he was going to be the one who finished it as the victor.

"Undress me, slave," he bid softly. Morrigan was too enthralled to think. She had been itching to explore him with her hands since the moment she saw his half-naked body standing in the bachelor line. Biting her lip, she carefully drew her hands to his shoulders. She quivered.

Ualan could feel her trembling as she ran her fingers along his tunic. His body burned where she touched him. Her chest heaved with deepened breaths, drawing his steamy eyes.

"You'll have to stand up," Morrigan answered, her voice husky. Ualan stood.

Morrigan was almost sorry she suggested it. He dominated the bathroom and everything in it, including her. Licking her lip where she had bit it, she reached to lift his tunic. She pulled it over his head with much effort. He refused to help, even when she struggled. Seeing his naked chest, she faltered. When his hands came back down, he purposefully grazed her breast.

"Ah," she began in question.

"The breeches, slave, or I will have to send you to the Queen," Ualan said, thoroughly enjoying himself.

She lost her voice. She glided her fingers down his skin, flesh that was drying with the sweat of his excursions. Reaching side laces that bound the breeches to his waist, she pulled them loose. She didn't push the material down.

"Your boots," Morrigan whispered, doing her best not to look him over, and failing miserably. Ualan kicked the boots off his feet, followed by his socks. Flushing, she turned her eyes away and quickly pulled the black material of his pants to his ankles. Refusing to look, she stepped back. "There. I'll just get going now."

"You will bathe me, slave," Ualan stepped forward, running his hand over a panel on the wall. Instantly, water cascaded down the rocks in the shower, forming into a pool at the bottom. He stepped into the water, proud and unashamed of his taut nakedness.

Ualan closed his eyes. Already the sweet perfume of her desire was filling his head. This was going to be the kind of torture even the most war-hardened warrior might not survive. Opening them when she did not readily obey, he watched her. She was shivering.

"Come and rinse, the water is warm," he said, as he turned to lay his hands beneath the rocks by the falling torrent. He leaned against the stone, resting his neck forward to let the currents of warm liquid glide over his head. He heard a splash behind him but didn't move.

Morrigan looked warily at his back, refusing to take off her uniform as she stepped in. Every inch of him looked like it was carved stone. She watched his thick gladiator body. The gold band on his arm glistened in the light from above the waterfall. His bronze skin shone slick.

Reaching to his arm, she gently pulled the bracelet from his bicep and set it behind her on the floor. He lifted his arm back to the wall, rolling his head on his shoulders, and letting water fall and run out of his mouth.

"Soap?" she asked, panting.

Ualan smiled. Her voice was rough with the effort it took for her to speak. Motioning his head, he nodded to the side. Morrigan blushed, seeing the bottle sitting in plain view of them.

She grabbed it and lathered up her hands. Gingerly, she began to scrub him, running her fingers over his taut back and shoulders. Ualan groaned as she rubbed at his neck, easing the tension from him with her fingers. He felt the soaked skirt of her gown slapping the back of his legs as she worked.

She tentatively continued to move her hands over his form, touching, squeezing, and unconsciously testing the firmness of him. Already she was driving him mad and she had only reached his back. When her soapy fingers found his hips he almost jerked painfully. Eyes tight, body stiff, he let her work over his buttocks and down his legs.

Morrigan was enchanted by him. The texture of his skin fascinated her. The look of him heated her blood. Her lips parted, wanting to taste him. He didn't move to encourage her and she held back. She had to remember this was a chore, not a pleasure.

But, oh, was it pleasurable!

By the time Morrigan worked her way up, her fingers turned from scrubbing to caressing. They glided over him in long strokes, reaching over his legs and buttocks, up his sides, and along his arms. She couldn't reach his hands without dipping around to the front and soaking her gown completely.

Without thought, she followed her restless fingers to his chest, blocking the water from him with her back. It soaked her clothes and hair, plastering the velvet locks to her shoulders. Ualan's eyes bore into her as she worked over his arms and neck. The wet material clung seductively to her skin.

Timidly, she met his gaze, captured it. Her breathing deepened. She forgot who he was, where she was. All that mattered was the way he was eyeing her and the aching heat it created in her loins.

Keeping her gaze steadily on his bold, blue eyes, she slowly circled lower on his stomach. The muscles tensed, but he didn't move. She moved out to his hips, begging him silently to press forward, to trap her to the rough stone with his marble body. Her breasts arched, the warm water rushing tantalizingly over them, the rough material clinging to the heated points.

Having already gotten his legs, there was only one place left. She didn't look, but could feel the heat radiating near her centering hands. His eyes narrowed into concentrated slits, daring her to go on. She slowly moved forth. Gasping, her fingers glided onto his long, awaiting erection. The size scared her and she pulled back. Had he been that size the night in his tent? Why hadn't she remembered that?

"Done," Morrigan breathed. The feeble sound barely whispered above the noise of the water.

"You're dirty," Ualan growled. His devouring eyes did not look away, nor did they appear to want to. "Remove that dress and wash."

"You said that we … that slaves…." Her face reddened.

"Wash for me," Ualan ordered. He growled low in his throat like stalking beast. He inched slightly closer and whispered in a tone that was both deadly and exhilarating, "Strip."

Morrigan began to move to the side to obey. He lowered his hands on the rocks, trapping her.

"Here," he commanded softly, his tone ragged with promise. "Strip for me here."

Morrigan trembled, but she couldn't deny his eyes. Reaching to her apron, she untied it from her narrow waist. Drawing it forth, she leaned near him to throw it behind his back. It landed with a splat on the floor. His eyes moved to the gown, waiting.

The gown was lifted to reveal her naked body beneath and tossed aside. Her eyes dipped a little shyly before glancing up to see his reaction to her. She wasn't disappointed. His molten gaze moved to take in every line of her. The water coursed down her overheated skin. It did not cool her.

When he had looked his fill, he leaned slowly closer. Hoarsely, he ordered her, "Wash."

Morrigan blindly reached for the soap on the ledge. Taking some in her palm, she lathered her fingers. Gradually, she worked over her arms and shoulders. His eyes devoured her every move. Next, she scrubbed her face, leaning back to rinse it. When she could open her eyes, Ualan nodded down to her breasts. His lips parted and she saw his tongue lingering just beyond the inner rim of his mouth.

She again obeyed, looking down as she worked. It was a mistake. The proof of his male prowess was reaching for her. To his everlasting disappointment, she quickly finished the rest of her body and then rinsed, turning her back on him. Gazing at her firm backside, he nearly groaned at the torment of watching trails of soap move over the cheeks, down the crevice. He flexed his hands, wanting to let them grab ahold.

Without stopping to think of the dangers touching her would bring him, he scooped her tightly wrought, wet body into his steady arms. Morrigan gasped at the feel of feel him. Ualan's hands gripped her flesh to keep his fingers from exploring.

He carried her to the steaming spring before setting her inside the bubbling water. The warm water curled around her toes and simmered up her legs. Ualan reached for a bottle of soap and stepped in after her. Squirting the white, creamy liquid on his hands, he brought the soap to lather.

"You're still dirty," Ualan insisted, bringing the lather to her flesh himself. If she wasn't going to do a proper job, he would just have to do it himself. The hot spring steamed and churned around them.

Morrigan hungrily followed his lead, squirting some onto her palm as she began to wash him again. The soap glided over their flesh, aiding their searching caresses. Ualan lathered her hair. Morrigan's body sung with surfaced desire. Her fingers slithered boldly over rock-hard muscles, washing his locks for him as she explored. Pulling apart, they rinsed their hair and went back on exploring, getting more soap.

She rediscovered valleys and peaks with urgency. Her body pulled closer as she explored the length of his back, liking the way the soap made her nipples swish unhampered against him.

The agony of her longing was still imprisoned in her flesh, waiting for release from the moment she saw him. Her mouth kissed his thick neck. She let loose a light, feminine moan.

Ualan almost died, pulling her away. The slave/master laws were old and clear. He could not bring her pleasure. For as a slave she was beneath a Prince. But, she could willingly give it to him.

He lifted his soap-covered hand to her lips, running a finger across the swollen parting. Then, leaning over he kissed her deeply, showing her the soap was safe. The taste sweetened their kiss. She moaned against him.

Morrigan's hands became more insistent. They slid down his body, over his hips. She wanted him to be as urgent as she. She wanted him writhing in desperation. She wanted it to end.

At his hand's bold urging, her mouth tasted him, moving over his nipples, nipples that were sweetened by the soap. By the gentle force of his fingers, her kiss continued its way down his stomach. Morrigan dropped to her knees in the large bath. Suds drifted from her skin on the water. Her hands glided over his buttocks, grasping and squeezing in slithering delight.

Stopping, she glanced up at him. His eyes were closed. With a growl, he shot her an impassioned plea and lowered himself to sit on the edge. Taking her arm, he forced her kneeling body before him and pulled at her hand so that she could discover the heat of his desire. She boldly wrapped her finger's soapy length around it. The soap was like a drug in her mouth, exploding on her taste buds, urging her to again kiss his stomach.

Ualan spread his legs, allowing her closer, and with a firm hand on her shoulder urged her mouth downward to his heated erection. He was overconfident, unashamed as he drew the tip of his member to rub at her lips. One hand stayed on her shoulder, the other found itself winding in her hair. Her breath deepened. Her locks tumbled wetly around her shoulders. He locked his fingers on her head, and he pulled her lush mouth onto him.

Morrigan gasped, unsure what to do. But as the sugary temptation of the soap entered her mouth, she sucked the sweet taste from him. Ualan groaned loudly in approval. Firmly, he used her hair to control her, forcing her mouth to journey over his erect member. Morrigan smiled against him, reveling in the size and taste, addicted to the control she gained over him. She dug her fingers into his thighs. She sucked harder, learning from Ualan how to please him.

Morrigan was surrounded in sensations--the warm, gentle caress of water, the hardness in her mouth, the firm insistence of the hand in her hair. Ualan's passion was loud as he groaned and shouted without inhibition.

Sliding her hands, she grabbed tensely at his hips and began commanding his thrusts. She was lost to Ualan and she knew it. No other thrill compared to what he did to her. He took her desires, taught her how to fulfill them. Nothing mattered. She couldn't think, couldn't act beyond the will of his body and she loved it. With him there was no shame, no stopping.

Suddenly, he tensed, jerking her off before he exploded. With a moan of release, he spilled himself into the water. A contented growl escaped his parted lips and he lowered himself into the water to wash off. Morrigan's hands reached for him. Without pausing, he grasped her firmly by the hips and turned her around so she was on her hands and knees before him in the water.

Leaning over her shoulder, he gently ran his fingers down her spine. She moaned, waiting. Her body was fevered, ready. To her horror, he said, "Thank you, slave, for the gift. You can stay in my home."

When Morrigan looked back over her shoulder, it was to see his arrogant, naked body striding from the bathroom. She choked on a wretched sob. He had done it again.

Chapter Nine

The next few days did not pass in pleasantness. Morrigan refused to speak to Ualan, shying to the other side of his home whenever he was near. He didn't dare ask what she did all day by herself and her silently festering anger didn't allow for conversation. He knew she spent every moment alone, for slaves were not allowed company, aside from their masters and other slaves. There were no other slaves in the Draig keep.

After discovering that his wife's cleaning was definitely worse than her dirtying, he had sent a group of servants to go over his home. They were instructed to only speak in the old tongue so Morrigan sat quiet the entire time, not understanding them.

The truth was that he left his home to avoid her accusing glances. He made sure to send her food through a silent Mirox. The servant had told him that she tried to talk to him on several occasions. Ualan could tell the man hated not being able to respond in kind.

A few times he thought to sense tears in her wide gaze, but she turned too quickly for him to see them. Her pain was a chord of discontent within his chest. The crystal had joined their feelings so that their marriage may be blessed with understanding. He had accepted it by accepting the marriage. She had not.

His wife would never understand how hard it had been for him to leave her in that needy condition. Until she accepted him freely, she would never experience his feelings as he did hers. Forcing himself away, the sweetness of his release had been dampened by the bitterness of her unfulfilled desire.

He knew well her anger was just a defense, hiding the deeper rejection she felt in his betrayal. He cursed himself for his weakness in accepting her slave-gift. He should have known better. But when she kissed him so willingly with lips that were made for giving him pleasure, she had weakened him and had taken a good part of his sense. Now, it was all he could do not to go to her again. And, however much she was hurting, he was hurting tenfold, for guilt was a heavy burden for a warrior to bear.

"You missed practice again, brother," Olek said, looking down at where Ualan sat against a giant tree. Olek looked much like Ualan, with the same build and same brown hair, though he chose to wear his sides in braids. Olek's soft green eye were strained and tired, but he managed a wry laugh.

Ualan raised a hand in greeting, not bothering to stand or explain. The soft, murmuring rhythm of Crystal Lake's waters lapped nearby. The green skies were light and blew stirrings of clouds over the distance. The trilling call of the blue sofliar nesting overhead filtered down to them. Taking a seat beside his brother, Olek lifted a weed from the patch of grass and thoughtfully plucked it into his mouth.

"I see we are both cursed," Olek grumbled. "Lest you would not be avoiding your duty or me mine."

Ualan didn't even try to deny it. "My wife has proclaimed herself a slave. Since she is the one to indenture herself, I cannot release her."

"Yes, I cannot help you there. The law states clearly that only she can seek the royal pardon."

"She won't," Ualan said to the unasked question in his brother's eyes. "And I have no idea how to persuade her."

"Does she know who you are? Does she know it is you who can clear her?" the green-eyed ambassador Prince queried, curious.

"No, I have no wish for her to know, not before she admits she is my wife. I would not have her considering my royal birth. It would defeat the purpose of the masks. Gardener or King, it is the same to the crystal bearers."

"I think our King is considering never doing business with Galaxy Brides again." Olek chuckled, though Ualan could tell he was depressed. "For they have sent all his sons mor-forwyns."

"That they have."

"Is it true she announced she was leaving you right after breaking your crystal?" Olek asked.

"Woe that Morrigan should find a spaceport," Ualan grumbled by way of an answer accompanied by a weary nod.

"Woe that she found a spaceport of our enemy," Olek added. When Ualan glanced over in surprise, he continued,

"There have been rumors that our brides have not been seen within the castle."

"And who would dare to spread such a rumor?"

"Supporters of the Var would be my guess. Our father has decreed a festival in honor of his new daughters to coronate them. We have a week to convince them."

"I do not relish the idea of our brides meeting. I should not like to see them banded," the blue-eyed Ualan grumbled somberly. "I can't hide the fact that she is a slave. I can't bring her out."

"Ah! Our mother has started the rumor amongst her maids that she does it out of embarrassment for how she acted after binding you with the crystal. Soon it will be common news. She will be respected for purging her honor."

Ualan had to concede to his mother's silent tactfulness. Her diplomatic ways were a great complement to his bold warrior father.

"The King fears that the Vars have spies within our walls," Olek answered.

"And you?" Ualan asked. A week? Thinking of Morrigan, he grew dejected. It wasn't likely.

"I was to head to the shadowed marshes before the festival began. They were uncommonly bold," Olek admitted. "I could sense it on them. They plan something."

"Hmm."

"I know something that will cheer you, brother," Olek chuckled. "Yusef's bride turned his own blade against his manhood. He was honor bound to put her in chastisement."

Both brothers shared a hearty laugh and breathtakingly handsome smiles. Their merriment echoed around them in the trees.

"Did she...?" Ualan asked.

"No, just a nick."

"I heard Zoran's wife screams like a tree witch every time he's tried to touch her," admitted Ualan. "It is glad I am that he lives in the far side of the palace."

"Mother is quite upset by it," Olek answered, taking the grass from his mouth and throwing it to the water. He watched it float away. "It seems Zoran felt compelled to disfigure his wife and cut off all her hair. The castle is abuzz with the rumor and no one has seen her about."

"That makes no sense. Zoran would not shame his wife."

"Our father says he saw it," Olek answered with a shrug. "He's upset because of the celebration. My wife has these contraptions, I will see if one won't grow the poor woman's hair back for her."

"Yeah, if what you say is true, we cannot let more shame come to the family. We'll be lucky to get through the night without one of our brides trying to kill us."

Olek wearily chuckled.

"And you, brother?" Ualan asked. "What ails your bride that she won't have you?"

Olek frowned, moving to stand. He held his hand down and pulled Ualan up to join him. "I truly do not know. But I think I am the most accursed of us all. My little solarflower wants nothing to do with me. At least your women fight you. Mine won't even speak to me, let alone yell. How can I fight a battle that will not be fought?"

* * * *

Three days of silence was more than enough, Ualan decided, even if he wasn't bound by his father's decree to make things right before the festival. Besides, a warrior did not avoid battle and the time for strategic planning was over. His wife would come around, he would see to that.

Standing, hands on hips, Ualan could see his 'slave' did not feel the same way. She looked as if she would be perfectly content to keep lounging on his couch, staring at the round fire as if he wasn't there. She was still dressed as a servant, her hair tied into a knot on the back of her head. He frowned, hating the style for it kept the locks from readily falling into his fingers.

He knew she kept the uniform as a silent protest of him, since he had not decreed that she should continue to wear it and her own clothes were in the closet, untouched in her bag. The uniform was clean and pressed, but he wished for a moment she would let him buy her the fine dresses of a lady. In the village, the tailor and his seamstress wife had many bolts of cloth that would fit her coloring better. With a wicked smile, he acknowledged that it would also fit his very male desires to see her better attired--or not attired at all.

Ualan knew she felt him coming closer. Her breath deepened, but then caught and held, and the telltale beating of her pulse in her throat began to race. He reluctantly had to admire her determination. She was a stubborn woman. From what he had seen, most wives would have been complaining at such neglect, being forced to endure days of isolation and silence.

Morrigan tensed, momentarily surprised when Ualan didn't continue past her as he had been wont to do the last several days. She knew he was giving her temper time to cool and possibly punishing her with the silent treatment. What he didn't seem to understand was that she had navigated the stars for months at a time by herself with only a computer to talk to. Three days was nothing. She could hold out for a year. She'd done it before.

"Enough," he said in displeasure, still standing. "I will have no more of your silence, slave."

"Would you rather I yell at you, caveman?" she growled. Her eyes instantly flashed with heat and Ualan thought maybe silence was more golden than speaking. "Or just slit your throat while you sleep?"

Ualan, whose lips had been tempted to form into a smile, quickly scowled. Darting forward with supernatural speed to where she sat on the couch, he took her throat into his palms and squeezed. Morrigan gasped in surprise at the unexpected attack, but held perfectly still, refusing to show fear. Ualan did not take the life from her throat. But, she could feel the power in his single hand to do so.

"You dare to threaten your husband?" he growled, incredulous. His eyes flashed a dangerous gold. Morrigan's eyes narrowed thoughtfully, detecting it.

Gritting her teeth, she seethed in return, "How many times do I have to tell you, cav--ugh!"

Ualan's fingers tightened, cutting of her words and part of her air supply. Her knot unraveled and the silken strands of her dark hair spilled over his hands as she struggled. Unable to resist, her fingernails clawed into his arm, trying to draw blood but merely scratching the surface. He shook her. When she stiffened, flinching in fear, he loosened his hold. "Call me that again, wife, and I will have your head. I have dealt with your insolence, but no more. Do you understand? I will have obedience and order in my home."

Morrigan's lips trembled. Foolishly, she slapped his face, yelling, "I am not your wif--ugh!"

The hand tightened. He didn't even flinch as the sting of her hand imprinted red on his face. "Do you understand?"

When he didn't let go, Morrigan quickly nodded, though her eyes shot daggers. The hand softened, releasing her.

Morrigan pulled back, gasping and feeling her throat for injury. It was fine. Feeling the power of him, the steady control, did something to her though. Her insides melted and she almost fainted with her desire.

Ualan's eyes narrowed.

Taking several more breaths, she stated, "I am not your wife, ca--" She stopped herself in time.

Her words lacked the fire of conviction as her wide eyes stared at him. She saw longing deep in him. Or did she see it? No, his expression was blank, hardened. His eyes were glaring. Closing her eyes, she felt the wave of it again and it wasn't coming from her.

Unknowingly, she pulled him forward to her. Not with hands, but with her longing for him, with the desire he smelled building in her, beckoning. It had been so hard on her the last several days. After he left her in the tub, she had stayed there for nearly an hour, panting, raging, crying, plotting his death in a hundred ways. Her whole body craved him, more than the wanderlust, more than the adventure of traveling to distant galaxies. If he would just relent his stubborn ways....

Ualan was summoned by the tips of her angered nerves to her throat. He could see the mark of his hand on her and was instantly sorry for it. Closing his eyes, he lightly kissed her where his hand had been so rough, his lips naturally seeking to soothe her ache.

Morrigan gasped, but was concentrating so hard on discovering what that weird power floating around her senses was that she let him kiss her for the moment. His body leaned over her, trapping her beneath him without touching. He braced his weight on either side of her waist. She didn't move, frozen stiff as he gently brushed feathery caresses over the skin, comforting the dull ache. Her quivering fingers reached for his face where her angry handprint still glared.

His kisses drew along her jaw, light and airy. Morrigan sighed, forever tormented by what he did to her. He smelled so good. She knew he would stop before she found pleasure, hadn't he always? But that faint hope inside her told her to wait, that maybe, just maybe he'd finish it this time.

"I'm sorry if I hurt you," he whispered to the corner of her parted lips. "But you could be killed for threatening the life of … your master."

He had been about say 'a Prince', but thought better of it. She was too agreeable now for him to risk enraging her.

Morrigan kept her eyes closed, knowing that he was sorry. She didn't know how, but she could almost feel his heartbeat reverberate slowly in her chest. A fog overcame her brain like with the glowing crystal, connecting them, allowing them to sense each other.

"I didn't mean to slap you," she admitted honestly, before she could think to stop herself. "I was scared."

"I am the one person you should never fear," he whispered, brushing his lips closer to hers. It was a delicate truce and he was almost afraid to move lest he damage it.

"You're the one person I do fear," she said, her lips turning to speak against his. Her voice was whispery, as if in a trance. She sucked his breath into her mouth, feeling the connection deepen. It was almost like she could feel his desire. The truth rolled out of her unhampered. "You keep me prisoner."

Ualan sighed. Her words hurt him because he knew them to be true. She did fear him. How could he blame her? Every time she yelled, he yelled back, or much worse, he teased her into horrific, unrealizable passion and left her like that.

Ualan frowned, knowing what she was doing. She was trying to feel him as he felt her. She was trying to build the connection that would join their emotions together as only a wife and husband could. It would allow her to read his feelings, and with enough practice and years, she could read parts of his mind. He wasn't ready for her to connect, not like this, not with the rift between them. She could not feel his vulnerability to her. If she did, he would be lost. She would know how to manipulate and control him. Ualan had no doubt that this woman of his would do so mercilessly. If she got her way, he would be damned to walk the rest of his long years alone.

"You keep yourself prisoner," he said. "Say you are my wife and you will get your freedom. My home will be your home." He couldn't keep his kiss from firming against her mouth. "My world, your world." Another kiss. "My bed…."

This time he kissed her deeply, searing her, probing her, leaving him unable to finish the words. Morrigan gasped. In his touch there came an electrifying rush of emotions she couldn't process.

"What…?" Morrigan began to question, pulling back from him both physically and mentally. She blinked several times. The connection broke and the fog lifted.

Ualan knew she couldn't take the rush of himself he had given her. It was too much too soon.

"I cannot be a wife, Ualan," she said, her eyes honest and sad. "Even if I wanted to stay here, I can't. I have a home of my own, friends, a job I'm good at. What would you have me do? Stay and be a housewife? I can't do it, Ualan. My life would be hell and so would yours. Besides, you're so young and," she almost said handsome but hesitated. His brow rose, knowing the word even though it went unspoken.

"These duties can be learned. In fact, you will start training immediately with Mirox."

"What?!" she hissed, all traces of feelings, save for the most base, were severed between them. "Do you even listen when I talk to you?"

"I listen, Morrigan," he said softly and with a smile that was all devil. "But your words make no sense. You will be a wife to me, make no mistake. Your honor is of utmost concern for it will reflect on mine. So even if you don't take your vows to me seriously, I do."

Morrigan gasped. Ualan insolently winked at her and strode up the stairs to his bedroom.

"Caveman," she hissed under her breath, making sure the word was too quiet for him to hear.

* * * *

"I understand now, my lady, why you have enslaved yourself," Mirox said with a firm nod as he showed her how to sweep the floor with a broom. She was anything but an enthusiastic student and he caught her eyes rolling and wandering more often than not. He chose to politely ignore her ill humor. "It is a noble thing for you to do. You will make your husband's name proud."

Morrigan frowned at the man. He didn't speak to her for days, though she had desperately needed a friend to talk to--anyone who wasn't a seven foot tall barbarian with the sexiest blue eyes, and the firmest ... Argh! She was doing it again.

"It must be hard not being able to have anyone talk to you," continued Mirox, handing the broom over.

"You're talking to me," she grumbled. Morrigan made quick work of the floor, glaring at the marble the entire time--hating it for being dirty.

Mirox scratched the scar on his nose, not giving her ill humor any mind. Moving to sit on the stairs he pushed out his legs, crossing them at the ankles and watched her work.

"I was granted permission to speak so that I may instruct you," he answered happily. "It is a great honor for me to have been asked."

"Yeah," she mumbled sarcastically under her breath. Teaching her to clean up after her caveman lord--great honor. Instead, she glanced at him and inquired aloud, "So that's why you have been ignoring me? Because you had to?"

"Yes, my lady."

"Morrigan is fine," she dismissed absently, before angling the broom at him. "All right, this is finished. What next?"

Mirox hid his amusement. Perfection wasn't one of the lady's fine points.

"Mop," he commanded. He pointed to the water bucket. Morrigan looked as if she wanted to dump it over his head, but she went and grabbed it and brought it to him without comment. He smiled. She was a stubborn one, never complaining--well grumping, but not complaining. When she set it on the floor, Mirox said, "I must address you according to your rank, my lady."

"My rank?" Morrigan asked, whirling around.

He nodded.

Morrigan narrowed her eyes and probed, "So I have a rank? What? Am I nobility? Do I have a formal title?"

Mirox artfully avoided answering as he plunged into a long explanation of the fine points of mopping. Morrigan was soon distracted as she worked up a sweat, tediously sliding the mop where she had swept moments before.

"This really is hell," she muttered. "If I ever get my hands on Ualan's Gods...."

"My lady?" Mirox called, not hearing her.

"I think I'm done," she answered wryly in return.

* * * *

If she didn't know how to clean before, she definitely knew now and she hated it with an even greater passion. She had no idea that dust could collect on so many things. She was almost grateful she couldn't leave the house, because Mirox called several maids to tend to the laundry and to beat the fur rugs. It just made for one last thing she really didn't want to do.

"I quit right now," Morrigan said firmly, eyeing the toilet. "I did not spend six months dredging through the Luxes mudlands to clean that. Haven't you ever heard of a space-port? They clean themselves, you know. It's why we call it social advancement."

Ualan chuckled, hiding around the corner of the bathroom and listening to his wife and Mirox fight. He had been pleasantly surprised to find his house in such great shape. He had almost expected to see Mirox strung up by his toes over the fire pit and his furniture ripped to shreds.

"My lady," Mirox began.

"No," she said darkly. "I've done everything else that you have asked me to. I'm tired. You can tell your lord to…."

Ualan smiled as he came around the corner to look at her. Her face flushed red in embarrassment but she quickly caught herself. Even disheveled, she was beautiful.

Mirox bowed instantly, "My lord."

"Mirox," Ualan returned. "Why don't we let the slave take a break? She is looking rather worn."

"Yes, my lord," Mirox bowed, moving to leave. "I will be back in the morning, my lady."

When they heard the door closing behind the man, Morrigan frowned. "Don't do me any favors, master."

To Ualan's surprise, she grabbed the toilet brush and began scrubbing the porcelain bowl with a renewed fury. Hiding his laugh, he shrugged his shoulder and left her to her work. His wife had spirit, he'd give her that.

* * * *

When she came out of the bathroom nearly an hour later, Ualan was sitting on the couch with a book. To his surprise, he saw her eye it with a hunger. Then, seeing him studying her, she blinked and turned her attention away.

"Would you like to see it?" he asked softly, angling it towards her in hopes of a truce. It was not to be.

"I can't read your accursed language, master," she snarled. "And I have no wish to learn."

Ualan sighed. It seemed 'master' was taking the place of 'caveman'. Her lie was obvious. She had a curiosity that ran deep. He could see it in her eyes as well as feel it in her.

"I know you're interested, Rigan," he said affectionately. He motioned for her to sit next to him. "Take the book. I'll teach you to read it."

He might as well have offered to give her the blue plague.

"I don't want to read your stinking book," she hissed, though her gaze did dip to it again. "I don't want anything to do with you, master."

At that he grinned. Morrigan gasped at the openly seductive look he gave her stating that he knew the words were an obvious lie. She wanted a lot to do with him.

"Oh," she huffed, turning away to walk back to the bathroom. "You are the most incorrigible...."

The rest of her insult was lost and the chuckling Ualan was secretly glad he didn't have to hear the brunt of her words.

* * * *

Morrigan should have locked the bathroom door. She knew she should have, but the water of the natural spring was too inviting and by the time she remembered it, it was too late. Ualan was standing in front of her, his eyes narrowed in unabashed interest.

"Don't even think it," she hissed. Her eyes glared in warning as she sunk deeper into the bath, trying to hide.

"What?" he grinned, his eyes leisurely trying to see into the bubbling water.

"You will be bathing yourself tonight, master."

"No gift then?"

Ualan almost cringed at her heated look. He had expected it but he couldn't help himself. She was too beautiful when she was angry. Besides, with enough commanding he could wear her down. It worked on the warriors he and his brothers ruled.

Ualan shrugged, turning away from her. Morrigan's relief was short lived when he began disrobing.

"You're not getting in here, master. You can wait until I'm done!"

"It is my home, slave," he answered. But he didn't crawl into the spring. Instead he went to the shower, quickly washing away the day's work.

Morrigan's eyes didn't look away as he showered. Her body sang with liquid fire, remembering all too well what his skin had felt like to her hands. Ualan did not turn to her again. By the time he was finished, she had not moved.

Flicking his hand, he shut off the water and reached for a towel. Holding it before him, but not wrapping it around, he turned to her and winked. Morrigan blushed in mortification. He wiped off his dripping face.

"See that you don't boil yourself, slave," he said glibly, striding naked and wet from the room.

Morrigan yelled at the top of her lungs the only thing she could think of. "Stop messing up my floors!"

"Spoken like a true wife!"

Morrigan gasped, swearing if she ever got her hands on a knife, she would cut his sorry tongue from his barbarian mouth.

Chapter Ten

Cleaning was bad. But this, this was intolerable.

"I'm not wearing that," Morrigan said, brows raised, hands on her hips. "And you can't make me."

Morrigan looked at the costume the dance instructor was holding out for her to try on. If the outfits of the Breeding Festival had been bad, these harem garments were simply horrendous. From what she could see, the thing would barely cover her most private of parts--and nothing else. Was that string supposed to go up her...? No way.

Cordele, the dance instructor sent to teach Morrigan the traditional wife's dance of pleasure, looked in confusion at Mirox.

Mirox sighed. Turning to study his charge carefully, he said, "My lordship instructed that if you did not wish to learn our traditional dances today, that I was to have you re-clean the entire house--starting with the bathroom."

Morrigan balked. Dancing sounded so much better than cleaning again. She would do almost anything to avoid that task. Her muscles were only a little stiff this morning, thanks to the hot spring.

"I didn't say I wasn't dancing. I just said that I wasn't putting that on." Morrigan pointed at the skimpy outfit Cordele held. "I'll wear what I have on."

The woman lowered her arm with a shrug that said suit yourself.

Cordele flicked her hand over a unit on her wrist. Instantly Qurilixian music sounded in the front hall. She lifted her hand and began to sway them, along with her hips, nodding at Morrigan to do the same. The woman wasn't allowed to speak, except to issue instructions like a drill sergeant, which made for a long day of lessons.

"I don't know why he wants me to learn this," Morrigan said at one point to the watching Mirox. She dipped forward, copying Cordele. She had taken off her apron and rolled up her sleeves. She could see why the skimpy outfit would have been more comfortable on her heated flesh, but she was too stubborn to change.

"It is pleasing to a husband to have his wife dance for him," Mirox said as if such a thing were common knowledge. "You are doing very well."

"What if I told you, Mirox, that I don't really care about pleasing Ualan?" Morrigan laughed when Mirox actually fell off the couch in his amazement.

"My lady," he said as he righted himself. Shaking his head at her, as if she were an insolent child, he said, "You should not say such things, even in jest."

Morrigan's grin widened as she flicked one wrist and then another. Cordele nodded in approval. Cocking her head, she queried, "The other day, why did you say that being a slave was a noble thing for me to do? It doesn't feel very noble. I mean, I'm a slave."

"You purge your reputation, my lady," Mirox answered. Then, seeming to understand her confusion, he said, "The slave is the lowest rank. We much respect you for choosing it. It shows you have self-discipline and will make your husband proud."

Morrigan didn't think correcting Mirox would solve any of her issues, so she let the reference to her 'husband' slide.

"It is a cleansing time, a selfless time," Mirox continued, absently scratching the scar on his nose.

"How do you mean?" Morrigan asked, leaning to the right and arching her back as her hand circled above her. She then folded her arms about her chest and wiggled her hips. Her journalistic curiosities were piqued.

"Well, you deny yourself bodily pleasures. A slave cannot partake of the common meals, cannot be spoken to, cannot copulate or be given pleasure."

"You mean no sex whatsoever?" asked Morrigan, thinking of the tub.

Mirox wondered at her blush as she turned away and then back again. Cordele stopped the music, shook her head, and made Morrigan try the move again.

When they were again dancing, Mirox said, "To do so would insult the slave's chosen station and their reason for denial. It is our law. It is considered a great lack of honor to the person giving them pleasure."

"And what happens if you break this law?" Morrigan asked, a plan of blackmail forming in her brain.

"The person will be stripped of title and be made a slave themselves until they have repented and been forgiven. The master becomes the slave."

"And if the slave gives the master pleasure? Does the slave become the master?" asked Morrigan, completely enthralled with the custom she stumbled upon. If she could control Ualan and make him a slave … She grinned. There were a lot of things she would want her little slave to do for her. Oh, yeah, and she'd make him break up with her too. Pushing those thoughts aside, she forced herself to hear the answer.

Mirox cleared his throat, slightly embarrassed by the forward question and the look on her ladyship's face. But she had asked, so he couldn't deny answering.

"It is allowed," Mirox said. "It is a great honor for the master to receive such a gift."

"So they can't demand it?"

"No, they cannot," he agreed. Then, smiling, he said, "If the master is particularly persuasive, he can convince the slave to please him. But he can never force her."

"If what you say is true, then your law does not apply to royalty?"

Mirox furrowed his brows, not following her.

"I mean, if the Queen is displeased with her slave and can make her whore for the soldiers … what?"

Mirox chocked on his own spit, coughing at the very idea. Chosen women could never be made to whore. No woman could ever be made to whore.

Morrigan knitted her brows at the look he gave her.

Cordele clapped her hands for attention, secretly saving Mirox as she waved him away from her student. Morrigan shrugged, following a twirl. Mirox had given her a lot to think about. If she could just enslave Ualan, then she could make him let her out of the house.

Cordele smiled at her student. Morrigan was doing rather well, for a beginner. Her husband should be pleased enough with her efforts this day. With a little practice, she would be able to dance for him in the common hall for all to see. It would be a great honor for both of them if she did well.

It was probably a good thing Cordele couldn't share her thoughts with her student, for Morrigan was determining that dancing might be great exercise, but Ualan would never be seeing her talent for it first hand.

* * * *

She couldn't have been more wrong.

Standing, barely clad in the disgustingly revealing dance costume, Morrigan scowled in displeasure. It seems Mirox neglected to tell her that at the end of the lesson, she was supposed to give a little dance recital for her husband to prove she had been working.

"I should have chosen cleaning," she growled bitterly.

The costume was no more than a pink gem-studded bra and a matching hot pants that formed at sort of g-string in the back. A long veil was pushed into her hair to hide her backside--that is until she swished her hips to the side.

"I'm not going out there like this," Morrigan told Cordele who was smiling at her like a fool.

Cordele didn't answer as she placed a music bracelet on Morrigan's wrist.

Morrigan frowned. She was going out there. She knew she was. Ualan's decree had been clear and there had been just enough threat in his gaze, daring her to disobey.

Become the master, chanted Morrigan silently. Make him the slave. Then you will make a deal for your freedom.

Hum, maybe dancing would be a good thing. Already she knew that such an idea would be easier said than done. She would just have to keep her wits about her.

* * * *

Ualan's body was already tense. He knew this was going to be one of the longest nights of his life. He'd caught just a glimpse of Morrigan's shaking waist when he came home. It was enough to make him regret what he was forcing her to do.

She's got to learn her place is as my wife if we are to have any chance at a happy marriage, he told himself.

He was sitting on the couch, facing the center firelight. When Morrigan disappeared into the bathroom to change nearly a half hour ago, he had dimmed the lights and set the mood. He had changed into loose cotton pants with a drawstring tie in the front. The dark charcoal color was a nice contrast to the lighter cotton shirt he wore. His bare feet flexed in front of him, and his arms lifted to the back of the couch. If he had anything to do with it, she would be repenting her slavery tonight.

By all that was sacred, he wanted her. She haunted his dreams with the memory of her lush lips. She haunted his days with the persistence of her stubborn fire. Ualan was fast learning that he wasn't a patient man. He wanted her and he meant to have her.

Ualan nearly jumped up in anticipation when he heard footsteps. Looking over his shoulder, he saw Cordele and nodded. The woman smiled secretly back at him.

"She will be out in a moment," she whispered in the Qurilixian tongue. Her words were well pronounced, but the accent of her birth still carried with them.

Ualan nodded at her. His throat was too dry to thank the woman. He forced himself to hold still as she left.

"Should we get this over with?"

Ualan froze, forcing himself not to whirl around to see her. Lifting his hand, he motioned her forward with the tilting of his fingers.

Morrigan made a face at the back of his head, mocking him with silent curses. Taking a deep breath, she went forward. She wished she could have been more confident, but inside she shook. It angered her, but her eyes sought desperately for his approval. Standing before him in the center ring, but not too close, she waited. His eyes stayed with the fire, as if he was being forced to do an unpleasant task. His disinterest stung and made her waspish.

Become the master, she chanted silently. Make him the slave. Then you will make a deal for your freedom.

"Ready, master?" she murmured with what she told herself was false sweetness.

Ualan's neck almost snapped as he turned to look at her. Her words were husky, excited. He swallowed. Her round eyes were looking at him expectantly. Her lush lips were parted in even breath, tempting him to her. He held back. He had to.

"Proceed," he answered, keeping his tone hard. As she moved to stand between him and the center flame, his voice was lost. He couldn't have spoken more if he wanted to.

The firelight outlined her body, haloing around her barely clad hips, sparking like stars off the crystals of her bodice and panties. Her feet were bare, as was tradition. The little dancing lights hypnotized him and he stared at her chest and waist with an intense male hunger growing within him. His loins, which seemed to be in a constant state of half-arousal at all times anyway, gladly stirred as they hardened with lust to torment him.

Morrigan watched as his eyes flashed with liquid gold before he caught himself. He didn't move. His hard tone was just an act. She grew empowered. Soon, he would be eating out of the palm of her hand.

Ualan's feet were still lounging forward crossed at the ankles. His clothes were comfortable, hugging carelessly to his strong flesh. She never in her life saw a man who made clothes look so … so delectable.

Morrigan had the strangest urge to kneel before him and run her fingers up the strong legs. Making him her slave would have its privileges, she decided, so long as he finished what he stirred so easily in her body. Maybe then she would not be tormented by thoughts of him. He would be out of her system.

"Dance," he whispered, aware of the sparks between them. His arms stayed lounged over the sides of the couch. He gripped his hands to keep them there.

Morrigan smiled, she couldn't help herself. Running a finger over her wrist, music softly sounded. It was archaic in its primitive rhythms and she felt like she was before a sultan. At first she was a little nervous and her movements were stiff. But, remembering what Cordele had told her, she closed her eyes and imagined she danced alone. When her body loosened and she could feel the seductive music inside her, stirring up a primal passion, she looked boldly at Ualan.

He was frozen, his chest heaving in animalistic pants. As she turned away from him to shake her hips in undulating motions, his jaw dropped and his eyes widened in bewilderment. Her nearly bare backside peeked from the sides of the long veil. He gripped his fingers into tight fists. He quickly snapped his jaw up and loosened his hands before she could see his dumbfounded expression.

The music continued. When Morrigan saw she had Ualan's undivided attention, she slowly worked her way forward. A battle lit in his narrowing eyes, to match the look she gave him. A half smile curled his masculine lips as she danced within his reach. Twirling, her legs spread over his as she turned from him.

Morrigan hid her mischievous expression. It was time to add her own moves to the routine. She was suddenly thankful she had made friends with the exotic dancer she lived with while being undercover for a month in the Zigar complex. She had been investigating a secret romance between the Zigar president and his brother's wife. What a mess that situation had been!

Morrigan suddenly leaned over, tossing the long veil over her shoulder to expose her back as she dropped to a crouch. Knees to the side, she leaned over to dance astride Ualan's feet. Her buttocks came up before her head, making slow circles as it climbed.

Ualan's hands shot forward in surprise. He almost came completely off the couch. He'd never seen anything like it before. His mouth opened, wanting to take a love bite into his wife's very luscious backside. Her long legs were bare, clad only in firelight.

When Morrigan moved her way back up she turned, swinging her legs to straddle him so she faced him. Ualan's hands were crossed over his chest. His eyes were transfixed on her, eager to see what she would do next. The smell of her engulfed his enthralled senses.

Morrigan knew the song was nearing its end. She worked her hips in agonizing circles, moving her feet and hands in waves as she made the journey closer. Ualan's head tilted back to watch her. With a swing, her hips dipped low, almost low enough to touch him. Ualan straightened, pulling his legs in as she wove her arms near his head. Her dark eyes glittered with the power of an enchantress.

The music faded. Her chest rose and fell as she tried to catch her breath. Seeing his passion-laden eyes, she was as seduced by her performance as he was. Slowly, she lowered her hands from near his head and pulled to stand before him.

Blinking heavy lids, she said, "Is my master pleased?"

Ualan's answer was a growl as he grabbed her and pulled her astride his lap. Instantly, he began kissing her neck. His fingers traveled her spine, forcing her forward. Morrigan grabbed his shoulders, frightened by the passionate press of his body to hers. Ualan didn't feel her struggle, thinking she knew what she was doing. Her dance said she knew what she was begging for. And so help him, his body wanted to give it to her.

Ualan released her neck pulse from his searing kisses. Taking her hips, he slid her forward to press into the hot, throbbing length of him. Cotton and a g-string was no match for the fire burning in his loins. It shot a potent spark along her body, filling her with moisture and heat.

Morrigan gasped at the power of him.

"Do you feel how pleased I am, Rigan?" he groaned, undulating into her.

She gasped again. Maybe her plan had worked a little too well.

When she didn't speak, he insisted, "Do you feel what you do to me, slave?"

Morrigan gulped, nodding.

His eyes flashed with golden fire, smelling her desire like an animal in heat.

"Where did you learn to dance like that? Cordele does not teach such a thing."

"Zigar complex," she said weakly, too far gone to lie.

Before Morrigan realized what he was doing, her top loosened and fell forward to bare her breasts. He pulled the studded material off her with a deft flick. Her hands didn't move from his shoulders. His fingers took to her hips. Massaging them gently, but unrelentingly, he urged, "Dance for me again."

Morrigan tried to stand. Ualan shook his head in denial. He moved his hand to her arm to start the music anew.

"Here, dance for me here."

The hands on her hips pulled her forward so she was intimately close to his fiery erection. His eyes bore into her, waiting.

Slowly, Morrigan began to move her arms. Ualan nodded, pleased. His eyes devoured her, starting with her breasts. Her hips circled near his waist in a slower mimicry of what she had done earlier. Her body brushed up against his erection in teasing strokes.

"Oh," he groaned, closing his eyes in ecstasy. To her surprise and pleasure, he growled, "You will be the death of me, woman."

He began to move his hands on her before his eyes again opened. His body swayed slightly beneath her, dancing with her in a private rhythm.

"You make me burn, Rigan," he sighed. His hair fell over his shoulders. He moved as if he would take her breast in his mouth, but then held back with a bite of his lips, denying them both.

Unable to stop the words, her body too on fire to think straight, she begged shyly, "Make love to me, Ualan."

She stopped dancing, her arms falling to his shoulders.

With a rip, he tore at her panties, opening them at both hips. Tugging them from between her thighs, he watched her tremble at the caress. It would be so easy to lower his cotton pants just so and slide into her.

Taking her now naked hips, he felt her buttocks, squeezing them as he pulled her to him. Blocked by the barrier of cotton, he slid her along his member, letting her get a feel.

She nearly fainted.

"Is this what you want?" he commanded with a tempered thrust, his voice leaving no doubt who was in charge.

"Yes," she said weakly. Her heart hammered in her veins. She clutched his shoulders, letting him control her movements.

"You want me inside of you, don't you, Rigan?" he whispered to her hotly. "You want to ride me?"

"Oh, God, yes," she pleaded, not completely knowing what she agreed to.

"Then say it, Morrigan, say the words."

"I want you inside me," she said, near frenzy. "I want to ride you."

Ualan grinned, satisfied. Leaning over, he nipped at her peaked and sweaty breasts. Growling against her skin, he demanded, "Who am I to you, Rigan?"

"My master."

"Who am I?" he insisted again, biting the solid nub slightly as punishment when she didn't answer correctly. He licked the hurt right after with the full press of his soothing tongue.

"My master!" she called louder.

Slowly, he pulled her away from his arousal. Morrigan blinked in confusion. Her hips strained against his strong hands. Their bodies heaved for air as he denied them both.

"I am your husband," Ualan stated darkly. "Say it."

Her lips trembled. But she shook her head in denial.

"Say it! Say it and end this, Rigan. Tell me I am your husband. Say you are my wife and end this."

"You," Morrigan gulped for breath. Her body hated her before the words even got out. "You are my master and I am your slave."

"Oh, but you are a stubborn woman!"

Ualan growled, tossing her off his lap onto the couch. He was so angry, his body shook and his eyes saw seeing red. How dare she do that to him without the intent of staying with him? He didn't understand her.

"Me?" Morrigan screamed. Her face was flushed as she tried to cover herself. Her hands were not very effective blockades. Denied passion made her quicker to anger. "You're the one who can't take no for an answer. You are not my husband! We are not married! Why can't you understand that, Ualan? I know your ego is hurt, but it shouldn't be. I don't want to be married to anyone. It has nothing to do with you."

"It has everything to do with me. I am your husband!" he bellowed.

"No, you're not! You are a lunatic who can't seem to understand when he's being dumped. I want to break this off Ualan. I want to go home!"

"This is your home, Rigan. Resign yourself to it!"

"But I don't love you".

His yellowing eyes narrowed. His nostrils flared.

"What is this?" Ualan asked with deceptive softness to his words as he motioned to the couch. "Tell me you didn't feel it. Try to deny it."

"That's just lust, Ualan. Pure lust. That's all. Don't confuse it for something it's not."

Ualan gasped. It was like a slap of cold water to his overheated body. He swallowed, knowing if he heard any more of her words, he would strangle her. Whipping around, he stormed into the bathroom and slammed the door behind him.

Morrigan dropped wearily to her knees. Realizing that her maid outfit was locked up with Ualan in the bathroom, and that she was standing in the front hall shivering and naked, she quickly ran up the stairs to his room. Going to the closet, she began reaching for her bag when she spied Ualan's large cotton shirts and pants neatly folded on a shelf. Knowing it would cover her better than any nightgown she owned, she slid them over her body. They smelled like him and she groaned.

When she ran back downstairs, tying the drawstring at her waist, Ualan was standing before her. He snarled at her, brushing past her to go to the stairs.

"Ualan?" she began, not knowing why she spoke. Maybe it was the smell of him on the clothes. Or maybe it was the feelings that refused to die in her stomach and chest.

"You wish to remain a slave," he said, turning toward her. Morrigan gulped. Ualan saw the fear in her eyes but couldn't force himself to back down.

Morrigan ignored the statement, and whispered, "It doesn't have to be like this."

You make it like this, wife, he thought.

"You will cook for me tomorrow, slave," he said sternly. Morrigan gasped, knowing it was another punishment. "Mirox will tell you what to do."

With that he stormed away. His body burned, and he knew it would be a long time before he slept. Glancing down at his treacherous member, he growled. If his aggravating wife wasn't going to relieve him, then he would just have to see to it himself--again.

Chapter Eleven

The next morning when Morrigan awoke from her troubled dreams, Ualan was gone. She was glad for it. But, like he promised, Mirox came to her bright and early to show her how to prepare a traditional Qurilixen dish.

Well, saying he was showing her would have been too generous. The man was sitting in a chair watching her do the showing as he instructed like a culinary sergeant from hell.

"Ah, you might want to add more honey," Mirox said from his chair. He couldn't help but notice her furious mood as she slammed stuff around.

Morrigan wrinkled her nose, making a face he couldn't see. As she squirted honey into the bread, she felt she had been kneading for at least an hour. The dark blue dough stuck to her fingers and she grimaced. Now this was slave work. Mirox watched as she poked a face into the bread's rising surface and then punched it repeatedly with a balled fist.

"This is fine," she grumbled, lifting her dough-covered hands in the air from the bowl. Blue clumps dropped on the clean floor. Mirox frowned. Setting forward, he took a towel from the counter and swiped up her newest mess.

Morrigan was hurt. Her body ached, her mind was overtired and she felt as if she was on fire all the time. One thought of her wayward 'master' and she would flush and her legs would weaken like a simpering female. And Morrigan Blake was not a simpering female.

She was more than a little upset that he hadn't finished what he started--again. Every time she remembered begging him for it, she punched the dough with renewed vigor. She had actually begged him!

Make love to me, her head mocked. How pathetic was she?

Become the master, Morrigan silently ridiculed herself further, her mouth moving to unconsciously mouth the words to the countertop. Luckily, Mirox was turned from her. Make him the slave. Then you will make a deal for your freedom. Not bloody likely!

"A little longer, my lady," Mirox suggested, seeing the dough wasn't thoroughly mixed.

"They should invent a machine to do this," she muttered. Mirox tried not to laugh. Right next to her on the counter was a mixer, but Lord Ualan had been very clear that she was to do everything by scratch and that included mixing the blue dough for the full hour.

Morrigan sighed as she began kneading again, making faces as she absently hit at the dough. This time she knocked sugar into the bowl with her elbow. Mirox frowned as she quickly righted it. After brief consideration, she kneaded the sugar into the dough too. Mirox grimaced.

Morrigan decided she was going to try again to turn the tables on Ualan. She was going to seduce him. Then let him be the slave to her! See how he liked being made to bow constantly at her feet. See how he liked having to cook her meals.

"Maybe we should start over," Mirox suggested, still looking at the dough.

"No, this will be perfectly fine. I'm not doing this for another hour. Besides, I wasn't sure which spices you were talking about when I basted the ... wil ... wilddeor?"

"Yes, my lady, wilddeor," Mirox said, growing weary.

"It seems to be smelling fine," she returned, shrugging.

Mirox swallowed. He should have been paying more attention to her--hovering right above her every move.

"I think this is enough mixing. Give me the pan you said to put it in," she ordered.

Mirox handed it to her, not saying a word. His lordship should have informed him his wife knew nothing about cooking before sending him in to help her. Instead, the Prince had only told him to instruct her how to prepare a traditional feast.

Morrigan washed her hands beneath the running water, smiling gratefully when Mirox pumped soap onto her hands for her. He watched her pour the dough without bothering to level it. She then stuck it in the oven without a backwards glance at the meat. Sighing, he went pull open the oven door. The meat was browning nicely, so he shut it again.

"I think you should get a salad ready now," he instructed. His gut pulled as he tried not to think of the disaster her cooking could cause for him. He hoped Ualan would direct his anger where it belonged.

Morrigan looked at the refrigerator and sighed, not feeling like it. Mirox began pulling out the salad ingredients.

He tried to smile, handing her purple cabbage and lettuce before retrieving a knife He motioned for her to cut. She stabbed the cabbage with a knife and brought the tip back up with the skewered vegetable embedded on the end of the blade. She painstakingly pulled the cabbage off and stabbed it again. Mirox took the blade and began nervously chopping with apt fingers.

Morrigan smiled wryly behind his back. Her ploy had worked. The man was taking over making the salad. Slowly, she moved back to his chair to watch him.

"Does this go in the oven, too?" she asked sweetly.

Mirox almost chopped off a finger. Glancing suspiciously around, he said nothing.

It was only after he dumped both the lettuce and cabbage in the bowl and was tossing it together, that he remembered she was supposed to be doing the work.

"Come, chop," Mirox said with a sniff, "just like I did."

Morrigan picked up the knife and, dropping the pretense of not knowing how to use it, she began to slice into a ripe tomato.

"Ah, well done, my lady! You are a very quick learner! You should be proud!"

Morrigan smiled wryly, apathetically throwing the tomato into the bowl. She was picturing Ualan's face as she sliced. Curling her lips, she growled, "Oh, you have no idea, Mirox, no idea at all."

* * * *

Ualan growled while he threw five knives at an already marred post. The blades hit dead center in a perfect circle with the last one embedding in the center ring. The accomplishment only caused him to growl again as he went to grab the blades. Ripping them from their post with angry jerks, he marched around and did it again. The young warriors, who were neglecting their own practice to watch the outraged Prince, grunted in awe of his skill. None were so bold as to approach him in his dark mood.

"Ach," Agro grumbled, coming to join the spectators. "But can he do it with his eyes closed?"

Ualan turned at him to glare. "Can you with blackened eyes?"

Agro's eyes were still bruised from Ualan's attack, though they stared to fade to a purplish yellow. The beefy giant scowled good-naturedly. He held no grudge.

"I should thank you," Agro called, his Qurilixian accent rising with a soft burr. "My wife has insisted she administer her special medicine. Tell me, would yours do the same?"

Ualan grimaced and swore a black curse upon the man, throwing the knives with even greater passion. They embedded to the hilt. Morrigan would more than likely have his head first. If he closed his eyes he could still hear her begging him to end their torment. She had asked him to take her. But what could he do? He had to refuse them both until she relented her hard-headed ways. He would not let her live with an illusion of leaving him. He would never let her go.

Agro was unconcerned with the curse as he went to retrieve the blades. Stalking past where Ualan stood, he put even greater distance between himself and the post. Throwing, he embedded the knives in a snakelike line.

"Blackened eyes," he announced with great flair. The spectator warriors cheered in approval. Knife throwing was one of their greater entertainments.

When Ualan went to the blades, Agro joined him.

Speaking low so none could here, Agro said, "Tell me, Ualan, do you treat your wife with the same delicacy you have been treating these blades?"

Ualan glanced at him, confused.

Agro took the last blade before Ualan could pull it. Bouncing it in his hand, the giant warrior said conversationally, "If you haven't noticed, she be a might softer than these fools out here."

He pointed the blade meaningfully at the crowd. Ualan frowned.

"Let me give you a tip, from one surly warrior to another," Agro said, handing the knife hilt to Ualan. Ualan took it. They began to walk. "What is softer on the outside is usually even more soft on the inside."

Ualan sighed, hating to admit that the man's words made sense. He walked away. Seeing Zoran coming to disperse the men and command them back to practice, he nodded to his brother. Zoran nodded back.

"Hey!" Agro cried to the pleasure of the crowd, before challenging, "What about eyes closed?"

Ualan stopped. Closing his eyes before he spun, he blindly threw the blades before he was even fully around. Four landed in the pattern of a cross on the post, the last landed in between Agro's feet. Agro jumped slightly back and let loose a hearty laugh. Ualan slowly opened his eyes, knowing the blades had made their target before he even looked. With a quiet nod, he thanked Agro for his council.

Agro smiled slightly back before waving him away with his impish grin. Before Zoran could speak, Agro commanded the watching soldiers gruffly, "Ach now, you pups, back to work."

* * * *

When Ualan emerged from his bathroom, his hair wet and his body wrapped in a towel, it was to the sound of his wife's laughter. For a moment, his body soared with the noise. It was so light, so feminine and soft. It left him longing to hold her. It left his heart hollow for what he didn't have with her.

Looking up, he saw the dome curtains were closed, leaving his house dim. It would be approaching the evening hour, though outside the world would be cast with daylight, albeit, the hazier daylight of dusk and dawn. Drawing his hand past the torches as he walked, he absently lit them to cast a soft, romantic glow over the front hall.

Quickly moving to his bedroom to dress, he found he was excited to see Morrigan. Agro's advice echoed in his head. He would not have thought of a softer control over force. It was such a simple concept. Trust that a man already married would come up with it. Morrigan hadn't greeted him when he came in the door and he didn't even know if she realized he was home.

In one fluid motion, he tore the towel from his naked body. Yawning, he scratched his stomach as he went to retrieve his clothes. Choosing a relaxed outfit of dark blue cotton, he tugged the shirt over his head and slid the loose pants over his hips. He tied the drawstring at his waist, not bothering with the Earth custom of underwear. His house clothes were much more casual than the tunics he had been wearing.

His bare feet took the stairs two at a time. As he neared the dining nook, his stomach growled. His meal was already laid out for him on the table.

Mirox was the first to leave the kitchen. Ualan smiled at the man. If the smell was any indication, he had done his job well. His smile faded when he saw the man's expression. It was pale and drawn. Bowing before him, the servant whispered, "I apologize, my lord."

Ualan watched, quizzical, as the servant quickly left his home.

Unable to resist, he stepped into the doorway of his kitchen. To his infinite pleasure, Morrigan was bent over wiping crumbs off the floor. Her luscious backside was to him, straining beautifully against the soft gray material of her uniform. The passions of his dreams renewed themselves full force. He must have groaned because she jolted in surprise and spun around. Having been caught staring, he shrugged, grinning like a schoolboy.

Morrigan swallowed to see him. His eyes lit with fire as he unabashedly devoured her with his senses. For a long time she stood, breathless, unable to move away. He was dressed comfortably, looking so warm and inviting in the flowing material that hugged each curve just right when he moved. His hair was wet, brushed back away from his face and left to hang.

Ualan was the first to look away. Glancing around, he wondered what Mirox was so worried about. His kitchen was as spotless as when she started and it smelled of food.

"I put the food in there," she said needlessly. Her eyes wavered, nervously as she glanced away to throw the towel in the sink. Wiping her hands on her apron, she said with a shrug, "It's done."

When Morrigan looked at Ualan, all half-baked plans in her head fell flat. She couldn't scheme, couldn't even think to remember her name, or that she was supposed to be breaking it off with him. Damned if he wasn't a persistently handsome suitor. Only the fact that she had spent the last four hours cooking kept her from leaping forward and begging him to keep her. She would not spend the rest of her days feeding him for one night of mindless, world blowing, galaxy destroying pleasure.

Nope, it didn't tempt her at all.

Liar! her brain scolded.

"Join me." The request came out like a command from his hoarse throat. He could see her mind working on her transparent face. If she kept eyeing him like he was the main course, he might just throw her down on the table and indulge her.

He pulled out a chair by the table, waiting for her to sit. Morrigan looked at him warily as if she expected he would pull it out from under her. He didn't and she relaxed. Mirox has insisted on placing two plates on the table, but she wasn't hungry. She found that seeing food in its raw form and smelling it for hours was more than enough to take away her appetite.

"You wouldn't happen to have any liquor? Something that doesn't require me to lose my complete free will?" she asked when he stepped away.

It took him a moment, but Ualan realized she was making a joke. He grinned.

"I could really use a drink," she said, unable to help a small smile in return. There was something to the way he was eyeing her. It was almost … gentle. She'd have to be careful. What was he up to now?

Ualan nodded. Going to the wall by the kitchen he ran his hand over an offset stone. The wall parted and opened, revealing a bar. Morrigan gasped. Hopefully, she asked, "Do you happen to have a food simulator hidden somewhere in here?"

His grin widened.

Morrigan's breath was captured by the look and she had to turn away. If she wasn't careful he would have her on the floor begging foolishly for his attentions like a lap dog. No thank you. A bit peevishly, she said, "You should consider it. Your next wife might want one."

Ualan's grinned faded, but he didn't rise to the challenge. He had decided he would kill her with kindness, even if it destroyed him. He never wanted to see fear in her face again, not directed at him. He glanced at her neck, remembering how he had nearly strangled her. Before Agro pointed out his treatment of the knife blades, he hadn't given the incident much thought. However, now, he tried to picture it from her side. He had to turn away.

"What would you like?" he asked.

"Scotch," was the instant answer. "Tall glass, no ice."

Ualan grinned, not letting her see it.

Looking at his firm backside, as he reached forward, she insisted, "tall, tall glass."

Grabbing a bottle of Qurilixian wine, he turned, smirking to see her eyes on him. "How about this?"

Morrigan shrugged, rolling her eyes in tolerance, as she nodded. "Fine, so long as I don't fall in your arms...."

She stopped, glowing pink with embarrassment. She really needed the scotch, a full bottle that could knock her unconscious so she would be free of him. Ualan took two goblets from the cabinet before motioning it closed once more. The goblets were of a simplistically carved silver metal. Morrigan chuckled inwardly to see that the carvings were of a dragon. Ualan was obviously obsessed with the design. Ah, trust a man to pick out such décor--not that her company spacecraft was much better.

"Mirox mentioned I might have a title," Morrigan said, trying to erase her last words. "What am I considered then? Besides a slave."

Ualan swallowed, hesitating. He didn't look at her as he filled the goblets and set one before her. Taking a deep breath, he said, "A Princess."

Morrigan smirked and shook her head. She didn't believe him for an instant. "All right, I deserved that."

Ualan became wary. Why she being so agreeable all of a sudden? He'd have to be careful.

After their plates were filled, Ualan looked at the thick slice of wilddeer. Its color was a little off, but he could contribute that to the low lighting. When he hesitated and looked up at Morrigan, her face was so open, so watchful that he couldn't decline trying it.

Morrigan watched his face carefully for a reaction. His hair was drying into soft waves, framing his masculine features in the torchlight. She held her breath.

He cut a piece of meat and stuck it into his mouth. The first blast of flavor was the last. The piece came flying out, across the table, and over her shoulder. Morrigan jumped in alarm, instantly irritated.

Ualan didn't care as he grabbed up the wine and began gulping. Not only was it not completely cooked, but also she had put a whole bottle of liquid Qurilixian pepper onto the meat. No one ever used more than a drop. Finishing his glass, he grabbed the wine bottle and began to chug it down. Red rivulets went down his neck, staining the cotton of his shirt.

Morrigan would have laughed if she weren't so hurt. Staring at him, she hissed: "Stop it! You're just being dramatic!"

A string of curses flew out in his native tongue as he stared at her. His mouth felt as if he ate flames. Panting, his accent was thick, as he accused, "You're trying to poison me!"

Instantly, he was sorry for the accusation. The hurt that flooded her face at the words was palpable. Tears entered her gaze.

"I should poison you, you big baby! Fine thanks I get working my butt off all day to cook for you! I did everything Mirox told me to do--everything."

"Oh, yeah?" Holding up a forkful, he demanded, "Then, you try it."

Morrigan looked at his flushed face, then to the red wine trailing over his neck. Slowly, she backed up and shook her head in denial. Through stiff lips, she muttered, "No."

Taking a deep breath, he sat back down. Looking guardedly at the ruined main course that a moment before had seemed so promising, he turned to eye the bread. It was a little lumpy but didn't appear so bad. Maybe that would take the flame from his throat. Taking a slice up, he sighed.

Morrigan sat down and watched him, almost flinching in horror as he bit into it.

Closing his eyes as the most flagrantly horrific combination of sweet and bitter rolled over his tongue, he stopped chewing and froze.

"Well?"

Ualan sighed. Taking up his napkin, he spit it out more politely than the last time and studied her.

"That bad?" Morrigan asked, growing dejected. She looked at her untouched food and pushed it away in despair. Weakly, she said, "I didn't make all the salad."

Ualan wasn't ready to chance it. When he saw her face, he knew she hadn't done it to him on purpose. She looked a combination of horrified and dismayed. Standing, he threw his napkin down and held out his hand to her. Morrigan eyed it despairingly.

"Are you going to give me to the soldiers?" she asked, as she took his roughened palm in hers.

Ualan chuckled. Shaking his head, he said, "No. Come on. Let's see what we can scavenge from the kitchen."

Chapter Twelve

"What do you want me to make now?" Morrigan asked in dejection, as he led her behind him to the kitchen. She thought of her failed cooking attempt with mortification. Well, in all fairness, she had warned him.

Ualan turned at the question to look at her. His expression declared an obvious, not on your life!

"You can keep me company," he answered more diplomatically.

Not touching her further, he stalked forward, forcing her to back around into the countertop. When she was trapped, Ualan grabbed her by the hips and lifted her up onto the counter. He held her like that for a spine-crackling instant. He massaged her skin, before releasing her and turning to the refrigerator.

Morrigan tilted her head to watch him lean over. She was like a parasite, dying to cling onto him at every turn. Ualan turned and winked at her, knowing she peeked at him. Morrigan sat up straight.

When he returned to the counter, he began slicing fruit with the expert hands of a knife handler. Morrigan suspiciously watched him working at her side for a long moment, before saying, "So are you a chef, then?"

"I will let you decide," was his only answer. When he finished, he quickly mixed a stiff dough with his pinching fingers and patted it into a flat bread. Turning on the stove, he lightly toasted it. Morrigan watched, amazed at his ease.

"Who taught you to do that?" she asked in wonder to see such a large man so apt at cooking.

"This is a planet of men," Ualan said, as if it was no big deal. "We have to learn to fend for ourselves."

Morrigan merely nodded, though she suspected there was more to his skill than that. He actually seemed to like cooking. She took her time studying him. His strong hands were so precise and sure in their movements.

His light brown hair held streaks of blond, as if burnt by the sunlight. It fell forward over his shoulders while he worked. His bronzed skin tightened and pulled naturally with each movement of his neck. Not for the first time she thought that this was a man who was built by physical exercise, not created by expensive body-enhancing machines. There was a definite difference in the way he carried himself--so primitive and sure. His was the kind of body that would follow each and every one of his orders to perfection.

Ualan winked at her as he finished toasting the bread and went to retrieve a can of cream from the refrigerator. When he came back, he started heaping piles of fruit and cream onto the top of the bread.

Morrigan was lost. He amazed her. This was a side of him that she would never have guessed at. She expected him to yell at her for messing up his dinner, not turn around and cook for her instead.

Without thought, she lifted her fingers and brushed back a strand of his hair so she could see his face. "Ualan?"

His name was heaven to his ears. It was searching and tender all at the same time. Her face was vulnerable to him. She couldn't speak. She didn't have to.

"Here," he murmured, lifting up a piece of cream covered fruit. "Try it."

Morrigan blushed. He ignored her outstretched hand and fed her himself. Taking the fruit, he rubbed the cream sauce over her lips.

She held very still, watching his eyes as the fruit slid between her lips. He briefly followed it with his finger, dipping beyond the edge of her teeth to pull out slowly. Morrigan chewed. It was delicious.

"Yeah?"

"Mm," she returned, her words muffled by the bite. She dipped her finger into the cream about to taste it again. "Really good. You should try some."

It was all the invitation Ualan needed. It took Morrigan several blinks to realize what she implied. However, when his mouth came to hers, she was glad for it. Her cream covered finger pointed up, falling to the side so as not to land on him. Smoothly, he licked her lips of the cream, trailing his tongue over them with a painfully unhurried speed, all the time staring into her eyes to see her reaction.

Her eyes fluttered closed, and she gasped for air. After trailing the inside rim of her lips in the same fashion, he dipped forward to swipe a deeper taste. The exotic pleasure of the fruit came between them as he stole her breath. When he pulled away, his eyes sparkled with ancient mischief. "Delicious."

"Aah," came tumbling incoherently out of her softly battered, aching lips.

Ualan, seeing that her hand frozen in air was beginning to drip, treated her finger with the same careful exploration. His thumb moved to gauge her pulse as he stoked his tongue to her flesh. Instantly, it jumped beneath her skin. She couldn't move. Her breath caught up in her throat. When had his kisses become so tender? When had his eyes begun looking at her in worship instead of dominance?

Something had happened to Ualan the moment he saw her vulnerability at the table. Agro was right. His vixen of a wife wasn't as tough as she tried to be. She wasn't immune to him. In fact, looking at her now with her trembling gaze full of unsure feelings, he would swear she had been very terrified by his actions in the past, though she had hid her fear amazingly well. Being a woman who claimed to have had many men, this surprised him. He would have thought her experience could handle his arduous onslaught. It wasn't as if she had no idea of what she was getting herself into when she looked at him with her big, round eyes.

Were Earth men as inept as rumored?

Could it be she didn't understand the game they played as well as he first thought?

"Ualan?" she asked when he stopped kissing her hand.

He waited, seeing what she would do if he didn't prompt her. To his disappointment and further amazement, she shyly pulled her wet finger from his grasp.

Looking over his shoulder, she mumbled, "Please."

"Please?" Ualan whispered back, sure she was going to ask for him to continue. He knew she wanted it.

"Please, stop, I beg you. Don't do this. If you do this to me again, it will kill me."

"You have the power to end it," he whispered. Neither one moved. She pressed her hands into the countertop, refusing to touch his silken hair that spilled temptingly over his shoulders in waves.

Morrigan misunderstood his meaning. She couldn't ask him. To again say the words aloud would mortify her. It would force her to accept that she wanted him. It would leave her open to his continued rejection. It was a chance she couldn't take, even with the tentative truce that was between them.

Picking her up, he slowly put her on the floor, letting her feel the strength of him as he lowered her down. Sweeping her into his steady arms, he carried her to the couch before the dim fire.

"Please," Morrigan begged, too weak to jump up and fight. She didn't know what she was asking of him. Please kiss me. Please stop. Please just let me go home. Please keep me prisoner forever.

"I cannot give you that, slave," Ualan said, seeing her ache and feeling it tenfold. He lowered her onto the suede cushions that had been her bed since her arrival to his home, only to sit next to her with distance between their bodies. "Not until you are pardoned. It is impossible."

"You mean you don't want to be my slave, don't you?" she whispered, curling her feet under her thighs.

"You're right, I would not indenture myself to you like that," he returned. Their words were softly spoken, without their usual malice. "I would dishonor us both, and that I will not permit."

"You have to always be the master," she mused, managing a wry smile. Her eyes were sad.

"Is that so bad?" Ualan asked, his Qurilixian accent rolling in a soft burr to wash over her. "Do you not wish for a husband who can make you proud? Men who are ruled too easily by women are not real men. Such a man could not protect you, provide for you, give you strong sons."

The last was rumbled out with an astonishing seriousness. Her entire being quaked. He did not relent. His eyes began to glow gold in the light. Morrigan felt as if the liquid depths were more than just a reflection of the fire.

"Tell me, Rigan, would you be proud to have a weak man as husband? A man who would hide behind your skirts when danger struck? A man whose sword arm would quiver at the first sign of battle? Would such a man bring you honor? Would he make you proud?"

Morrigan shook her head in denial. No words came out of her opened mouth.

"Then why do you resist your destiny? Why do you resist us? Do you think I would dishonor you in such a way? Do you need me to prove my worth to you?"

To Morrigan, it was a stupid question.

"Ualan, I know your honor is not lacking and with the right woman I know you would make a dutiful...." His look narrowed. "No, let me say this. I know you would make a wonderful husband. But I don't think this is my destiny. These last days should prove we are not meant to...." She paused. "I have a life...."

How could she explain?

"You mention this life and yet you do not live it. Why did you agree to be a bride?"

Morrigan wasn't sure how, but he had moved closer to her. She could feel his heat, smell his scent. It was as if he were in her head, making her answer truthfully.

"I wasn't ... I didn't...." Morrigan tried to pull away. "It's not like that."

"What is this job you hold so dear?" he inquired, frowning slightly as she backed up. Easily, he edged forward.

"It's ... it's freedom. How can you expect me to give that up to be your sla--?"

"Wife," he inserted firmly.

"Either way, Ualan, you would want me molded to your will--cooking, cleaning. It will drive me insane to be a housewife. I need more than that. I need...."

"Marriage is about compromise, Rigan. If you promise to try, I will promise to honor you as you are. A wife can enslave her husband in other ways. You do not need to be named my master."

He smiled, devilish and handsome. The idea had plenty of merit to Ualan, who instantly had visions of being strapped to his bed and at her mercy.

Morrigan was just confused. But his smile held enough hidden meaning to make her shiver. Enslavement? Is that what marriage was to him?

"No," he answered, not needing her to speak the words. He was focused on her feelings. It was a new sensation to him, to be able to feel someone so closely and purely as if both drew the same breath.

Morrigan blinked. The walls inside her heart might have had cracks in the mortar, but the bricks could still hold. "I didn't say anything."

"You didn't have to, Rigan." Ualan leaned back.

"Will you let me go? If I truly wanted it, will you let me go?"

"No." He didn't even need time to consider. "Never. We were chosen for each other."

Morrigan stared at him, wondering how chosen they would be in a few years when he grew tired of her independent ways. How would he feel after she'd spent every second of a week on a writing binge, forgetting to eat and sleep? How about in forty years when her looks were fading and her body was falling and he no longer could desire her? Or when she was thick with his sons, sore and bloated and emitting strange smells as she heard pregnant women often did? Where would his attentions be then? And what would she be left with?

Her face turned hard and he could feel her pain like it was his own.

"Then I have no say?" she asked.

"Not in this. Knowing or not, you bound yourself to me. It cannot be undone," he allowed. If she left him, he would be alone. Not even if he wished for it, could it be taken back. He wasn't ready to give her up and risk it.

"Why did you torture me that night in the tent?" she asked, suddenly having to know. If she were to agree to his role for her, then she had to have this one question answered. She already knew that in the tub he could not return her pleasure. But what about the tent? If she allowed him to get close again, she had to know he wouldn't keep hurting her.

"Torture?" he asked, perplexed by her choice of words.

"I understand the other night in the bath," she said. Instantly a blush lit her features, but she swallowed it back. "But why in the tent? Why was I being punished?"

"I thought you wanted me to." Ualan furrowed his brows in thought. "Amongst my people, when a woman is chosen, it is up to the man to prove himself worthy. We aren't allowed to use our words until the mask is lifted and we are deemed worthy of speaking, because--"

"Actions speak louder than words," she finished wryly, "and talk is cheap."

"Yes, precisely," he nodded, glad she understood. "And when you did not remove my mask and accept me, it was up to me to continue. If you would have taken my mask off right away, we could have talked through the night, ate, bathed, whatever you wished. Breeding is not allowed during the festival. It is a sign of bad luck if you do. It angers the Gods and is bad for the marriage. Though we would join eventually, essentially we were still strangers until the crystal was broken."

"But I heard the others in their tents," she gulped. This time she did hide her face. She was remembering the couple before the throne, to her everlasting mortification.

"Certain discoveries are allowed," he grinned. Reading her thoughts, he said, "And married couples are not hampered by this rule."

"Oh," she mumbled, wrinkling her nose.

"You have no need for this embarrassment," he said. He stroked the dark hair back from her face with his hand. The bulk of it was still tied into a knot and he frowned, making a mental note to get her something prettier to hold back her locks. "You can say anything to me, Rigan. You can ask me anything. I will always be honest with you." When she made a sound that said she highly doubted it, he added, "That night was torture for me, too."

It was a good explanation and made sense. From what she knew about his culture, it fit. Swallowing, she said, her voice muffled into the couch, "Fine."

Ualan cocked his head, leaning closer to hear the rest.

Morrigan turned to look at him. Drawing a deep breath, she said, "Fine. I'll be your wife."

A grin spread over his features. Morrigan's expression was more guarded. When the time came to leave, it would be hard. But he left her no choice but to deceive him. He would never let her go on his own. He had admitted as much and she had given him chance after chance to prove his words wrong. No, this man of duty and honor would not recant his word. The only way for her to get her freedom back was to take it, by any means necessary.

"But I'm not promising--." Her words were cut off as he yanked her forward. He kissed her with a swift passion that left her weak and breathless. When she tried to further the embrace by touching his face, he pulled back.

"We can't," Ualan denied her. His body hated him, but was comforted by the fact that soon he would be able to possess her completely. And she was willing! If only he had realized earlier that the way into her heart was to kill her with soft words and kindness. She was such an aggravating vixen at times that he naturally rose to her challenge. "You need to be pardoned."

"How--?" she began, not sure her body could stand another month of waiting. It stirred restlessly on the couch.

"The royal celebration." Ualan smiled. Oh, but it was a gorgeous smile. Morrigan stared at the fire, doing her best to block her every emotion from him. It would not do for him to discover her plan. She knew she could never stay, but the idea of leaving him was killing her too. "It's in a few days. I would be honored if you attended it with me."

Morrigan thought of her assignment. It would be the perfect time to take pictures of the royal couples and learn their stories. Her editor would be thrilled--four Princes at the cost of one marriage of inconvenience. She swallowed, taking a nervous breath. But did she really have a choice?

Her eyes were hollow. Her heart refused to beat as the guilt tried to choke the breath from her constricting lungs. Quietly, she answered, "Yes, husband, I would love to go to the celebration with you."

* * * *

Still in the haze of sleep, Ualan reached out across the mattress to feel for Morrigan. In his dreams, she had been there and closer. They were joined as one, no walls or barriers between them. Groaning, he came to full wakefulness, his body tensed and readied with his passions. Realizing she wasn't by his side, his groan turned tortured. Soon, he told himself, never imagining he could be so happy. Very soon.

* * * *

Morrigan grumbled sleepily as she felt something poke her in the ribs. Swatting, she turned her back to whatever it was and tried to burrow once more into her dreams. The images that cocooned her were so real. She could feel Ualan's lips pressed into hers. His eyes were gentle as he looked at her, adoring and demanding at the same time. His arms protected her throughout the night. It was heaven. She did not want to leave it.

Hearing a chuckle and feeling another poke, Morrigan grunted. Lifting her arm from over her eyes, she glared. Ualan stood above her. He was handsomely dressed in a long tunic shirt of black wool, the blue insignia of the dragon in the center of his chest. The sun from the dome above haloed around his head like an angel.

A damned fine warrior angel, Morrigan thought, trembling with the leftover influences of her dreams.

Glancing down, she saw it was his hand that poked her. With a dark grumble, she said, "I already agreed. Go away before I punch you. This slave is on strike."

Ualan smirked. His poking fingers turned soft, trailing over her loosened hair to her back. Fitting his fingers by her collarbone, he leaned over and whispered hotly, "When your slavery ends, I will have to work on waking you up in a way that is more pleasurable for both of us."

"Caveman," she mumbled without thinking. She stiffened, but relaxed when he chuckled at the insult.

Reaching down to nip the tip of her ear with his teeth, he whispered, "If that is what you wish … mmm."

This time Morrigan did hit at him. Her aim was weak from her position on the couch and it only glanced at his shoulder. But he had won. She was awake.

Lifting his hands in mock defeat, he backed away. Morrigan tried to glare through her tired yawn. He chuckled again, his smile light and carefree. She waved her hand in his direction trying to wipe him out of her vision. Why was he in such a good mood this morning? She was sure she preferred him surly. At least that way he left her alone.

"I hate this accursed planet," she grumbled, though her voice lacked conviction. "I can't even tell what time it is by the light." Putting her hands in her hair, she rubbed her temples. "You need a food simulator, barbarian. I need to materialize some coffee."

"It is around noon," he gauged, looking up at the dome. "What is coffee?"

Morrigan studied him in disbelief. Shaking her head, she said, "Poor, poor, backwards people."

Ualan knew she was teasing him. He grinned like a fool. He couldn't help it. He was so happy.

"It's a drink and it has a lot of caffeine in it and I don't like to wake up without it," she grumbled. His grin struck a nerve in her chest, and she hid her reaction by rubbing at her eyes. This man was really too handsome for his own good.

"Ah," he smiled, "sloken. One moment."

"Sloken?" Morrigan mumbled as he strode to the kitchen. "Whatever."

But upon hearing noises coming from within, she couldn't resist getting up. Her maid's uniform was crumpled but she knew she would find another in the bathroom. She stumbled to lean against the doorframe.

Ualan was taking a few ingredients out of the fridge and placing them absently on the counter. Morrigan had the wildest urge to go up to him and run her hand over his spine.

"You are still a slave," he warned, unable to hide his grin at her gasp.

Ualan had smelled her longing long before she awoke from her dream. Whatever it was in her head, it had been giving her much pleasure. It was only too bad he couldn't get inside her mind with her. He'd give his sword arm to know what she fantasized about.

"So," Morrigan said, not realizing he could sense her longing. "You're still a caveman."

"Then we make a perfect pair, don't we?" Ualan mused, winking as he shut the door. Within seconds he whipped her up a drink and handed it to her.

Eyeing the dark green liquid warily, she asked, "Sloken?"

"Drink," he commanded as he brushed past. Morrigan blinked at his fast movements. He caressed his fingers over her neck as he left her, saying, "The dressmaker will be here soon."

"Wait, dressmaker?" she asked. Sniffing the green concoction, she wrinkled her nose and set it down on the counter without tasting it before chasing after him. "I don't want a dressmaker. I want a tailor."

* * * *

She got a dressmaker. The woman was a kind sort, with deft, precise hands that measured and stitched quicker than Morrigan could think. She came supplied with half-made garments and bolts of material and a handful of dutiful assistants--mostly men. She didn't speak directly to Morrigan, and Morrigan wasn't sure if it was because she didn't speak the language or because she couldn't speak to a slave.

Ualan stood by and watched, speaking to the dressmaker in the Qurilixian tongue and pointing at Morrigan with amused looks of concentration. Once, he moved his hands as if to signify the curves of Morrigan's hips. Morrigan blushed. He insolently winked at her when the woman turned.

"I want an upload of the Qurilixian tongue," she mumbled pointedly to Ualan. "And this dress better be decent."

The dressmaker laughed, forcing Morrigan to lift her arm higher.

"We don't upload," Ualan said off-hand. He stated a suggestion to the busy woman and she nodded in agreement, pushing at Morrigan's breast to lift it up.

"Hey, watch it," Morrigan warned. Ualan's grin widened. The dressmaker ignored her. When the woman again turned to Ualan and spoke, Morrigan asked, "Why does she keep calling you Draea Anwealda?"

Dragon Lord. Ualan waved his hand. "It is just an address of sorts."

"Like a title?"

Ualan gave one last order to the dressmaker before stepping up to his slave-wife. Kissing her cheek in an act of public affection that took her off-guard, he whispered, "I already told you, Rigan, you're my Princess."

Chapter Thirteen

The days before the royal celebration passed in a blur of dress fittings and etiquette lessons. Mirox brought two women for the task--Lyna and Mary. Both women were from an Earth quadrant and very pleasant when it came to explaining the Qurilixian customs.

Morrigan found that the more she learned about her husband's rich culture, the more fascinated she became. It would seem they were creatures of very old tradition and exact habits. There were several small ways in which you could insult honor, most of which Morrigan thought she could easily avoid. She didn't think she would be kissing anyone's boot in public anytime soon.

By the time the dressmaker finished her gown, it was the day of the celebration. Morrigan was very excited, despite herself. She had been cooped up in Ualan's home for nearly two weeks and thought she would go mad if she had to stay a minute more indoors. Her curiosity was killing her.

Her blue-gray ball gown was a slinky medieval affair made from a thin silk-like material. It had sloping shoulders that greatly exposed and displayed her lifted cleavage, long flowing sleeves that nearly touched the floor, and a high waist that gathered beneath her breasts and pulled seductively at her backside when she walked. Ualan's symbol of the dragon was fitted in the valley of her breasts to hold the gathering together.

The material was so light that she felt naked. Morrigan nearly fainted when she discovered that Qurilixian women never used undergarments--except for the bustier that was sewn supportively into the chest--and she was to be left bare beneath the gown.

A hairdresser was sent to fix her hair. He brushed the sides up and let ringlets of curls fall over her shoulders. A circlet of silver with a little dragon pendent was placed low on her forehead, the delicate chains sweeping up into her locks. When he was finished, Morrigan hardly recognized herself.

All week Ualan kept a respectable distance. She assumed it was because the house was always full of the company of her instructors. Whatever the reason, she was glad for it. His heated glances and few stolen touches were full of promise and had made for a very long, painful time for both of them. When he spoke, his words were bold with hints of passion and invitation. He made sure Morrigan knew that, after the celebration tonight, he would be coming to claim his wife--completely.

It was that 'completely' that left her shaking in her delicate slippers. For with the words there was delivered a present. It was a nightgown of silk and lace straps. It was lingerie like she had never seen before, with barely enough material to cover her most private of parts. She was very embarrassed and couldn't look Ualan in the eye for the better part of a day.

"You're beautiful."

Morrigan turned from where she sat on the couch, quickly getting to her feet. Ualan's words sent a rush of pleasure through her, as did the look of desire that flooded his features as his eyes roamed freely over her form.

"You're not so bad yourself," Morrigan said huskily, eyeing his tunic jacket. It was bound together with a cord that matched her headpiece. She could see a lighter shirt beneath the jacket. It was thin and hugged each of his muscled curves like air. His hair was brushed back, out of his face, framing his strong features with its golden brilliance. The breeches he wore were tight and clung to every dip and curve of his legs in harmonious precision. Morrigan gulped, thankful that the jacket and shirt pulled low enough to hide his more significant parts from view.

"If you keep looking at me like that, slave," he said softly, coming forward. "We will not make it to your pardon."

"I--" Morrigan flushed, realizing she was staring at his groin and panting. "I have to get something, one second."

Ualan watched as Morrigan ran up the stairs as delicately as she could in the tighter dress. When she returned seconds later, she was slipping an emerald on her pinkie. Ualan raised his brow in question.

"It's for luck. I always wear it when I go out."

As he led her from his home, Morrigan's eyes devoured everything. Tapestries, paintings, and statutes decorated the hallways. The wide passages of red stone continued in various directions. Ualan explained that they led to different suites and parts of the keep. Pointing to a symbol on the wall that looked like a bunch of lines and dots, he said, "This is how we tell where we are going. I will teach you to read them for yourself so you don't get lost. But, for now, do not wander anywhere alone."

Morrigan stopped and looked at the design. Pointing to a line with a curve, she said, "This must be a dragon … and these dots must mean…."

"Later," he urged, amazed she had got that far with the hieroglyphic code. "You are expected before the festivities to receive your pardon. Do you remember what you must do?"

She nodded weakly. Her fingers began working on his arm, clutching at him.

"Good."

Suddenly, he stopped at a set of high arched doors. Morrigan could hear the murmuring of laughter behind the thick oak barrier. She studied the carved hatching on the wood before looking at Ualan. His eyes were liquid pools.

"You must enter alone for this," he whispered, brushing one of her curls onto his finger so it clung to him. Leaning over, he could not keep from lightly kissing her cheek. "You'll do fine."

Morrigan swallowed and nodded. Then he stepped back, and she bravely pushed her way in. The heavy oak was pulled from her grasp and two servants bowed silently as she entered. She was too nervous to study the main common hall, as she stepped down three stone stairs onto the main floor. The crowd grew quiet at her arrival. Morrigan found the head table exactly where it was said to be. Going forward, she bowed to the King and Queen who she barely recognized from the crystal crushing ceremony.

"Queen Mede, King Llyr," she said, curtseying. Her voice wavered and she swallowed.

The royal couple both motioned their hands in acknowledgement.

Morrigan had been told they were also honor bound not to speak to her until she begged her pardon. Keeping her eyes down, as instructed, she mumbled the words Ualan taught her. "I come to you as a humble slave, begging for your royal pardon. I have restored my honor and wish to seek your blessing."

The Queen and King shared looks.

"Prince Olek?" the Queen asked.

"Yea," a man to the Queen side said.

"Prince Yusef?"

"Yea."

"Prince Zoran?"

"Yea, my Queen."

Morrigan stood tense, her fingers itching to snap a picture of the royal table. But she couldn't photograph with her eyes pointed down. She needed to get a picture of the Princes and their brides. She wondered which of the girls from the ship would be with them if any. Hopefully it was someone she got on with so she would have an excuse to question her extensively.

"My husband?" the Queen continued.

"Yea," the King answered. His booming voice was full of authority.

"And I say 'yea'," Queen Mede stated. "She has spoken well."

Morrigan began to curtsey at the compliment when the Queen's words stopped her.

"We have agreed. It is up to you, my son. Will this slave receive her pardon, Prince Ualan?"

Morrigan's sharp gasp resounded over the hall. Her eyes darted up of their own accord to stare at the royal table. There, standing by his mother, a crown of silver metal atop his head, was her husband. The blood drained from her features.

Ualan stepped down the platform at her attention. How did he dare to smile at her? You didn't just smile innocently after a public bombshell like that! Morrigan was mortified. As soon as her senses recovered, she would be livid and there would be hell to pay.

The hall was quiet in respect as he stepped up to her.

"Tell me you are the royal gardener and this is a joke," she said through her tightened throat.

"No, my Princess," he answered, low so none could hear.

Morrigan panicked. It would be much harder to bail on a Prince. Ualan would have the resources to send many nations to go and find her. If he wanted, he could have every military and police force in the galaxy armed with her picture.

So much for her career as an undercover reporter.

"Do you still wish to be pardoned?"

She nodded. How could she not?

"Yea," Ualan announced. "I shall pardon my wife. She has proven herself very worthy of her title and of my family's honor." Cheering and pounding erupted at his words.

Ualan led her forward to the royal table. Morrigan's eyes flew over the royal couples. A Prince who looked much like her husband sat next to Nadja. She blushed, recognizing him from his tent. Another crowned brother sat next to Pia. She didn't really know the woman, but nodded when Pia acknowledged her attention with a strained smile. The fourth Prince, and ungodly dark specimen of male splendor, sat alone.

"It is glad I am that all my sons have found brides. We are a house blessed," the King announced when Ualan and Morrigan were seated. "Preosts, crown the Princesses."

Morrigan arms trembled with outrage. She numbly felt a crown being fitted on her head as she refused to look at Ualan. If she did, she just might kill her Royal Highness of a husband in front of a hall full of witnesses.

* * * *

A grand meal was served to the hall. Morrigan couldn't eat. Looking around, she saw Ualan wasn't the only son with the dragon symbol. It was the royal seal. Cursing, she thought of the upload that claimed the seal was a tiger. She was definitely going to write a story about the shoddy business practices of the Galaxy Bride Corporation.

Clicking the emerald several times in her ire, she made sure to get many pictures of the dragon emblem. Musicians played lively tunes. The crowd laughed, breaking into spontaneous song at the oddest moments.

Suddenly, a hand found its way onto her knee. Morrigan tensed, her eyes shooting daggers at Prince Ualan.

"Relax," he urged, kneading her thigh muscle through her thin gown. "Eat something."

"Is that a royal order, Prince Ualan," she ground out angrily through the side of her lips. She was very aware of how on display they were.

"You're upset," he answered seriously.

She shot him a look that said, no kidding, caveman.

He took his hand away. This wasn't the time to discuss it.

"What are the Var doing here?" Ualan turned to ask Olek.

"They are our guests," Olek answered. They still spoke in English and Morrigan's ears listened intently to every word. Ualan sounded concerned. She turned to study the blond men at a distant table. They seemed to be the only ones not enjoying the lively celebration.

"See that they are watched," Ualan said. "I will not have their deceits in the House of Draig. There will be a big price to pay if we must punish them."

"Yusef is taking care of it," Olek answered. He glanced quizzically at where Morrigan was staring at him. Switching purposefully into their native voice, he said, "I wanted them to see the royal marriages for themselves."

Morrigan scowled when Ualan answered in the same tone. Out of spite, she took a grand picture of Prince Olek and his bride. Nadja tried to smile at her. Morrigan just nodded stiffly in return.

Is it just me? Morrigan thought. Or do all the royal brides look peeved.

"I want to leave," Morrigan said when Ualan finished his lengthy, serious conversation with his brother. "I'll find my way back."

"You cannot go. It is your coronation."

"Your dark brother's wife isn't here," she pointed out with a stiff nod of her head at Yusef. The tall, serious Yusef saw her dark look and scowled back.

"That is because she in chastisement. She isn't allowed," Ualan said. He lifted his drink, allowing his plate to be taken by a servant. Morrigan lifted her full plate and handed it directly to the man. The man seemed surprised to see her clearing her own meal, but when Prince Ualan nodded him away, he took it and left.

"Well, I want to get put in chastisement, too. What do I have to do?"

Ualan glanced down, thinking he didn't care to have a knife taken to his male-defining anatomy. So instead, he teased, "You forget already, wife, I have given you punishment aplenty. But if you insist, I will give you more. After all, I am an honorable man duty bound to see all is in order."

Morrigan read the fire in his gaze as his hand reached beneath the table to touch her most intimately. He slowly gathered her dress in his palm, pulling the slinky material up until his fingers were rewarded with warm flesh. She tried to swat him away, while retaining her dignity. He squeezed tighter, sending a chill over her nervous system. The more she hit, the tighter he squeezed until she was forced to give up. Gradually, he slid his hand higher, finding the place where her thigh connected to her center. She was on fire for him. He smiled, pleased by the response.

"Stop, brother."

Ualan blinked, dropping his hand as he tuned to Olek's knowing smile.

"Before the whole hall smells her desire," Olek added, so the brides couldn't understand. Nadja looked at him quizzically, but hastily turned away before he saw her watching him. "Let it not become one of those celebrations. I have no wish to share."

Ualan smiled and shrugged, unashamed, but properly reined in.

Morrigan's attention was drawn to a shout of laughter that sounded over the hall. She leaned over to see a little boy sprawled on the floor. Several large warriors watched him from the table, laughing harder when he limped to his feet. One foot turned in slightly and started to drag.

Suddenly, Pia jumped up from the table and rushed to the boy's side. He seemed surprised to see her standing by him and tried his best to bow before the Princess. It was awkward moving on his foot.

"Leave him be!" Pia ordered to the table of warriors. They quieted to look at her in question.

Pia looked back to her husband who seemed surprised by her outburst. Morrigan watched the interplay quietly, pushing the recorder on her finger out of habit and letting it run.

"What do you want with Hienrich, my lady?" a burly man with a beard asked. "Does he offend you? I will have him removed."

Pia turned red, her blonde hair flying as she spun to glare him down. "He does not!"

There was a commotion and Morrigan couldn't hear what was being said. She unconsciously leaned closer to Ualan. He glanced at her in surprise before putting his arm around his waist. Then, she heard Pia shout, "Well, I am a Princess and he will be my personal warrior."

"If my lady wishes for a warrior, let us battle for the position. Do not insult us by naming a boy," the burly man said in return. Pia's husband came down the platform, going after his wife. The warriors gathered around the burly one growled in agreement to the idea and shouts were called for a tournament.

"Do you dare to question a Princess?" Zoran began, Pia's husband.

"He is my warrior too," Nadja yelled, standing. Olek looked at her in amazement, choking on his wine.

"And mine as well," Morrigan piped in, rising to her feet. Her gown fell back down over her leg and she was glad for it.

Ualan merely smiled up at her, not caring. Let his brother Zoran deal with this problem.

"There you have it," Zoran said. Morrigan saw he was trying not to laugh. "You cannot deny the wish of three Princesses. Heinrich is now under royal protection and will be treated according to his new station."

The three Princesses glanced at each other, a silent understanding formed between them. Pia nodded her thanks for their support. The stunned hall picked up its celebration once more.

Morrigan felt Ualan's hand taking advantage of her standing position, sliding the tips of his fingers near the sensitive back curve of her knee. She quickly sat back down. Ualan flashed an innocent smile.

The feast was cleared and after dinner drinks were poured aplenty. The musicians kept playing. The quiet Yusef strummed a few tunes with them on a guitar looking instrument and proved himself to be quite up to the task. Someone sang in the Qurilixian language. It was a beautiful sounding ballad.

Morrigan noticed that her husband's race was much freer with their affection than most humanoid cultures. They openly kissed and caressed their lovers as if it were no matter. To her relief, nothing got carried too far.

Ualan spent the better part of his evening trying to obtain feels of his wife under the table. He burned with desire, wanting to touch her as electricity shot throughout his whole being. He knew that only a few hours separated him from his release. Morrigan shivered despite herself and clamped her legs tightly in irritation when Ualan's venturing became to bold.

Whispering into her ear, he offered, "If you want me to quell that flame burning in your thighs, I can disappear beneath this table. I would be very pleased to lick the fire from your wet, parted loins."

Morrigan shot him a horrified look and he chuckled loudly. When his laughter subsided, he pulled away to once more settle close to her ear, breathing hotly onto her skin. She tried to push his hand away for the thousandth time. He took her hand in his. With the speed of a striking snake, he brought her fingers to his solid erection and held her hand to him. He smiled around the hall as if nothing was amiss. Morrigan paled, not as stealthy as her waywardly randy husband.

Still leaning close, he forced her fingers to curl around him. He held her hand to him and began to stroke long and slow. Morrigan's body jerked of its own accord, feeling the size and power of him. His breath caught and became ragged as he quietly let her hear what she was doing to him.

Ardently, his words a low bestial groan of pleasure and approval, he urged, "Or perhaps you could be persuaded beneath the table to tend to me."

Morrigan gasped, too weak to pull away at the moment, as she was made to stroke him over the material of his breeches. Emboldened by the smell of her response, Ualan flicked the tie strings holding his pants together and moved her hand to touch directly onto his fiery arousal. The danger of it excited her in a way she had not thought possible and she did not resist as much as she should have.

"I would love to feel the soft suckling of those sweet lips once again," he implored her. His breath hit her earlobe and it was as if he nibbled it without touching.

Morrigan flamed in embarrassment and roughly jerked her fingers from him.

"Ah," he sighed in disappointment. Really, he had been toying with her. However, if she had wanted to try and get away with his naughty plans he would have wholeheartedly agreed, despite the unfavorable circumstances and the unaware crowd. With disappointment heavy in his words, he shrugged, "Tonight then."

Morrigan spied a new goblet placed near her empty one the table, full of a yellowish liquid. Grabbing it up without thought, she gulped the sweet contents down. Instantly it made her head buzz and she was happy for it.

Observing Zoran escorting his wife to the floor for a dance, Ualan leaned in to ask Morrigan, "Would you like to--?"

"Try it and I will have your head," she growled in return.

Ualan blinked in amazement, but laughed when he realized she thought he meant to propose they have sex right there on the table. He let silence fall between them once more.

"King Llyr."

Morrigan turned to see one of the blond Vars standing below the table. As he bowed, she could detect the pattern of a tiger on his chest. She frowned, trying to get a picture of it.

Morrigan couldn't understand his words, but Ualan could and he listened intently.

"Many blessings on your unions," the stranger said. "May your reign be long."

"As may yours, King Attor," the Draig ruler returned, standing to show a respect that did not reflect wholeheartedly in his eyes.

Morrigan shivered. The blond Var shot her a heated, sidelong glance. He bowed once more and left, his band of troops behind him.

"What was that all about?" she leaned forward, her curiosity momentarily getting the best of her anger.

"Politics," Ualan stated darkly, turning to keep his eyes on the Vars. Some of his humor faded as he suspiciously watched the man. Prince Yusef passed his instrument off to its owner and followed quietly behind the departing men.

* * * *

Morrigan felt terrible when walking home with Mirox. Her stomach churned and she was sweating profusely. Ualan had to oversee some urgent royal matter of the court with his father and had sent his man ahead to escort her. Mirox said nothing, respecting Lady Morrigan's quiet. It didn't take a genius to figure out what this night would mean for the couple. They had all seen well the heated way they Prince and Princess looked at each other all night.

Once alone, Morrigan stumbled to the bathroom. She was nervous about her night with Ualan. Her heart beat wearily within her. He was so bold. What would he expect of her? She couldn't even repeat some of the things he said to her with his firm lips and bold tongue.

Shivering, she wondered if every bride was this nauseated when faced with the prospect of bedding a Qurilixian warrior. The chills didn't stop, but grew by bounds.

"It's not that," she muttered to herself. "It's because he is royalty. How can I dare to escape royalty? I am truly trapped."

Morrigan tugged the crown off her head and set it on the floor as she fell to the ground. Crawling on her hands and knees across the bathroom's marble floor, she barely made it to the toilet before she stared to throw up.

Chapter Fourteen

Ualan frowned, his excitement severely dampened by the night's events. Yusef had been attacked while seeing King Attor out of the keep and off Draig land. His brother was brought to a medical ward where all the latest technology had been employed to save his life. He was in bad condition, unconscious. The doctors said he was still in danger, but they were hopeful for a complete recovery.

Guards were already being sent to gather Yusef's wife at the Outpost and bring her into the safety of the castle walls. It was clear the attack had been to his back for Yusef had not been given time to shift into his warrior form. If he had, the knife wounds would not have penetrated so deeply beneath the surface.

Coming into his home, Ualan glanced around. Morrigan wasn't on the couch. With a soft smile, he glanced up the stairs. His body sprung to automatic attention, seeking fulfillment. His mind craved her nearness to chase the demons from his thoughts. There was nothing she could do, but the idea of her gentle hands holding him was comfort in itself.

"Rigan?" he asked, taking the stairs to his bed two a time. To his surprise, she wasn't there. Frowning, he searched the closets and balcony before rushing to check the downstairs floor. Heading to the kitchen, he stopped, hearing a sound in the bathroom. Smiling, he imagined her in the bath--warm and naked. But as he neared the closed door, his senses pricked. Something was wrong. The door was locked.

Pounding on the door, he called, "Rigan?"

He was answered by a cough, before she moaned: "Go away."

"Rigan, what is it?" Ualan called. Surely she wasn't this upset about being a Princess. When he felt a wave of pain overtake him, radiating from her body to his, he stiffened. "Open the door."

There was only silence. Cursing, he leaned back, slamming the wood with his shoulder. It splintered in several pieces allowing him to charge forth.

"Rigan…?" The question died on his lips as he stumbled on her discarded crown. She was lying on the floor, spots of yellow patches forming on her overly pale skin. He could see a trail where she had thrown up before she fell helpless on the floor.

His blood ran cold.

"Rigan," he urged, sweeping her up into his arms. He crushed her crown, splintering it under his boot as he rushed from the bathroom. "Rigan, wake up."

She stirred. Her eyes blinked wearily to look at him, and she mumbled, "Cavema…."

She was out.

Ualan ran from his home, pulling her close to his chest as he sprinted to the medical ward. Calling desperately for help before he was even in the door, he saw his brother's prone body on one of the beds. Soon, Morrigan was whisked from his arms, her near lifeless body flopping as the doctors carried her to a private room in the back. Turning, Ualan growled to the stunned doctor's wife and yelled, "Get my family."

She ran off to do as he commanded.

Ualan was still staring helplessly at the door leading to where they took Morrigan when the royal family, Princesses and all, were ushered into the room. Only Yusef's bride was missing. The frightened Princess Pia and Princess Nadja were escorted into a separate room to be tested for poison and the men were left standing alone with the Queen.

"If any in our family die," Ualan swore to his father, his voice deepening into a growl as his face began to harden with a shift. His eyes glowed with a deadly yellow as fangs extended into his mouth. Resembling the beast he could become, he roared, "There will be blood."

* * * *

Morrigan was very ill and did not stop throwing up, even in her sleep. She had been poisoned. Her body fought with a bravery that made her husband swell with pride and in the end she won the battle for her life. The doctors told him that if he hadn't found her when he did, she would be dead.

Yusef and Morrigan had both yet to wake up. The family stayed close to their sides, plotting retribution throughout the night as they waited for a sign of life. To their alarm, they discovered Yusef's bride had been taken. Already their best trackers were going after her kidnappers. As soon as their location was determined, Olek, Zoran, Ualan, and the King would be leaving to reclaim her.

Ualan felt useless waiting around at Morrigan's side. He was a man of action, not waiting, and it tore him up. He was secretly glad for the mission to find Yusef's wife, eager to pound out his fear and helplessness. Retribution and rage were the two best outlets for hopelessness a warrior knew.

The servant responsible for serving her the drink had been dealt with. It was soon learned he wasn't at fault. One of King Attor's men had distracted him as he was preparing to serve the royal drink. The drink had been meant for the King and Queen, but when King Attor went up to speak, the servant had placed the goblet before Morrigan instead so as not to get in their way. He never realized Princess Morrigan wouldn't recognize the King's seal and would indeed take the drink for herself.

Ualan frowned, taking his forehead to Morrigan's fingers. If he hadn't embarrassed her, she would never have taken the drink. But he also knew that, if it had been his parents, they would have died instantly. The poison worked slower on humans.

"Mm," came a light moan. Ualan felt a hand lift from under him to stroke back his hair. "Hey."

Morrigan's voice was cracked. Ualan's head shot up to stare at her. His eyes were sunken into the depths of his face. He had not eaten and had barely left her side. He had gone once to meet with his family and once to bathe and retrieve his wife a change of clothes so she didn't have to sleep in a vomit-stained dress.

When he looked into her eyes, he could see the powerful drugs the doctors had given her were still influencing her and her mind was hazy. He didn't care, so long as she was safe. For the first time since finding her nearly dead on the bathroom floor, he felt as if he could breathe.

"Hey," she murmured again. She was too weak to keep her hand lifted to him and it fell to the mattress. "What happened? I can't feel anything."

"That is the medicine," he whispered softly. "It is to keep you from hurting."

Morrigan nodded, blinking heavily. She almost drifted off before catching herself. Her wide eyes shone brightly as she looked at him.

"I was dreaming of dragons," she said, her voice hazy. The medicine lowered any filter between her head and mouth. Ualan chuckled to himself. He didn't care, letting her ramble.

He smiled tenderly, teasing her in a low murmur, "Just dragons or one dragon in particular?"

Her eyebrow rose but could not hold the pose.

"What did you do to me, caveman? Hit me over the head and drag me home?" she muttered.

Ualan's relief intensified. He heart soared to hear her quick wit. He had been so worried she would hate him for not protecting her better, as he hated himself.

"You were butterfly poisoned," he answered. "But don't worry. The doctors said you would be fine so long as you rest."

"I don't have butterflies in my stomach," she protested, her mind drifting as she mumbled, "I'm not too nervous to sleep with you."

He would have grinned like a fool if her skin wasn't so yellow. "I'm glad to hear it, wife."

"Who?" she asked suddenly, trying to get up. "Poison?"

"Easy," he said, urging her back. "They will be dealt with."

"Oh," she mumbled, with an amazing show of trust. "All right."

Ualan glanced over to the table by her bed, moving to get her a drink. She took it gratefully before closing her eyes. Seeing the small eye camera lens the doctors found in her eye next to the emerald trigger, he couldn't help but asking, "Why did you have the camera, Rigan?"

Morrigan sighed. Before falling asleep, she murmured, "It's my job. I'm going to expose you after I leave you."

* * * *

Ualan growled like a thundering brute. Gripping the center horn of his mount, he swung up behind the beast's bare shoulders. The ceffyl's wide back shifted low at the weight of its warrior rider, used to the rough handling. His fanged mouth darted open with a hiss of its long tongue. It had the eyes of a reptile, the face and hooves of a beast of burden, and the body of a small elephant. It was wickedly fast for an animal of its size and equally deadly.

Adjusting the long blade at his side, Ualan grunted.

"There will be enough blood for all of us," Zoran growled, seeing his brother's mounting rage, though not exactly disapproving of it. He too swung up his animal.

"Your wife will recover," Olek said, joining them. "Her mind is well."

"Not if I strangle her into the grave," Ualan roared fiercely. His face shifted briefly in his rage.

Olek and Zoran exchanged weary looks as the King rode up beside them.

"For there is not enough blood in all the land to kill a husband's wrath when he has tasted the bitterness of his wife's deceit." Ualan hit his steed, murder flashing in his yellow eye as the ceffyl took off.

The King looked at his sons. They merely shrugged in return. Kicking their mounts, the three men were quick behind Ualan.

* * * *

"They've gone where?" Morrigan looked wearily at the Queen from the depths of Ualan's couch. She hadn't seen him since his brief visit in the medical ward that morning. She could barely remember it, for the drugs the doctors had given her to flush out the poison had been strong. He hadn't been back since. So much for a caring husband, she frowned.

"To give justice," Mede answered calmly. She was dressed simply in cotton slacks and a shirt, not looking anything like royalty in her attire. It was her intelligent eyes that gave her position away.

Mede was visiting her sick daughter-by-marriage, as she had promised her son she would do. She wondered what Morrigan could have said to Ualan to make him so angry. Even though she could read the fury in Ualan when he said this woman's name, she could tell he cared for her and would never really hurt her. He had been a wreck since finding her poisoned and no amount of comforting would ease his pain or his guilt. So they did what was best and left him alone.

"Who? Where...?" The young woman tumbled forward in confusion. Her eyes shone with concern. Mede considered her carefully. "Will there be danger?"

"Most certainly."

Morrigan stared at the woman as if she had grown another head. She said it like it was a good thing.

"Where is he? I've got to see him," she said, trying to fight to her feet.

Mede stood back, refusing to interfere with the woman's will to stand. Though she knew Morrigan would be better off seated.

She was right. Morrigan trembled and fell back into the couch with a huff.

"You are in no position to ride out. Do not fret. None of the other Princesses have gone to battle. You are not being left out."

"Gone to battle?" Morrigan squeaked, staring in horror at her mother-by-marriage. Were Qurilixian wives expected to go to battle with their men? She turned her eyes to look at the dragon beasts on the blue tapestry. She knew a lot of races believed in such things. Did this one? "I don't know how to fight."

Mede smiled. "You do not know your own strength, daughter. Only a fighting spirit could have withstood the butterfly's poison. And I am guessing that only a fighting spirit could have resisted her husband with slavery."

Morrigan thought about that. There was approval in the Queen's words. When she called her 'daughter' Morrigan nearly teared up. She'd been on her own for a long time. She had no family. Suddenly, it hit her. Here she had a family, a strong, close, protective family. And they all wanted her.

Thinking of Ualan, Morrigan knew the Queen was right. It was much harder to resist him than it had been to fight off death. How did she ever do it? Why had she even wanted to try? None of the rest seemed important anymore. Not if they had a chance of working it out and being happy. Would it be so bad to be the barbarian's wife?

Mede waited patiently as the girl collected her thoughts. She watched as the discovery of Morrigan's feelings crossed over her pale face. That was one thing the warrior men of her race never understood. It took much more than crystals and destiny to win a woman's heart. It took patience and time. And, sometimes, it took almost dying.

"Are all men on this planet as stubborn as your son?" Morrigan asked quietly.

The Queen smiled. "Only if you're lucky, dear. Only if you're lucky."

* * * *

Morrigan looked up from the table in surprise. The news arrived more than an hour ago that the men had safely retrieved Princess Olena from captors and were heading back to the keep. Morrigan was too tired to go to the courtyard to greet them, but she sent her blessings down through the Queen.

Seeing Ualan, she darted to her feet. She wobbled slightly, still weak from her ordeal. Her pleasure turned to horror when she saw his blood splattered face. His clothes were soaked to crimson, his hair matted to his head with dirt and sweat. Trembling, she stumbled forward.

"Are you hurt?" she rushed.

It was an insulting question and Ualan didn't answer it.

"Ualan?" Morrigan breathed. She let her fingers roam over him, searching for wounds, glancing at the gore-covered sword that hung at his waist. He winced once when her fingers skimmed his ribcage. Satisfied that it was only the one injury, she demanded, "Why weren't you wearing armor? Are you insane?"

"Stop pretending," he fumed bitterly. "What would you care if I were slain?"

"Ualan?" she gasped in surprise at the personal attack. Seeing his tired eyes, she forgave him. She had been sick with worry and was too happy to see him well and together to give his surliness much mind. "Come on, let's get you cleaned up."

Ualan shrugged out of her grasp. "I do not require your help, wife."

"But--" Morrigan began, her eyes round.

"Quit coddling me, woman," he growled, withdrawing his arm from her achingly tender hands. His body tingled with treacherous desire. He didn't want to feel anything for her. Roughly, he pushed past her, spinning her weakened body on its heels as he stormed into the bathroom. He would have slammed the door for good measure, but it was still broken off its hinges.

Morrigan waited. After a minute, she heard splashing in the hot spring. Putting her hands on her hips, she shook her head, "Oh, no he did not!"

With her limbs empowered by determination, Morrigan went in the bathroom after him. She placed her hands mincingly on her hips and stared him down. Ualan looked up in surprise to hear her. His nostrils flared and he had been poking at a gash on his side like a wounded animal.

"First you want a wife," she yelled angrily, "and you get mad when I want nothing to do with you. Now you're yelling at me because I was worried about you? I think not, caveman."

"Rigan," Ualan said. His tone warned her to use caution.

"Quiet," Morrigan warned, her eyes flashing unafraid. "You wanted a wife. Well, guess what buddy, you've got one."

"Have I?" he inquired softly, watching her raging eyes.

Ualan knew the deceit that lingered there and yet she drew him in. He wanted to believe her. He wanted it more than anything.

"Oh, yeah, and so help me, you are going to let me tend that wound, help you with this bath, and then I am going to make you dinner if it kills both of us." Morrigan dared him to disagree, before adding, "And with my cooking, it probably will."

It took all of Ualan's strength not to laugh. The fact did not make him happy.

Although he was stiff and unresponsive, except in the basest of manly ways, Morrigan managed to wash his skin and hair. Ualan nearly went mad when her hand dipped to clean his hard stomach. Her fingers faltered almost shyly as she neared his erection. His eyes flamed with liquid fire when she finally ran her soapy hand down the length of him. She swallowed, waiting for a sign of his approval.

Standing, abruptly, Ualan said, "I think you're done."

Morrigan drew back, mortified.

He climbed out of the bath and wrapped a towel around his waist, shielding the obviousness of his desire from her view. Morrigan wasn't so easily put off once her mind was set.

"Where is your first aid?" she asked.

Ualan, who had been concentrating on smelling anything but her clean scent, looked at her in confusion.

"Bandages," she ordered, pointing to his seeping stomach. Now clean, it wasn't so bad. She pushed his bloody clothes onto a pile on the floor with her kicking foot.

Soon they were on the couch, his arm lifted over his head as she poked at his wound. Ualan glared, but said nothing. Lightly, she asked, "So are you going to tell me what happened?"

"No," he answered darkly. He couldn't speak, couldn't concentrate with her so near. When she lay dying, he had been so scared. He never prayed for anything like he prayed for her safety. Then she awoke and had said those words that replayed in his brain a thousand times. She was planning on leaving him. She had lied to him. She had no intentions of staying and being his wife. It was a most cruel betrayal.

Standing as soon as the bandage was finished, he announced, "I'm going to bed."

Morrigan glanced at his towel where the heavy protrusion still vied for her feminine attention.

"Would you like me to come with you?" she asked, rising to touch his arm. Her body was weak, but she didn't care. She had been so scared with him gone and would be content to just hold him. Slowly, her fingers trailed to touch his bandaged waist.

Ualan took her hands in his. He could see what she was offering. It shone tentatively from her wide dark eyes. For a moment, she was sure he would kiss her. To her astonishment, he put her away from him and let her go. Without a word, he walked alone to his bedroom, leaving her to sleep alone yet another night.

Chapter Fifteen

That first night of rejection could have been battle fatigue. The next day? All right, Morrigan could buy that it was still battle fatigue and maybe post-rescue contemplation. But the second night and third day? Morrigan shook her head. No. Day three was definitely heading into rejection territory.

Now that she was a free woman, Morrigan was given leave to explore her new home. The palace keep was a dazzling place. There were five wings build into, up, and around the tallest mountain on the planet. She was told that each Prince had designed his own section. To her amazement, and judging by their homes, she discovered that the brothers were anything but carbon copies of each other.

Whereas her home with Ualan was all fire, marble, and fur, Zoran and Pia's wing was constructed with a wood finish, giving the place a real oriental lodge feeling to it. Olek and Nadja's home had a giant water fountain in the front hall, surrounded by high backed, comfortable chairs and exotic fish tank walls. She didn't see Yusef's and Olena's section, but she guessed it would be equally marvelous. Yusef was still in the medical wing. He was recovering, but she hadn't heard much else.

For a palace designed and decorated by a race of antiquated, warrior men, Morrigan thought it was fantastic.

When she saw the courtyard, she discovered the palace made for a flawless fortress. From the ground, because of the angle, you couldn't see the windows or balconies that were adjoined to the royal family quarters. They were carved just so, that even from a distance it looked just like a mountain cliff. It was impenetrable.

Within the surrounding valley, near the breeding festival grounds, sat a small village under the protection of the House of Draig. The roads were of rocky earth, smoothed flat and even. The village was kept immaculately clean, built with almost a military perfection of angles.

The houses were of rock and wood, so that even the poorest of families looked to be prosperous. Everyone wore light linen tunics during the day much like the royal family, but minus the dragon crest and finer embroidery.

With the three suns shining overhead, she expected it to be hotter than it was. The bright village sported a cool breeze. The evening hours, when the sky turned to a brilliant shade of blue dusk, were reserved for the more comfortable cotton pull-string pants and shirts. They provided protection from any night chill, which to Morrigan wasn't much.

She adopted the more comfortable style immediately, having, at the queen's insistence, ordered more gowns to befit her new station. To her disappointment, Ualan merely grunted sourly when he saw them and turned to seek his own bed.

She took her meals in the common hall along with the rest of the family. A high alert had been set on the kitchen and staff, so it was a little more stressful than usual when they gathered together. The men did not join them often, taking their meals wherever they practiced and strategized.

Morrigan missed Ualan more and more each passing hour. She wondered how, in a few short weeks, he'd grown to be such an important part of her life. She ached for his wicked words that made her to blush. Without him, she didn't feel right inside, like a piece of her soul was missing. It was a hollow, sick feeling.

Each night Ualan came back to the house, worn from training with his brothers, or whatever it was he did while he avoided her. He looked at her as if he was surprised to see that she was still there. Then he would go to his dining table and pore over maps and charts until the wee hours of the morning. Morrigan peeked at them once, but couldn't read the script or understand their meaning. Not once did he offer to explain them to her.

When she spoke to him, his responses were curt and his actions uniformly more so. He refused to tell her of his plans. Ualan never voluntarily talked, except once to ask after her health when she had a passing moment of dizziness and to make sure she was seeing the doctor for her daily check-ups.

Morrigan again found she was alone in their home, as she came back from shopping with the Queen. Pia invited her to spend the evening learning to defend herself and Morrigan readily agreed. Anything was better than being alone.

The Queen was only too happy with the plan and told Morrigan to get a dirk from her husband's closet. Looking at the array of weaponry, she wasn't sure which knife was the dirk. So, instead, she chose one for the prettiness of the hilt rather than the deadliness of the blade. Smiling, she strapped it to her waist.

If anything, thought Morrigan, I can learn to beat my husband into submission.

She grinned. The idea had real merit. She wondered if she could take him.

Reaching to the back of one of the shelves, she pulled out an old intergalactic communicator. Drawing the knife from her waist, she set it aside, before sitting on the floor. Next to her, buried beneath the skirt of one of her hanging gowns, was her bag from the Galaxy Bride's ship.

Pulling the bag to her and unzipping it, she realized she hadn't looked in her suitcase since arriving. It was surrealistic to see her clothes again. She pulled out a hooded sweatshirt, some socks and her underwear. Feeling nostalgic, she shook off her boots and slipped her feet into the socks. Before she realized it, she had changed her clothes completely. The bra felt different than the built in bustier of her Qurilixian shirts and her panties were oddly constricting to her hips.

Morrigan sighed, shivering and feeling suddenly very alone. She hadn't allowed herself to think about it before. But now, alone in the closet, her insecurity would be held back no longer. If Ualan had grown tired of her would he tell her? Was he getting bored with her? Did he not desire her? Tears in her eyes, she sniffed. Now that she wasn't a challenge, was the thrill gone?

Seeing her computer port, she checked its power. The lifecell lit up without a problem. Her article flashed open before her. With a click, the air screen floated up with the words she had written on the spacecraft. They begged for an ending.

Swallowing, she took up the communicator and stuck her adapter into it. The unit lit up showing that it still worked. With only minor hesitance, she hit the keys for her editor.

Click. Click.

Morrigan sighed, tense as the signal blinked. For a moment, she considered pulling the plug. But, by the time she moved to end the signal, it was too late.

"Rigan? Rigan?" came her editor's gruff male voice. He seemed worried. "Rigan, are you there? Damn it, girl! Come in. Rigan!"

Taking a deep breath, she said with a wry tone she could not so easily feel, "At ease, Gus, don't bust a plastic artery."

* * * *

"My lord, your presence is requested in communications."

Ualan looked up from were he held his knife to a young soldier's throat. Sighing, he tapped the soldier's neck, indicating the kill shot. Standing, he nodded at Zoran before tossing the blade to him. Zoran caught it with one hand, barely blinking as he turned back around to watch a practice fight.

"What is it?" Ualan asked as they crossed from the practice yard into one of the palace's secret tunnels. They walked several feet into the mountain, through the bare passageway, before loading onto an elevator. The young soldier pushed a button and they began to rise with lightening speed.

"Our sensors have picked up a communication signal, my lord."

"Who hails us?" Ualan asked, watching the metal door slide open. He was at the top of the mountain in a glass pyramid. From the bottom of the mountain and from space, the peak was camouflaged to look like the red rock. However, inside, it was as transparent as glass.

"No, my lord, it is one of our communicators," the soldier said. "The signal is trying to connect to the outer galaxy."

"Have any requests been made to call out?" Ualan asked. He knew he hadn't approved any.

"No, my lord," the soldier said. He looked wearily at the tall Prince as he stepped aside to grab an earpiece.

"Whose signal is it?" Ualan asked.

The man gulped. "It is yours, my lord."

"Signal connected, my lord," said another man in front of a floating screen. He touched it in the air, causing it to flicker and change.

Ualan's heart beat dully. The last time he saw his communicator it was in his closet.

"Closed circuit," he ordered, hooking the earpiece to his ear. He threaded his hands behind his back, and looked up at the sky. Through the solar shielding on the panels, he could see an expanse of stars. He ignored them and he listened.

"Yes, my lord," the man said. "Intercepting now."

"Rigan, are you there? Damn it, girl! Come in. Rigan!"

Ualan stiffened. His jaw was tight. He refused to move or show emotion in front of his men. Inside him, his stomach turned in on itself. His heart squeezed to a vicious stop. For a moment, he didn't think she would answer. He hoped she wouldn't. He was disappointed.

Clear as day, he heard her sultry voice answer, "At ease, Gus, don't bust a plastic artery."

* * * *

Morrigan took a deep breath. She didn't wait long.

"What the hell is going on, Rigan?" the man's tone turned from concern to annoyance. "I send you to do an exclusive story on a royal family, not to get yourself married. I contacted Galaxy Brides and told them I was your uncle. They told me my niece was lucky enough to find a life mate--whatever the hell that means!"

Gus had been married thirteen times. He didn't believe in life mates.

"Gus--" she began, but his frustration wasn't vented. She knew he was just blowing off steam. The man was worried about her, though he wouldn't admit it.

"What the hell happened? You got the breast enhancement, didn't you? I told you not to do that!" Gus wheezed as if pain. "What they do? Carry you off into the sunset like some damned fairy tale?"

"Gus, this is no fairy tale," she interjected, thinking of her unfulfilled body that seemed to ache all the time, no matter what she was doing. Just sitting in the closet, surrounded by Ualan's clothes made her body shiver and pulse with wicked thoughts.

"If anything," he said, as if he didn't hear her, "you should have had them take your breasts off completely until your trip back."

"Take it easy. Grab a pill, Gus, you're about to keel over."

"I'll take it easy when you tell me what the hell is going on!" The words were followed by a fit of coughing.

Sighing, Morrigan lied, "I've got detained. It's nothing, Gus, just a minor inconvenience."

It was easier than explaining that she was married and the guy wanted nothing to do with her. Not to mention more diplomatic to her bruised ego.

"You got something don't you, girl!" Gus exclaimed. "I can practically smell the story in your voice. What is it? The virgin trading practice piece you were working on? Did they offer to fix you up?"

"No, they did not! Stop being lewd or I'll hang up."

"Easy, girl," he coughed, hacking viciously. "What's got your goat?"

"My goat, Gus? You haven't been gambling with the Slayers in Valex Ten again, have you? I told you they are mind readers."

There was a long, silent pause. The communication reeked of guilt.

"Never mind," she said. "I don't want to hear how you lost another wife to them in poker."

"She wanted to go," the man protested.

"Listen," Morrigan broke in before he could defend himself further. The old communicators were unstable sometimes and could disconnect at any moment. "I need a favor. I want you to look up the contract I signed with Galaxy Brides. See if they've altered it in any way." She paused. "And see if our galactic lawyers can find any loopholes in it."

"Loopholes?" Gus said, understanding dawning in his voice. "You did get married, didn't you? I was just kidding about that. I never thought I would see the day you'd be leaving me, Rigan. Makes a man almost want to cry," Gus grumbled. He coughed, refusing to get too much more emotional. "I can tear up your contract if that's what you're asking me. No need for the lawyers. You just tell me you're happy and I'll mail the shreds to you myself." Another throat clearing. "That is after you get me that piece on those barbaric Princes."

"Damn it, Gus! Put your damned glass down and listen to me. The Galaxy Bride uploads are inaccurate. They're tricking … they're not right. It's like someone just filled in the blanks with guesses."

"What do you mean?"

"I got married by accident. Galaxy Brides has the uploads all wrong, almost all the minute details are inaccurate."

"Do they? Now this could be interesting. What angle are you going for? Poor star reporter gets trapped? Or the evil greed behind intergalactic marriages--what corporations will do to save a few bucks?"

"Slow your wheels," she broke in. It was good to hear his voice, even if he was frustrating.

"So you're not married?"

"Only technically by their laws. That is why I need you to get my contract. Use Harcy. He's fast at retrieval. Tell him I'll clear his Quazer poker debt if he does this for me."

"So, you're not leaving the paper chip?"

"No," Morrigan said, "I am not leaving the chip."

"I knew it," Gus exclaimed. "I knew my top girl would never settle down. That is what makes you the best, Rigan. I'd kiss you if you were here! Now, about those Princes--"

"I'll get you the story, Gus. You just do your job and get me the hell off this forsaken planet of barbarians."

"Will do, girl, will do!"

"Thanks." Morrigan began lifting her finger to end the transmission. His voice stopped her.

"Is he that bad?" There was a pause and a snicker. Morrigan rolled her eyes. Once she got back to the office she would never hear the end of this. "Your husband I mean?"

"He's not my husband, Gus. He's just a lead to a story." Her tone was dead and the lie left her hollow. It would be better not to think about it.

"Damn, you're cruel hearted. I always thought so, now I know. But, for now, why don't you send me your pictures. I'll expose them and get them ready for copy."

Morrigan froze. Closing her eyes, she lied, "The camera got broken. I'm trying to repair it but it might be unusable."

"What?! I should leave you there for that. Do you know how much I paid--?"

"Stow it, you owe me at least that. Besides the camera was ten years old and I bought it myself. Now come and get me you stubborn--"

"I'm on it," he answered, sternly. "Call me back in two days. Can you have the story by then?"

"Sure," she mumbled. "Oh, and Gus?"

"Sure, girl, what is it?" His words were soft.

"I'm never taking another assignment like this again."

Morrigan hit the button, breaking the communication. Her heart trembled and she began to sob.

* * * *

Ualan handed the earpiece to the watching soldier. He had listened in silence to his wife's voice. He was an inconvenience to her, a way to get her story. The Gods had indeed cursed him. Stiffly, he nodded at the awaiting soldiers.

"She called her uncle," he lied. "I will speak to her. She won't be making unauthorized communications again."

"Yes, my lord," the men answered in unison, taking the Prince at his word.

* * * *

Morrigan was drunk. No, that wasn't true. She had hit drunk and surpassed it about and hour ago. Stumbling back to the liquor cabinet, she studied the line of remaining bottles. It was hard to see them in the dim firelight. Opened containers spread about her on the floor and table. Glasses were lined up with strangely mixed concoctions swirling beneath their rims.

Taking a particularly attractive purple bottle, she stuck it beneath her arm and grabbed an ugly red one to go with it. Stumbling back to a clearing within the field of half-drunk glasses, she slumped to the floor. Taking her last clean cup, she pulled the cork from the purple and poured. Capping it, she studied the red. Twisting the cap, the red soon joined the purple. It clumped like mud but she was too far gone to care.

"This should be pretty," she mused drunkenly, swirling the mixture together and gulping it back. It wasn't. Morrigan spit the contents back into her cup with a gag. She was surprised she could still taste after so much boozing.

"What the...? Rigan?"

Ualan looked at his wife. The house smelled of liquor. Glancing around at the bottles, he saw she had nearly wiped out the cabinet. Corks and ties were littered around the floor. Some of the bottles weren't even meant for drinking. Cups, attesting to her hours of experimentation, were scattered about, some on the table and chairs. Ualan noticed that the more 'interestingly strong' blends were barely touched. He even saw a couple leading into the bathroom door. More worried about her than his liquor collection, he scowled.

Morrigan looked up and scowled drunkenly back. Ualan stood before her swimming eyes, dancing in and out of blurred vision. Oh, but he was still handsome. He had a great waist, a great chest. Morrigan hiccupped. He looked upset. His hands were on his hips, as he stared at her in disbelief. What was new? She snorted, picking up the last mixture and trying it again. Seeing the taste had not changed, she spit it out and cursed.

"The red is Qurilixian rum and the purple is a cooking spirit," he offered. "They don't mix."

Morrigan frowned, lifting the purple and trying to read it. She had no luck. It wasn't her language and it wasn't in focus.

"What do you think you're doing?" he demanded, looking at the mess she had made of his marble floor.

She flinched and wobbled to her feet. Slurring, she said, "Doon't worrry, your grace, I, Mooorrigan, your humble and most obedient servant will…."

She tipped over when she tried to bow, hiccupping again. Her head spun in momentary circles but she was too drunk to notice. Ualan started to dart forward, but stopped when she righted herself holding his ceremonial knife.

"Give me that before you hurt yourself," he demanded, getting worried by the way she was swaying with it. If she fell over, she could do herself harm. His heart leapt in his throat when she stumbled again and the knife dipped low, nearly slicing through her thigh.

"No," she said. She had been using the tip of the blade to open bottles, now she pointed it at him.

"What do you think you are going to do with that?" he snarled in warning. His eyes flashed and his nostrils flared.

"I'm killing you!" she shouted.

Morrigan's mind spun. The liquor only intensified her pain. She thought that if she just got drunk she would be able to block him out. But none of the bottles had worked. He was here, and he was so handsome. She just wanted him to look at her like he did the night of her coronation. She just wanted him to end the torture she felt. She just wanted him to want her again. Tears clouded her dark eyes, burning her nose. She wanted him to give her soul back.

"Rigan," he warned, starting to take a step forward. He thought better of it when she fearfully stumbled. Agony overwhelmed, intensified by the knowledge of her words to that man on the communicator. His gut had been rock-hard with pain ever since and now, to see her ready to kill him to be rid of him, it was the ultimate betrayal. "If you are going to strike me, then strike. But you best make the blow count, wife. You'll only get this one chance."

Morrigan looked numbly at him and blinked. She couldn't feel the teeth in her gums and she gnashed them together violently. The knife gripped in her hands. All she knew is that her soul had a hole in it and it was beginning to eat up her heart. She had to stop it. She had to stop the pain.

"I will," she said with another hiccup.

Ualan sensed what she was going to do, right before she turned the knife to her chest. Instinctively, he shifted. His skin hardened, turning a dark brown beneath his clothes. A line grew out from his forehead, pushed forward to make a hard plate of impermeable tissue over his nose and brow. His eye yellowed, able to see down to every microscopic movement of her tittering body. Talons grew from his nail beds and deadly fangs grew from his mouth.

With supernatural speed, he struck forward, throwing his own wrist before her heart to stop the blade. Since she was drunk her thrust was weak and the blade skidded off his armored skin, barely scratching him.

He ripped the blade from her fingers. Morrigan's grasp had weakened to such a degree that she let him take it. He threw the knife behind him, ignoring its noisy crash on a wall. His dragon-like nostrils flared as he studied her.

Morrigan's heart raced in excitement and fear. For some time she had been suspecting something like this, but not to such an extent. All the Qurilixian men's eyes glowed eerily at times and once she had see Zoran's skin shift slightly in color. It wasn't as if shape shifting was all that unusual in the galaxies. She met several species that had the ability to some degree.

Her eyes blinked, trying to focus on his face in an attempt to take him in. Ualan forced himself to be still, bracing for the scream that would, must come. He couldn't have been more wrong.

Morrigan's breathing deepened. She didn't care that his features had shifted and changed. She didn't care that his skin had hardened to press even more firmly than his muscles usually did. He was handsome to her. He was holding her. That was all that mattered.

His eyes, though different in color, were the same eyes she had fallen in love with. His chest heaved as he held her in his embrace, arms so strong and safe, arms she wanted to spend a lifetime in. She longed for him and it was painful, more painful than the wanderlust that normally consumed her.

Drunkenly, she grabbed his face in her hands and kissed him. Ualan stiffened. He was stunned that she would so readily accept his shifting. Feeling her soft mouth pressing forward, he changed back to human form to better taste her offering. She tasted of liquor, but he didn't care. It was sweet and her body was so soft.

Morrigan moaned. She felt him shift and ran her tongue to deepen the kiss. His skin became more pliable beneath her fingers. She jumped up, winding her legs around his sturdy waist, pushing naturally into his rising erection. His arms wrapped firmly about her buttocks to keep her there. Morrigan ground herself to him, rubbing passionately into his erection, trying to end her torment.

Ualan grunted to feel her damp heat searching for him. Nothing mattered, not her deceit or lies. She was a part of him, and he a part of her. Tomorrow would be for fighting. Tonight would be for....

"Upstairs," she growled in command, her lips bruising. Ualan didn't need to be told twice. With all the pent up frustration and anger he'd felt since meeting her, he dashed up the stairs, carrying her easily in his arms.

Morrigan was tearing at his clothes before they even reached the top. He scorched her, made her lightheaded with his passion for her. She loosened her legs and Ualan dropped her to the floor. While she tore at his pants, sending excitement through his entire being, he backed her towards the bed.

Her hand froze around his hot erection, halfway curled over the rigid tip. Ualan pulled back in surprise just in time to see her eyes roll dangerously in her head. If he hadn't been holding her, she would have dropped to the floor, completely passed out.

Ualan gulped, panting wildly for breath, and trying to adjust to another let down of his desires. Shakily, he pulled her hand away from his arousal and lifted her up to set her tenderly on the bed. He was still trembling when he drew back to study her.

Tonight would be for...ever.

Chapter Sixteen

Morning was cruel and afternoon was nor much better. Morrigan woke up alone in Ualan's bed instead of on his couch. Her head pounded in white-hot agony and she was lucky she remembered her medicine downstairs. She might not be suffering from butterfly poison, but according to her throbbing head, it was a poison that afflicted her.

Ualan was gone, but she saw the crumpled pillow on the couch signifying she had again slept alone. Vaguely remembering her degree of inebriation, she was surprised to find the house in order and the liquor cabinet completely locked up. Eyeing the laser lock silently, she laughed, and then winced at the pain the action caused. It wasn't as if she would be trying that failed experiment again any time soon.

To her amazement, when she went back upstairs, she saw that Ualan's weapons were gone from his closet. She frowned, recalling the knife she'd taken. Surely the whole scene in the living room had been a dream. But, wait, the kisses had been real enough. Was the other stuff real as well? She didn't actually try to stab herself in the heart, did she? Morrigan shook her head. No, it was impossible. She'd never do anything that stupid.

Refusing to move much further than the bed, Morrigan fell into it and soon was back asleep.

* * * *

"None of the men will fight us," Zoran said darkly to his brothers. He glanced from Ualan to Olek and then back again. "They say our mood is too black. They are frightened we will kill them."

Ualan looked over to the men who had carefully edged farther across the exercise field to get away from the angry Princes. He couldn't say he blamed them. But it didn't mean he had to like it. His lips curled into a snarl. Morrigan had pushed his body to the limit and he needed release--any kind of release.

Saying what they were all thinking, Olek growled, "What the hell are we supposed to do now?"

* * * *

Olek and Nadja's home was filled with lush plant life that grew from the sunroom to wind around a door and part of the trellised ceiling. A giant fish tank took up two walls, one clear with a giant pink sucker fish adhered to the glass, the second with dark murky waters they couldn't see into except for hints of life that fluttered past the glass. In the center of the hall was a water fountain, relaxing and calm in its resplendent beauty. It too had plant life growing in its stone crevices.

Stretching her arms over her head, Morrigan yawned. She felt better, though her body ached when she moved and her head wasn't quite right. Nadja and the other two Princesses were nice enough not to mention her unusually pale face and red eyes. At one point in their marriages to the Qurilixian Princes, they had all felt like doing the same.

"Hienrich is now training as a soldier. I released him from his duty to us," Pia said in answer to a question about the boy.

Olena didn't understand, but the others nodded in agreement.

"So, have any of your husbands lied to you about whom they were?" Olena asked. Her red hair was pulled back into a bun, and her green eyes flashed with continuous mischief, even when she wasn't up to something. She looked none the worse for wear for her ordeal with the kidnappers, but she also wasn't speaking of it.

"I thought mine was a prison guard," Pia chuckled.

"I use to call mine a gardener," Morrigan mused, tucking her hand beneath her head on the high-backed chair. "And a caveman."

The women laughed lightly. Nadja just blushed shyly, and admitted, "I call mine a dragon."

"They're all dragons, if you ask me," Morrigan winked at Nadja.

Nadja giggled as she rose to answer a summons from the door. Blinking in surprise to see the Queen, she allowed her in.

Mede stepped into the intimate circle of women and nodded. "I heard you all were hiding out here."

"How's Yusef?" Olena asked, suddenly blushing at the outburst. She refused to glance around at her comrades.

"Still awake," the Queen answered. "And still with his brothers. They speak of fighting and fighting always makes warriors happy, for it is something they know how to do."

Olena nodded, leaning back in her chair and trying to pretend she didn't care either way. No one was fooled.

Mede glanced at Morrigan and raised her delicate brow slightly. Morrigan had to turn away. There was too much knowledge in that look. But, to her credit, the Queen said nothing.

Nadja suddenly asked if anyone wanted something to drink. Morrigan balked and instantly declined, turning a shade grayer. They all laughed.

"No, dear, we're fine," the Queen answered. Silence followed. Mede was disappointed the women weren't going to continue to talk freely with her present. She had heard their laughter and had been anxious to be a part of it. But, she also knew the women were troubled in their own ways. She couldn't blame them. Her sons were great men, but were sometimes too stubborn for their own good. Announcing, she said, "Daughters."

The Princesses looked at her expectantly. Mede took a seat next to them.

"Enough of this. This planet is in desperate need of more women and I intend to see that each of you explore the power you possess. Your husbands are warriors. I expect you have a clear idea now of what that means. Just because they made the rules, doesn't mean you can't use them. You have more power than you think. So, tell me your problems with my sons and I will give you the Qurilixian solution. I think it's time that the royal woman had the upper hand for once."

Slowly, one by one, the women smiled, growing more and more trusting of the earnest Queen. The Queen nodded, happy. Yes, this was how it was supposed to be with daughters. She had waited too many years to let her sons ruin her plans for a giant family.

"Pia," the Queen began, looking pointedly at the woman closest to her. "Why don't you go first?"

* * * *

Morrigan couldn't believe it, but she did indeed feel three-hundred percent better after her afternoon chat. The Queen was a great source of information and had been only too glad to inform her daughters in how to receive the upper hand. The chat made the women closer too--like family. Morrigan smiled. A girl really could use a family. Now, all she had to do was get her husband in line. But, first things first--it was time to ease their marital tension.

"Rigan?" Ualan called, stepping hurriedly from the door. It slid shut behind him. The lights were dimmed, but he had noticed his wife usually preferred the torches to the top dome light.

He clutched the missive he'd received in his hand. It said there was an emergency back home. The guard could tell him nothing else, even though the Prince had nearly shaken him with worry. When he left that morning, his wife had been breathing and appeared to be fine. Looking around the hall, he frowned. "Rigan?"

"Here."

He heard her voice call overhead. Taking the stairs two at a time, he began, "I got a message that there was an emergency."

"There is an emergency."

"Are you ill?"

Ualan's feet slowed to a stop as he reached the top of the stairs. His heartbeat ended completely. Lounging on his bed, her silken body indecently clad in the strap negligee he had bought her, was his wife. His mouth went dry and his brain went momentarily dumb.

The white lace straps ran over her chest, crossing to barely cling to her budded nipples. The silk underneath kept the lace in place, though not at the expense of covering the valleys of her delightfully naked skin. Darting low, one lacy slash made its way between her legs, legs parted slightly in natural invitation.

"Rigan?"

Crawling up like a cat, Morrigan said, "Yes, I am sick and I am tired, Ualan. And so are you."

Ualan gasped. The mirrored headboard gave him a lush view of her backside. By all that was sacred, his wife was exquisite. His eyes roamed the back of her thighs, only to find their way over her back to stare at her lovely breasts turned gold by the firelight.

Morrigan slowly crawled to the end of the large bed, letting him look at her, liking the way his breath deepened and his stomach tightened. Her dark hair spilled over her shoulders, coming forward to brush the sides of her breasts, framing her dark eyes. Leaning back on her heels as she hit the edge, she spread her thighs and beckoned him closer.

Ualan swallowed to see the naughty expression on her face, revealing her plans for him. His body could not take getting interrupted again. It had taken all his might to leave her passed out on the bed. Not that he could have done anything with her lying unconscious.

"Rigan, no," he said to both their surprise. Was he insane? Everything his tight body desired was right before him, wrapped up like a deliciously wicked present. Ualan gulped, his eyes trailing of their own accord to where her breasts lifted with gentle breath. Blood rushed from his head, down his body to fill his loins with liquid fire. Shaking his head to stop the daze her pale skin was having on his body, he added hoarsely, "It's not working with us. Maybe we should stop trying to force it."

Morrigan wasn't so easily dissuaded. She saw the passion in his eyes. Licking her lips in appreciation of his carnal pleasure, she shook her head. "No, it hasn't been working. But that's going to stop right now." When he would protest, she scowled at him and demanded in a loud voice, "I invoke the right of inn makti murr."

Ualan was shocked. She was demanding her marital rights from him?

"Only men," he began, putting his hands on hips. Though a soft smile began to form on his lips at dominating stance.

"No. Did I ever tell you that I was a reporter, Ualan? And like a good reporter, I did a little research," she said, flicking a strap off her shoulder while she spoke. It slid leisurely over her skin to rest on the top of her breast. If she were to move, it would fall completely away. She held still.

Ualan couldn't breathe. He already knew what she did, but this was the first time she had ever admitted it to him. Did this mean she was changing her mind? Thinking of 'Gus', he doubted it. Still, he watched her every move, too far gone with lust to do anything else.

"You don't have to be male to invoke the right," she purred knowingly. "A wife has every right to her husband's bed and if he refuses to fulfill those rights, she can demand them. If he still refuses without good excuse, he will be thrown into the dungeons for thirty days to rethink his decision."

Ualan's gaze steamed over. He knew the law--knew it very well. Swallowing, he could barely listen to her words.

"From where I'm at, you don't have a good excuse," Morrigan said, with a meaningful look at his arousal.

Ualan's body tensed.

"What say you dragon Prince? Am I to call the royal guards?" Morrigan lifted up, sliding her feet onto the floor to stand before him. To his shameless disappointment, she pushed up the strap to her shoulder, but she did give him the sexiest pout of her lush lips he had ever seen.

In the back of his mind, Ualan thought that maybe she was trying to seduce him for her own purposes. But, seeing her creamy skin reflecting golden in torch light, he ignored the feeling. There would be time for listening to annoying little voices later.

"Do you wish to be imprisoned?" she whispered.

Ualan shook his head, his eyes hungry as he devoured her.

"Then undress."

Morrigan's gaze was unabashedly staring as he obeyed. With a graceful sweep, the tunic came off his shoulders. Kicking his boots, he brushed them aside before slipping completely out of his pants. Boldly, he stared at her, his eyes glinting with his inner fire. He knew no embarrassment, standing proudly before her.

Morrigan was at a loss for words. He was so handsome. His darker skin lit with fire, the flames dancing wickedly over the contours of his muscles. He didn't even have to touch her to make her body lurch. Sparks, fire, flames of lust, or whatever that was shooting through her heart and limbs, it was potent with its heady force and it was all for him. The hole inside her chest began to mend. She knew this was the piece she was missing.

"Do I meet my lady's approval?" he growled huskily, coming forward with an urgent need to touch her. His muscular chest heaved with animalistic breaths. His head lowered, as if he were ready to pounce.

Her lips parted at the boldness of his form, the freedom of inhibition in which he walked. She tried to nod to answer him, but she could barely move.

Ualan saw her matching hunger and took his opportunity to regain control. "Now you, wife, let me see what you claim I have been neglecting."

Morrigan shivered. When she didn't move fast enough, a smile formed wickedly on his tantalizing lips.

Ualan's hand darted forward, pressing instantly to her heated center. He stood away from her, pleased to find her hot and ready for him. His fingers were hard against her flesh, dipping into her through the silk barrier. "Now who resists?"

"Ah," Morrigan titled her head back and moaned. Delicately, he stroked her mound, finding her wet, making her more so. Her breath caught in ragged, openmouthed gulps. Her hips searched for something more.

Keeping his distance, save for the undulating fingers, Ualan leaned to breathe fervently on her neck, leaving trails of passion to run rampant on her fevered skin.

"So hot," he whispered in dominating pleasure, "so moist."

"Ah-hhh," she gasped, thrusting more insistently in her mindless torment. She instinctively tried to get his fingers to dip inside, past the lips of her opening.

"So ready for me."

"Yes." Morrigan's thigh lifted to restlessly rub Ualan's outer leg. His arousal hit near her stomach, touching intimately, branding, scalding.

Feet planted firmly on the floor, Ualan swiftly lifted Morrigan by her buttocks. Forcing her legs to spread wide, he wrapped them around his waist. He held her easily with his strength, shifting her weight so he could claim her. Morrigan held on to his shoulders for support. Her breasts bobbed before his face causing him to growl and nip at the air.

He held her to him, leaning her back slightly in his passion. Morrigan clung on to him, trusting him completely with her body. She arched to receive him, naturally seeking what only he could give. Without delay, Ualan guided himself to her, stoking his tip on her wet opening to part her delicate lips. Morrigan moaned loudly, feeling the hard heat of him hovering at her brink. Inside, she quivered and tensed. He felt much bigger than expected. Outside, she offered her hips to his seeking fire.

"Oh, ye ... ah," she swore she heard him pant shakily under his breath as he aimed.

Like a man possessed, the warrior deeply thrust himself into the slick offering of the temptress before him. It was sweeter than anything he could have ever imagined. The heat of her stunned him, halting the groan from his opened mouth. Her gripping muscles were almost painful in their hold.

Morrigan cried out in pain before freezing. Her eyes teared slightly. Sucking in a breath of air, she was amazed at how deeply he conquered. It burned like a flash of searing heat. This was nothing like what she had expected. She took a deep breath and then another. She had waited for so long, been teased to such an unimaginable point that the pain of it was only a minor nuisance. Ualan looked in surprise when she tensed, feeling her stretching muscles around his shaft.

Weakly, he breathed, "I thought you said you were not pure. Have you been with a man?"

Morrigan thought of the emotionless, almost medical puncture of the human-like droid. She had chosen a beginner's model to make it easy, one with a little endowment and a quick one-time poke. The machine was nothing like the man before her now. Slowly, she shook her head in denial. Ualan smiled, leaning down to nuzzle her neck.

"Ahh," was his only answer, as if that one revelation answered many of his questions. He began to walk her towards the bed. The motion caused him to thrust inside her in shallow strokes. Morrigan whimpered softly at the stinging pleasure. Laying her tenderly on the bed, he left her thighs off the edge of the soft mattress, wrapped about his waist.

Standing, he took her thighs in hand. Morrigan watched the hard lines of his body move. His flesh rippled with muscles, with control. Ualan kept his feet firmly planted, as his hips tested her, pulling out so he wasn't so deep. He had yet to give her his full length.

"Does this hurt you?" he asked, his words a low whisper. He kept himself from delving too deeply. The mirror on the headboard gave him the most erotic view as he watched them unite.

Morrigan shook her head. "No."

Slowly, he began to move. Taking it easy, he glided, fitting himself deeper with each thrust. It was warm, moist heaven. Morrigan didn't protest as the passion built inside her skin.

"How about this?" Ualan gulped. Oh, but it was hard to hold back. He wanted nothing more than to give her his full length. "Am I pushing too deep?"

"There is more of you?" Morrigan asked, understanding his comment. She looked down in amazement. Ualan grinned, still careful not to embed too deeply.

"Yes," he grunted, thrusting in shallow strokes within her heat.

"More," she demanded, as she relaxed to him. Oh, how she wanted this to work more than anything. His fullness conquered her. "I want more. I want it all."

His eyes were closed to her, but Morrigan kept her gaze fixed firmly on him. Watching his body was almost as pleasurable as feeling it. The hands on her thighs began to move, urging her legs up onto his shoulders. Her polished toes curled next to his head. Ualan growled, going even deeper as he leaned forward.

"Ahh!" Morrigan screamed, pleasure ripping through her as he gave her everything of himself.

Ualan grunted at her cry of pleasure. Her muscles spasmed, accepting him. Suddenly, he couldn't hold back. Hearing her continued cries of pleasure, he quickened his pace. His thrusts became more powerful and urgent in his hunt for release. His hips pumped faster, testing her reaction, harder, yet mindful of her newly altered state.

Morrigan tensed, grabbing onto the silk beneath her back. She couldn't move, couldn't fight. She could only let her giant warrior ride as he took complete control. Her legs trembled, her body quivered and shook. A whimper of budding pleasure escaped her lips. Ualan didn't stop. He found the sensitive nub guarding her entrance, circling it in fast strokes with his fingers as he pushed her onward, hammering his violent need into her slick core, forcing her to face her pleasure, pushing her over its trembling edge.

Morrigan's body racked, exploding with the force of her climax. Her back arched. Soon, Ualan's conquering yell joined hers. Ualan's body jerked violently as he spilled his seed into her. He stood frozen like a statue, releasing himself completely. Morrigan panted, too weak to move, sure she was near death. Growling masculine approval, Ualan dropped her legs and dragged his heavy limbs on the bed, forcing her up with him as he stayed embedded intimately inside her.

Ualan stared deeply in her eyes when he pulled himself free. She winced a little, but gave him a shy smile. For a long moment, he stayed poised atop her, stroking her tousled hair with the backs of his fingers. His eyes dipped over her negligee. Leaning over, he kissed her nipple lightly, before finding her lips to do the same. Then, rolling off, he pulled her into his arms.

"Did I hurt you?" Ualan asked.

"Not too bad. It just stings a little."

"It will get better."

Morrigan stroked his face. Trailing a line over his forehead, she whispered, "Does it hurt when you change?"

Ualan looked down in surprise. He had thought she didn't remember.

"Ualan," she began at his look. "I am a reporter. I have been all over the galaxy. I've even seen giant slugs get married. I've seen birds that could speak seven languages. I've seen--"

His lips cut her off. Pulling back, he said, "I get the point."

"Anyway, I don't know why you would think I would be shocked by a little thing like shifting." Dipping her eyes shyly, she admitted, "In fact, it was kind of neat."

Ualan saw the light in her eyes when she spoke of her adventures. Never could he realize that the light in her was put there by him. It tore at him, believing she longed for something he could not give her. His life was here as was his destiny. The House of Draig needed him. He was the future King. He could never leave. Aside from a very few ambassador-like duties, he would live and die on Qurilixen. Until now, he had been content with that future.

"You love it, don't you?" he asked quietly.

"What?" She nuzzled his jaw, her whole being singing with contentment. His warm flesh felt so right against her skin. She began to roam her hands aimlessly, unable to get enough of him. There wasn't an ounce of fat on his muscular frame. She lightly trailed each and every indent of his chest, skating across it with her fingers. Ualan's stomach tensed as she went over his ribs. Morrigan smiled, absently clarifying, "You mean reporting?"

"Yes." The word was low. He tightened his hands slightly on her in possession.

"I'm good at it. I get to set my own schedule, see the universes. I've learned different customs. I even get to set my own pay. I've worked hard for what I have," she said. She slowly ran her fingers lower. A part of her pulled, eager to see how better it would get. "It's been my whole life. I don't really know how to do anything else."

Ualan said nothing.

"Hey," she whispered. The pit of her stomach churned. "I've been meaning to ask. How old are you anyway? The uploads that Galaxy Brides gave us were inadequate at best, but they said you lived for five hundred years or so. Is that true?"

"Writing a story?" he queried softly, remembered her conversation on the communicator.

"Maybe," she breathed, thinking he was teasing her. She had wondered if he had been married already. If what was said was true then he could live long past her death. Would he look this beautiful when she was wrinkled and old? How soon would he replace her with another wife? To think it was agony. She didn't want there to be anyone else for him, but she knew she would never curse him to live hundreds of years alone.

She wanted to ask, but her treacherous eyes were drifting to his lips and her mind began to wander as she felt him stirring against her leg.

"Then close your eyes wife and I will give you a story to tell."

Morrigan gasped as his body came over her. Soon his lips were caressing every inch of her form, licking and tasting, kissing and biting. Then, when he licked the center of her hot desire to soothe the ache his body had wrought in her, he brought her to climax with his mouth and she screamed anew, overwhelmed by the sensations. Nothing mattered at that moment of ecstasy but her warrior husband. She was where she wanted to be. She was finally home.

As Ualan held his wife afterwards, he knew that she was what completed him. He would pledge himself to her always if she demanded it. He would crush kingdoms at her command. He'd even buy her the damned food simulator she seemed so desperately to want. But, the one thing he couldn't bring himself to do was let her go.

Morrigan stirred his arms. Her mind was wide-awake on her recovery from her trembling journey. She knew his needs weren't satisfied. She could feel his erection still firm to her thigh. Not knowing the thoughts that troubled his head, she began kissing his ear, and asked, "Can I try being on top this time?"

Chapter Seventeen

Morrigan's body couldn't have been more pleased with its mistress. It hummed with a gentle fire throughout the night and allowed her to face the morning rested and completely sated. Thinking of Ualan, she reached her hand over to search for him. Well, maybe not completely sated....

"Ualan?" she asked under a yawn. She felt an empty space beside her on the bed and wrinkled her face. Her voice rocky with sleep, she asked louder, "Ualan?"

"Yes," came the solemn answer from their closet. His words rolled over her and she nearly blushed to remember some of the wickedly delightful things he had said to her in the night hours. Her husband really did have a naughty way with words.

"Come back to bed," she urged shyly. "It's too early to get up."

"Its noontime," he answered and Morrigan swore she heard him chuckle.

"Noon?" She shot up and mumbled, "Accursed planet. I can't keep my hours straight."

The chuckling stopped. Inside the closet, Ualan took a deep breath. He heard her words clearly.

With a grumble, she asked, "What are you doing in there? Come back to bed by order of the Princess! You're a Prince and it's not like you have anything important to do anyway."

At that he came around the corner. Morrigan gulped to see him so handsome in his formal wear and crown. The crown circled around his forehead, pushing his hair flat at the sides. The long black tunic he wore hung down past his knees, splitting open in the front to reveal his black breeches. The family emblem surrounded by a shield was embroidered on the front in blue. She quickly grabbed the covers and hid her naked body. His eyes dipped in disappointment, but he didn't stop her.

"What's going on?" she asked, moving to stand. "Why are you all ... princely?"

"There is a meeting with some of the other kingdoms," he answered, smoothing down the longer sleeves of his formal tunic. It was the uniform of the Draig war council.

Morrigan's brow furrowed and journalistic instinct kicked in. Seriously, she said, "Attor."

Ualan nodded.

"I want to go with you," she said, dragging his gray coverlet with her in her attempts to scurry to the closet.

"You can't wear that," he laughed. His eyes weren't so joyous. More fodder for your exposé, wife?

"Just give me a second," she said. She came rushing back around to look at him. Her hair was beautifully tousled around her face and shoulders and her features were still rosy from the warmth of sleep. Frowning, she admitted, "I don't have anything to match that."

She wouldn't, thought Ualan, slightly amused. He was dressed for the war council and women were not allowed entrance. Occasionally the Queen would come to give her opinion, but that was rare.

"Sorry, Rigan. You can't come this time." Ualan brushed past her to take a sword from a locked truck he pulled from the closet. Strapping it over his shoulder, he took a knife and hid it in his waist. Then, he strapped one in each boot.

"Are you expecting trouble?" she asked, growing worried. Her round eyes looked him over.

"There is always trouble when warriors get together," he replied, amused.

"You...." She paused, her face becoming terrified. Her dark eyes frantically searched his. "You won't get hurt will you?"

"I thought you trusted me," he answered softly, not pleased with her concern. It showed a real lack of faith in him as a warrior and protector.

"You can put them back. I'm not going to do anything foolish. I only had the knife because Pia was supposed to teach me how to knife fight."

"I know you didn't intend on acting that way. I found one of your concoctions. You mixed Tetrex with Mifol. They are opposing stimulants that are harmless apart, but make you crazy when put directly together." Ualan closed the lid, leaving it unlocked. "I put these up before I found the bottles."

"Oh, but I am still very sorry about that. I didn't hurt you, did I?"

"No," he answered. Softly, he leaned to kiss her cheek. "Just stay away from drinking things that you have no idea what they are, all right?"

"Sure," she agreed with a dutiful nod. "Why can't I come with you, Ualan? Please. I won't say a word. I promise."

"We are giving King Attor the right of defense. If it was he who poisoned you and stabbed Yusef there will be justice and possible war." Ualan made his way down the steps. He didn't want to tell her that Attor would assuredly deny everything and war was inevitable.

Morrigan trailed behind him, dragging the coverlet.

"Shouldn't I be there? I was the one who was poisoned by him."

"No, Princess," he said, turning to wrap his arms around her. Morrigan snuggled naturally into his strong chest. Ualan's breath caught at her easy affection. Concern shone in his gaze when he looked at her. "You stay here today. Attor's men are here and everyone is instructed to stay within their homes. We will not have blood shed. We aren't going to risk losing anyone."

Morrigan frowned, ready to protest.

"Shh..." he whispered when her mouth opened. "Promise me you'll stay here."

Slowly, she nodded. "All right, I promise. Can I visit the other Princesses?"

"It's not a good idea to be out walking the halls," he said. Going to the door, he commanded it open. "Food will be sent around in a moment. Only Mirox is allowed to enter."

Morrigan nodded.

Ualan didn't want to tell her that spies may possibly be afoot in the palace. Whoever stabbed Yusef knew the back passages well enough to escape through them. Even as he wanted to protect her from worry, he also knew he could not publicize his family's affairs at such a delicate stage. This was a Qurilixian conflict. He did not want her attracting intergalactic attention to an age old feud. Others would only try to step in and help, causing more problems than solutions.

"When will you be home?" she asked, hopeful.

"As soon as I can," Ualan answered. "It depends on what Attor has to say."

"Wait," she called when he went for the door. He came to her, brushing his finger over her lush lip when she would plead, "Just...."

His gaze glittered as he studied her.

Just be careful.

Morrigan didn't know what else to say. She didn't want to insult him by implying he would be outdone and she didn't want him to go. He smiled slightly and ran his fingers from her lips to her cheeks to give her a gentle caress. He kissed her with tender lips that held promises of later things. With a soft nudge of his forehead to hers, he let her go.

"Bye," she whispered breathlessly, her knees weak.

With a shut of the door, Ualan was gone.

* * * *

King Attor denied all charges with a smirky grin. He knew so long as he was under the protection of justice, he would not be touched. Nothing was accomplished during the seven hours of talks. But, then again, nothing had been accomplished in the centuries of fighting that had occurred between the two kingdoms. Death attempts on both sides were nothing new, though none had occurred for over a hundred years.

After the meeting, it took another four and a half hours to insure that Attor and his men were gone. A thorough search of the castle revealed nothing and the alert was taken off the village. By the time Ualan dragged his feet home, he was too tired to think.

Ualan knew that soon they might be facing another war with the House of Var. Wars were terrible affairs for their kind, lasting sometimes for fifty to a hundred years with many deaths and seldom any clear progress or victory, just an uneasy truce while each side replenished their warriors and concentrated on rebuilding the population. The Var were worthy opponents, powerful.

Seeing his wife already asleep, Ualan stripped off his clothes and crawled into bed next to her. She stirred when he wrapped his arms around her waist. Blinking, she smiled at him. Then, seeing his tired eyes, she asked, "Long day?"

He nodded, leaning over to kiss her. They made love slow and leisurely, taking their time, trying not to think of what separated them. Morrigan thought of her limited years, of growing old and out of Ualan's interest. Ualan thought of her leaving him, sentencing him to a lifetime of loneliness and hollow solitude.

* * * *

Ualan awoke the next morning instantly reaching for Morrigan at his side before his eyes were even open. His touched an empty bed instead of her warm flesh. Frowning, he opened one eye. She never woke up early.

He dressed and rushed downstairs, expecting to see her on the couch. Quizzically, he smiled, going first to the bathroom and then to the kitchen. His smile faded. His heart squeezed painfully in his chest. She was gone.

* * * *

The warriors cheered good-naturedly as the four Princesses, wearing dark breeches and tunic shirts, aimed knives at the practice post. Olena was the first to throw. She did fairly well as each knife made it into the center. The gathered soldiers clapped and stomped. She glanced at Yusef, trying to act like she didn't seek his approval. A white bandage slashed across the Prince's arm but he looked well.

Nadja was hopeless, missing the target completely on all five tries. She glanced at Olek in embarrassment. The men applauded anyway.

Morrigan managed to hit the post on her turn, though they weren't centered. She curtsied as she received her cheers.

She had gotten up early, unable to sleep as nightmares invaded her dreams. Pia had sent a servant around with a missive, requesting she 'get her lazy butt out to the practice field for some sport'. Morrigan could hardly refuse. Ualan looked so handsome, his arm resting above his head, his brown hair splayed messily around his face, a strand of which slashed over a closed eye. She didn't have the heart to wake him, knowing how hard he'd worked the day, and night, before. Morrigan grinned to think about it.

"Maybe you ladies should let a man show you how it's done," called a voice from the crowd.

Morrigan rolled her eyes at the others, retrieving the silver blades for Pia's turn.

"Ach," Agro cried. "You're hardly a man, Hume!"

Pia took the knives, weighing them carefully in her hand. Getting to the third one, she lifted it and studied the blade.

Frowning, she went to her husband and handed it to him. She took a knife from his waist to replace it, testing his blade as she did the others.

At his curious frown, she announced loudly, "You need to check the balance on that one. It will pull a fraction to the right."

With hardly moving a muscle, Zoran threw the blade over her shoulder. It stuck just to the right of the target. The men laughed heartily. Morrigan stared at Prince Zoran. He was even larger than Ualan. She shivered, thinking her husband was definitely the better proportioned and better looking.

Not turning around, Pia said, "Told you."

Zoran's lip curled up at the side.

Going before the target, Pia took a deep breath. Flinging one of the blades, she rapidly dropped to the ground to throw two more in roll. Then, coming to kneel, she threw the last two. The fourth blade struck against Zoran's to knock it free, before sticking in its place. The fifth, she turned her arm and it missed the post completely. The warriors watched in stunned silence, their eyes following the path of her last throw. It was a foot before Hume.

"You missed," said Hume, to break the silence. The men went wild cheering. Pia took a graceful bow. The woman jumped in excitement, basking in Pia's victory.

Ualan ignored the commotion as he came to the field. He had checked everywhere and couldn't find his wife. At first, he suspected she tried to leave him. But, after questioning the guards at the spacecraft dock, he saw everything was in order.

Morrigan turned, seeing Ualan going towards his brother. A bright smile lit her face.

"Careful," Olena teased, bumping into her arm. "Or else we might think you actually like the barbarian."

Morrigan blushed, turning her eyes away, only to peek again from beneath her down turned lashes.

Zoran frowned at Ualan's fevered whisper. Without uncrossing his arms, he nodded his jaw to where Morrigan stood with the other Princesses.

Ualan felt instant relief when he located her. But worry made his face look harsh as he came to claim her. Seeing Olena with the blades, he said to Morrigan, "Come."

"What?" she whispered in question. "We're still practicing. Pia is going to show us how to roll while throwing."

"Don't argue with me," he hissed. "Come, now."

Morrigan was embarrassed. When she looked over her shoulder while being dragged roughly away, she received looks from the other women that seemed to say they understood her situation completely and were sorry for it.

Morrigan's embarrassment turned to anger as he dragged her along a path that would take them closer to the village. "What in the hell do you think you're doing?"

Ualan turned, making sure no one watched. They kept their voices low. Morrigan did not want to create another scene.

"Where were you this morning?"

"What? Is that what this is about?" she asked in disbelief. "You're mad because I wasn't in bed when you woke up. I'm sorry, I didn't realize it was my duty to see to your...." Morrigan looked down at his pants and said, "...your release each morning."

"Rigan," he warned. That's not what he meant and she knew it.

Ualan, not wanting to draw attention by standing so close to the village, grabbed her arm and dragged her deeper into the forest. Morrigan trailed along in silence, hurt by his attitude. She'd thought that after what happened between them in the night hours he would trust her more. Obviously, she was the only one deeply affected by their joining. The realization stung.

"Rigan," Ualan began again when they came to halt. The hairs on the back of his neck stood on end. She was so damned beautiful and even more infuriating.

"No," she growled in a heated whisper. "I didn't realize I had to check in with you whenever I wanted to do anything. You don't want a wife, you want a cook and a maid and ... You want a slave. Well, I'm sorry master. I didn't realize I had to be there for your pleasure each morning. Should I relieve you right now? Right ... here?"

A dart shot out from the trees, hitting Morrigan in the neck. Her eyes rolled in her head, and she fell forward. Ualan caught her with one hand, automatically lifting his sword with the other. Twelve light blond warriors jumped out from the trees, their bodies growing with fur as they shifted with the features of wild cats.

Ualan was forced to shift awkwardly, using his arm to deflect the enemy's blows. He tried to protect Morrigan, her feet trailing in the dirt as he called out to his brothers for assistance. Soon his brothers were by his side, shifting into the Draig while they fought against the Var. The one-armed Yusef bravely hacked forward with his sword, giving Ualan time to get Morrigan to safety.

Ualan dropped Morrigan to the ground behind his battling brothers as softly as he could before returning to the fight against the attackers. Pia ran swiftly to join the men, throwing a blade into one of the creature's throats. When Zoran swung his arm, she ducked beneath him, grabbing a knife from his belt.

Nadja stiffened in fear to see the fighting creatures--human dragons against human tiger-like beasts. Shaking herself at Olena's call, she darted forward to the fallen Morrigan. With Olena's help, they pulled the woman from the fray to safety.

Almost immediately the Vars retreated to the forest. Zoran nodded to his wife in pride, shifting back. Ualan turned, sniffing out Morrigan's trail and took off down the path, Yusef and Olek were behind him.

Nadja was by Morrigan's side, examining the wound. She jolted to see Ualan's Draig face before he shifted back to how she knew him. Looking around, she warily eyed Olek's human features.

Ualan began to reach forward.

"Don't," commanded Nadja. Ualan drew back in surprise. She nodded at his arm where red blisters were forming on his skin. "She is poison to you."

Ualan's jaw tensed, but he held back.

"You can't move her yet," Nadja said.

"But, the poison...." Ualan tried, desperate to help his wife.

"Quiet," Nadja hissed. Zoran and Pia approached from the battle, having checked to make sure none of the enemy remained. "Let me think. I need to concentrate."

Ualan looked at Olek who appeared as confused as he was. Olek shrugged.

"Give me your knife," Nadja said. She reached out with shaking fingers. Her eyes darted around the now silent forest. Pia immediately handed her blade over.

Taking a deep breath, Nadja cut into Morrigan's throat where the dart had embedded in the skin. Instantly, green began to drip and ooze from the wound. Soon, she had dug out the star tipped points of the dart.

Nadja dropped the blade and continued to bleed the poison out. When she had finished, she commanded Ualan, "Try touching her."

Ualan did. He was left unharmed.

"It's as I thought. I've seen this kind of poison before. Usually jealous old lovers do it for revenge. If you had torn the dart out of the skin, it would have released a poison into the blood stream. She would have lived but you never would have been able to touch her again. It's ironic really. That way it is the current lover that poisons the woman, sealing their fate. You should get her to a doctor."

Nadja stood, wearily trying to edge away from the Draig shifters.

"I would say that whoever poisoned her didn't want you to be with her," Nadja said, before turning and running away from them. Olek was right behind her.

Olena stood, watching the woman disappearing into the forest. Her eyes narrowed. Solemnly, she said, "She didn't know about the Draig."

Ualan picked up his wife, not caring about Nadja's fear of him and his brothers. She would get over it easily enough. All he cared about was getting his wife to safety. The others followed as he carried Morrigan to the medical ward. No one said a word.

Chapter Eighteen

"Why do they attack the Princesses?" Yusef asked with a frown. Olena stood by his side, her face unmoving. Nadja and Olek had not joined them, but Zoran and Pia stood next to Ualan. Morrigan was on the hospital bed, having been checked by the doctors and given some medicine to help along her recovery. If not for Nadja's interference, she would have been as good as dead. She couldn't imagine never being able to touch Ualan.

Ualan looked at his wife. Her face was pale, but was regaining color. The puncture on her neck left a small mark, but nothing that wouldn't be healed. His heart beat painfully with the thought that he'd almost lost her--again.

With sudden insight, Pia whispered, "Because without us, you will have no sons. Your line will end."

Morrigan blinked. Her throat hurt too bad to speak, so she held quiet. She watched the hard side of Ualan's face for a reaction. They had not spoken of sons.

Morrigan knew Ualan was mad at her. She couldn't blame him. She had said some pretty mean things. She just couldn't help it. His eyes had been so accusing, like she was up to something devious. Now, he barely even looked at her. Her entire body ached and she wanted nothing more than to be pulled into his arms and protected. Once, she saw his hand straying as if to touch her, but it changed course and only scratched the back of his head. Her spirit fell in disappointment.

Pia's lips stiffened, as she continued, drawing Morrigan's attention away from her husband to the problem at hand. "It makes perfect sense. I've seen you all fight. Especially with all four of you banded together, you would be a formidable opponent. You expect the attack. We are new here and it would be assumed that we had no clear idea of the dangers. Plus, we are women. Men ... ah, no offense to anyone here ... men, especially those from warrior classes, often misjudge women as unworthy opponents."

The Princes listened closely to her words, giving away none of their thoughts. Morrigan watched Ualan slowly nod in consideration of her words. She automatically sought him with her hand, but dropped back, unsure how he would take the familiar contact.

Pia gazed up at her husband. Her face was pulled with concentration. "If you were to destroy an enemy, Zoran, would you attack their weakness or their strength?"

"Only a fool would choose to fight a strength if a weakness was to be had," Ualan said, nodding to the woman's insight. Morrigan couldn't take her eyes from him. How she wished they were alone so she could talk to him.

"Only they have obviously underestimated the strength of our women," Zoran added.

Ualan glanced at his wife, wondering at the look on her face and dismissing it as part of her illness. He wanted to hold her, but knew after what she yelled at him that she would think he only sought to force her into his arms. True, this morning he had been ready to make love to her again. And why not? It was one of the few times they weren't strained emotionally towards each other. It was the one time when he knew her actions and words were pure and untainted by deceit. Besides, she was his wife. It was only natural that he wanted to make love to her. He refused to feel guilty about it.

"What better way to end this age old feud than to wipe out the leaders before they are born?" Yusef said. He frowned, unconsciously drawing Olena under the protection of his good arm.

"For, if we were to die," Ualan added, turning his eyes again to his brothers. He again resisted the urge to pull Morrigan into his embrace to convince himself that she was unharmed. But he did not want to risk her rejection in front of his family. "There would be an heir that could sometime rise against them. If they secure that our line is ended, when we die there will be no one to avenge us. With no King or protection, our people will be left without defense. Everything will be in chaos."

"It is imperative that we discover who is spying for the Var," Yusef said. Whoever had stabbed him knew the back passages well enough to escape through them.

"Spy?" asked Pia, blinking. She turned to frown at Zoran. "You said nothing of a spy!"

"Olena," Pia said. "You remember that servant at the festival, don't you? The one who spilled his drink? It has to be him. He was no more fit to be a servant than I am."

Olena shook her head, barely recalling anything but her husband from that night.

"What are you talking about?" Zoran demanded of his wife, turning to grab her arms and study her eyes.

"There are too many servants in the kingdom," Ualan mused. "For festivals many come to help. It would take forever to locate them all just to find this one."

"No," Pia said. "He was at the coronation. The spy would be here in the palace kitchens. I remember watching him fumble with some plates. He only carried two, unlike the other servants who carried four or more. It has to be him. He was graceless. Yet there was something different to his walk and his hand had a sword callous along the ridge. I would almost bet my life he was your man."

Morrigan, having an idea and desperately wanting to help, glanced hesitantly at Ualan. He didn't pay her any attention. Knowing that lives were more important than her pride or Ualan's anger, she said with her hoarse voice, "I recorded that night on my camera." Everyone turned to look at her.

Sheepishly, she admitted, "I'm an undercover reporter for an intergalactic newspaper chip."

Ualan stiffened but did not stop her. Morrigan's eyes searched his for a sign of anything. He was cautiously blank. She swallowed, nervously.

"I was supposed to write a story about the royal weddings," she continued softly. Turning to Ualan, her eyes pleaded with him not to be mad. But, her own discomfort over the confession would not stop her from helping her new family. Quietly, she admitted, "My camera will have recorded part of that night. Maybe Pia's servant can be found on the relay."

"It's worth a shot," Yusef said.

"I'll go find it," Ualan said stiffly. He went from the hospital room, his arms rigid with anger. His stomach tightened at how easily she spoke of exposing him and his family. Hopefully, his brothers would take little heed of her confession. Knowing exactly the container the camera was in, since he had been the one to put it up, he grabbed it. His gut ached and he paused taking a deep breath before returning to her.

Morrigan watched him leave, knowing he was upset. It was silent in the room and she couldn't meet anyone's gaze, afraid that they would be mad at her. When Ualan came back, he handed her a small eyepiece and the emerald trigger.

"Can you make it work so we can all see?" Yusef asked.

Morrigan nodded. "I think so."

She requested some saline and wetted the lens before sticking it into her eye. Slipping the emerald on her finger so it could react with her nervous system, she turned the stone. A light shone from her eyes, darkening as she blinked. They watched in amazement as they saw a picture of the Breeding Festival floating on the air.

Coming around to stand across from Morrigan, they eyed the round picture.

"Can you see it?" she asked.

"Yes," Ualan said, his tone stiff. He took a deep breath, trying to relax his body. It would not do for the others to see his fury.

"All right, just let me leaf through these," she murmured. Morrigan closed her eye and the picture disappeared. Instantly, she came across a video feed of Ualan the night of the Breeding Festival--his proud face, his delectably oiled body ... Gulping, she pushed the button, trying her best to get through all the naughty photographs to the important ones. She'd forgotten all that was on there and made a note to erase it--just as soon as she looked the fur loincloth over another time.

"Morrigan," Ualan began. He saw her turn bright red and wondered about it.

Morrigan blinked in surprise at the gruff sound of his voice. A flash of Ualan's naked backside came up bigger than life before his brother's faces. Ualan felt his stomach lurch with manly arrogance that she had taken such a thing, tempered with just a touch of embarrassment.

"Oh," Morrigan panicked. His discomfort left to see his wife's obvious panic as she squeezed her eyes shut and hit furiously at the emerald on her hand.

Suddenly, Zoran and Yusef began to laugh vigorously.

Wryly, Ualan stated, "I had no idea I looked that good from behind."

He was rewarded with punches from his laughing brothers.

Morrigan nearly threw up all over herself in horror. Olena and Pia exchanged amused looks, biting back their laughter in front of their husbands.

"Here," Morrigan said, getting back to business as she swallowed her mortification. A screen of the festival came up. "I can't play sound, but you should see the picture moving like a silent movie."

They watched in silence. Then suddenly, Pia pointed and said, "There, stop, that's him."

Morrigan froze the picture with a tap of the emerald. She couldn't see what they were pointing at.

"Yeah," Olena said, leaning forward to get a closer look at the corner. "I remember him. Now that you mention it, he was rather strange."

"He has the coloring of a Var," Yusef said.

"But not the scent of one," Zoran said. "Do you think he has found a way to mask his smell?"

"He wears the tunic of the kitchen staff," Yusef said. "We will find him and question him. If he is Draig, it will be easy for him to prove it. If he is Var, he will come up with an excuse not to shift."

Ualan nodded. Yusef and Zoran left with their women by their sides.

Morrigan shut off the camera and eased it out of her eye. Seeing Ualan's extended hand, she gave the ring and eyepiece back to him.

"Ualan," she began, weakly.

"I'll be back in a moment," he answered, turning from her. Morrigan paled horribly, watching his broad shoulders as he walked away. He was livid. When he came back, the camera was gone. She wondered where he put it and didn't really care, except for the fact she wanted to erase the pictures of him before anyone else saw them.

"I was going to tell you about the article," she began.

"It's fine," he cut her off harshly. His lips pressed tightly together.

She opened her mouth to say more, but the doctor came back before she could get a word in. Sighing, she watched Ualan step back to watch the doctor work. She looked at him in dejection, wondering what he was thinking behind his emotionless mask of a face. Whatever it was, it couldn't be good and her heart broke a little because of it.

* * * *

Morrigan was released into Ualan's care. He carried her home and laid her down on his bed where he watched vigilantly over her when she fell asleep, completely worn. She was going to be all right. Ualan wasn't. He felt horrible. It had been his duty to protect her and he had failed. Now, she was poisoned for the second time.

Going downstairs, he went to work on the food simulator he had bought for her as a surprise. Ualan really didn't like it and didn't know why he had bothered, as he installed it into the wall. If he couldn't protect her like he promised, then he couldn't expect her to want to stay. He cared for her too much.

"Coffee," he said to try the machine out. When the door beeped, he pulled out a cup of steaming hot black-brown liquid. Smelling it, he grimaced. That couldn't be right.

Closing the door, he said, "Sloken."

The door beeped again and when he opened it he eyed the green liquid. It smelled normal and he tried a little taste. It wasn't the best he ever had, but it was adequate. Maybe it was working.

Ualan frowned, drawn to check on Morrigan. Climbing the stairs, he joined her on the bed. Gently, he laid his hand on her hip, studying her pale, sleeping face in the darkness. If she was unhappy on his planet, then all he could do was give her what she wanted. Though it would kill him, it was time to let go.

* * * *

The news came soon after Ualan got his wife home that Pia's blond servant was apprehended almost immediately upon the Princes entering the palace kitchens. They found him hiding behind one of the big brick ovens, ducking from his work. Zoran's nose picked up the Var smell beneath an all too potent covering of Draig.

The spy must have known that he was found out, because he tried to run. It was no use. Yusef was standing in the doorway and with a swing of his good arm he punched the man square in the jaw and laid him out on the floor.

The Draig servants blinked in surprise at the sudden attack, but as they witnessed the lazy man sprawled on the ground, they began to cheer without knowing his deceit. As a fellow worker, the Var spy was not well liked in the kitchen.

The royal family was relieved as news was spread of the spy's capture. Olek escorted the man to the lower prisons and even now the Var was being questioned by Agro. Ualan had no doubt that the beefy giant would discover much from the man. When Agro chose to shift, he could be most persuasive.

* * * *

Unable to draw out his love play any longer, Ualan guided himself into his wife. With a firm stroke, he delved into her moist opening, gliding in her like he belonged there. A victorious shout came from him as he claimed her. Morrigan growled in exhilaration, not caring who heard her loud cries. Ualan plunged onward in excitement, compelling her hot center to open for him and accept him in her tight depths.

Sitting back on his feet, he pulled her up so she could ride him. Morrigan did so willingly, pushing herself up and pulling herself down in a frightfully decadent rhythm of searching lunges. Deeper he went, imbedded fully into the prison of her silky depths, only to be released and recaptured again and again.

Morrigan grabbed the sides of the bath, splashing water over the edge as she rode him faster and harder, seeking fulfillment to the torment he caused with his endless teasing and his … his….

"Ahhh," Morrigan shrieked her trembling freedom into the Breeding Festival tent. Ualan met her, his cry rivaling hers in passion and release. Her lips parted, and he heard her whisper, "I love you, Ualan."

It was only a dream.

Sitting up with a jerk, Ualan's body was drenched with sweat. He blinked, looking around the living room before realizing he'd fallen asleep on the couch. His head turned looking up to the bedroom. His body was hard, thumping against the restraint of his pants.

He would just go check on her, he assured himself, as he stood with a single-minded purpose coursing through his fevered blood.

"Ualan?" he heard her voice to call softly into the darkness when he climbed up the stairs. "Is that you?"

She seemed frightened. Maybe he should comfort her. A devil's grin came to his face. "Yes, Rigan."

He heard her sigh.

"I was having a nightmare. Where were you? I woke up and you weren't here."

"I fell asleep downstairs," he answered. Was that disappointment in her voice?

"Oh," Morrigan sighed. Then, timidly, she asked, "Are you coming to bed now?"

Ualan walked over to the bed. He could see her clearly with his Draig vision. She reached out for him. He tensed, moving over slightly so her fingers could find him.

Morrigan gasped. Ualan groaned. Her fingers had landed on his stiff member.

He watched her face carefully. She smiled, not knowing he could see her as she licked her lips.

"Ualan?" she whispered. Her hand didn't move. She edged timidly over the material to feel him. Her lips parted and she panted softly. Her perfume filled his nostrils. Suddenly, her hands were on his waist, drawing his pants down over his hips. The warm air hit him, fanning from her parted lips.

He saw her face hesitating, as if she waited for his response.

"Don't stop," he commanded. His stomach tensed. Morrigan leaned forward lightly kissing the dip of his navel. His arousal brushed her cheek and again she looked up at him, unable to see him in the darkness.

The images of his dream came floating through his mind, powerful and all consuming.

"Undress," he whispered.

Morrigan obeyed instantly. She knew she should stop and demand he listen to her explanation about the article--that she would only submit it after she had his approval. Morrigan knew it was against every journalistic code to give a copy of the piece to the subject before print, but she didn't care. It was a small sacrifice to pay if it would regain his trust in her.

Ualan watched the unveiling of her flesh in the darkness. Her breasts rose and fell--tempting his lips. Just seeing her heated his blood past boiling. His skin was on fire with the need to feel her. And, by watching her jerking, hurried movements, he knew that in this they felt the same.

"Turn from me and kneel," Ualan breathed.

Morrigan shivered, liking his steady commands, the assurance in his words as he spoke. She turned her back to him without protest, looking over her shoulder to try and see if he moved. She felt his weight shift the bed.

"Bend over."

Morrigan wondered why he did not touch her. Her body sang with liquid fire, emboldened by the darkness and the persuasively mysterious feel of his words.

Ualan knelt behind her, his eyes burning as he watched her. When she complied, Ualan said, "Now back yourself up until you feel me against you."

"Ualan?" she asked softly, but she did not hesitate to crawl back on the bed. When she was within grabbing distance, he sprang forward and firmly grasped her hips in his palms.

Morrigan yelped, startled.

Ualan pulled her thighs to part so that he could stroke her with his hand. She rubbed up against him, a low humming noise coming from her to drive him wild. His fingers gently parted her, sliding along her opening, stroking first one then two fingers up inside her. Her whimpering grew into cries of delight. Her opened mouth begged him for release. Only when he'd stroked her to flames, did he pull her back against him.

Ualan pressed her down, spreading her wider so she was the perfect height to accept him. He groaned to feel her wetness taking him in. With a mighty thrust he conquered her. Morrigan gasped at the fullness of him, still surprised each time that he could force himself so deep.

"Ualan," she shrieked, yelling his name, urging him on. She twisted her hands into the bed, clutching as she tried to hold on.

Ualan moved, spurred on by the thrusting image of her body before him. Her breasts reflected back to him from the mirror, teasing him with their bobbing movements. Her back arched. He ran his hands into her hair, pulling the tender threads lightly in his fingers.

Morrigan gasped, not minding his hold on the locks. Reaching a hand around her body, he stroked her womanhood as he thrust. Morrigan jerked, never having felt such pleasure as she did with him.

Their bodies built with the tension he created with his claiming. They panted, moaned, yelled in ecstasy. Ualan hit against her, delving harder, deeper. Morrigan trembled with violent gratification, her body tensing as she spasmed in pure pleasure.

Ualan grunted, loosing himself in to her. He hollered viciously, jerking his arms to slam her hips hard against him a last couple of times.

Almost instantly, Morrigan dropped when he let her go. She lay on her stomach, raggedly gulping for air. Her body waited for Ualan to come beside her, to touch her with tenderness and approval. Ualan dropped down to the bed, but his hands didn't stray to her body. Morrigan felt tears rise up in her eyes. He might desire her enough to come to her to slake his lust, but he wasn't speaking to her and he didn't move to hold her.

Ualan wanted to pull her into his arms, but he would not delude himself into thinking she cared when she did not. Didn't her mention of her story mean she was still thinking about her past, longing for it? The loneliness, which drove him away from her earlier, returned tenfold to haunt him.

Morrigan held still, her body still weak from his touch. She closed her eyes, listening until she heard him fall asleep. Then, when she was sure he slept, she softly lifted herself from the bed, careful not to wake him. Morrigan quietly dressed, sneaking down the stairs. When she made the bathroom, she locked the new door. Curling into a ball, she began to cry.

* * * *

Ualan felt his wife get up and heard her soft descent down the bedroom stairs. He wondered what she was up to. But, as he heard the bathroom door open and close, he shut his eyes. His heart ached even as his body sung with the feel of her. Feeling a deep pain making itself a home in his chest, he tried not to breathe. It was the feeling of his heart dying.

Chapter Nineteen

Morrigan sat, lounging across the arms of her chair as she lifted her bare foot to dangle over the side. Ualan had been gone for the last day with his brothers, plotting vengeance. She knew that he felt bad about what happened, but she didn't blame him. It wasn't his fault. He hadn't touched her since the night of the attack, but Morrigan hoped he was just giving her time to recover. It was sweet of him to give her space, but she wished he didn't bother. Biting her nails in away that really irritated her mother-by-marriage, she said, "I need a job."

"You have a job," the woman said calmly.

Morrigan looked at her. Reaching down, she picked her coffee up from the floor and sipped. Ualan had looked at her strangely when she thanked him for the simulator by sprinkling kisses all over his face and proclaiming him the best husband in the world. He had pulled away, mumbling something about needed to meet with Zoran.

Morrigan shook her head as she set the cup down. "Being a wife is not a real job."

"The others might disagree with you," the woman chuckled warmly.

"It's work," she said with a 'don't get me wrong' tone. "But it's not a job. I need something to do. I can't just sit around here all day waiting for Ualan to get back from whatever he does. I need more than that."

"What do you want to do?"

"Well, I am a reporter."

"We have no need for a reporter," the Queen said with a delicate shrug. "All news spreads by word of mouth or royal decree."

Morrigan frowned. She was restless. Ualan got to leave all day to do princely things. What was she supposed to do? Lie around and get fat? Not likely.

"I'm sorry I can't help you," Mede said, before scowling and motioning Morrigan's finger from her lip. Morrigan sheepishly obeyed, grinning like a disobedient child. "Have you talked to Ualan about this?"

"No," she said with a wry smile. "He seems to get all weird when I mention being a reporter. It's like he thinks I've suddenly contracted leprosy."

"What's that?" the Queen asked, unfamiliar with the term.

"An old disease, we eliminated it long ago, it's not important." Morrigan leaned forward, steepling her hands beneath her chin in thought. A heavy sigh came from her lips.

"Could it be he looks at you like that because you hide things from him?" asked Mede, her expression shining wisely.

"How are Nadja and Olena?" Morrigan asked suddenly. "Ualan said something about them having a scare?"

"They're fine," the Queen answered, not wishing to change the subject. For emphasis, she repeated, "Could it be he looks at you like that because you hide things from him?"

"Like what?" Morrigan asked, seeing Mede was getting to some sort of a point.

"Or maybe he's scared," the Queen continued.

"Scared? Ualan?" Morrigan grinned. Now, that wasn't likely.

"Morrigan, when you say you notice a change in Ualan when you speak of it, do you mean you see it on his face? Or do you mean you feel it within you as if the emotions were your own?" Mede leaned forward, seriously copying her daughter's pose.

"I feel it," she answered weakly, after consideration.

"That is because you do feel what he is feeling. And he feels what you are feeling. If you are discontent or wistful when speaking of travel and reporting, then he will feel your longing. He might even think you long to leave him." Mede smiled sadly as realization dawned on Morrigan's face.

"But, how is it possible?"

"Qurilixian men are given a crystal when they are born. It is their guiding light. When you were paired by the crystal, your lives became joined in such a way that can never be taken back. You exchanged part of your souls. By crushing the crystal, you assured that the exchange would never be reversed. In a way, you are now his guiding light."

Morrigan gulped, frozen.

"Do you understand what that means for him?" the Queen asked.

Morrigan shook her head, her wide eyes fixed on the Queen.

"It means his crystal is broken. It means he put his every chance at happiness on you. He gave his life to you, Rigan. There will never be anyone else for him as long as he lives. That is a long time for our people, and for you. By giving you his life, he shortened his and extended yours so your fates could remain entwined. If you were to choose to leave him, he would be alone for the rest of his days. Without the aid of our blue sun, your life would play out like normal, maybe extended a few more years than usual. When he took you to his tent, it was his choice. When you stayed, that was yours. You're it for him, Rigan. There will be no other in his bed or his heart. There simply can't be."

"You mean he was a...." Morrigan blushed, realizing she was talking to his mother.

The Queen merely laughed, not so shied by the revealing question. "I doubt it. The Princes have occasionally left our planet for ambassador duties. And, distasteful as it sounds, there are several roving bands of ... women with loose morals who make scheduled stops for the warriors. They are men after all."

Morrigan blushed.

"Don't think on it. It was before he met you. Once mated, they do not go back to such things-- ever. Besides, there is something to be said for a husband with training." The Queen smiled and winked to show she was teasing. Morrigan chuckled. The Queen continued, "He won't go to them now. He couldn't if he wanted to. You would know right away. Besides, if he wanted to, you would know that too. He doesn't desire anyone else, rest assured."

"And you've never regretted choosing one man?"

"Never, though around the one-hundredth year, they do start getting very inventive. It is something to look forward to." The Queen stood. "Now that I have you straight, I have other daughters to visit. I swear, when you have sons, Morrigan, be prepared. They will bring you a handful of problems. But, then again, occasionally they'll bring you flowers and it will be well worth the frustration."

"Just like their fathers," Morrigan mused, liking the idea of having Ualan's son very much. She wondered if he ever thought of it.

"Yes," the Queen agreed, thinking of her own stubborn husband. She kissed Morrigan's cheek. "Just like their fathers."

* * * *

The news came that night that the men were off to battle with King Attor and his Var warriors. Agro had discovered from the spy that King Attor did indeed plan on killing three of the four Princesses. Olena, he wanted for himself, thus the attack on Yusef. Agro also learned Attor's whereabouts and the Draig trackers soon had the position confirmed. It was a small encampment of Var on the southern borders of Draig land.

Morrigan was worried sick, but she had faith that Ualan would come out the victor. Besides, after what Mede told her, she was confident that she would feel it if Ualan was hurt.

The doctor came to check on her, reporting that all was well and she was nearly healed. She stayed up late, waiting until she could hardly keep her eyes open. No news came and she spent the night alone.

* * * *

"Here." Ualan's voice was stern as he handed his wife her camera. He was tired and worn from the battle. "This belongs to you."

Morrigan glanced up in surprise. Her hair was pulled back in a ponytail and she wore a simple linen shirt and relaxed cotton pants. She had asked Mede for any books she might have on the Qurilixian customs. To her delight, her new mother sent cartloads of information--history, law, art, trade publications, myths and legends. Nadja had lent her a translator so she could read them. It was slow going, but she was doing research and was having a ball. Besides, it helped the hours pass until Ualan came home.

The books were piled around her in a big mess, but Morrigan didn't care. She jumped up, stumbling over them as she ran forward to greet the tired warrior. Morrigan threw her arms around him.

To Ualan's surprise, she said, "I knew you were fine."

Looking over her shoulder, he was stiff and only half returned her embrace, holding back. It had taken him a long time to get the will to come to her. Ualan eyed the texts wearily, assuming she was doing research on his culture for her story. It didn't stop him from handing her the camera.

Ualan pulled her back. And, lifting her hand, he set the eyepiece and emerald trigger in her palm. Slowly, he stepped back.

Morrigan blinked, confused by the gesture. She eyed him as she set it down. "Thanks."

Ualan nodded.

"What happened? They didn't send word. Did you…?"

"King Attor is dead. We tried to arrest him according to our treaty and he called his troops to battle. Attor's son will take the throne. Olek is speaking to the new Var King, negotiating a peace. It looks like our battles have ended, hopefully." Ualan could not feel the pleasure such a revelation should bring. It would be slow going, but peace could be achieved. Some of the older nobles would protest on both sides. However, in the end, they would bow to the decision of their leaders.

"That is good news, Ualan," Morrigan said. "I'm glad there will be no more battles between you and the Var."

"What are you doing?" he asked, ignoring her comment.

"Ah, just some research."

"Hmm." He handed her something else. "This is for you, too."

Morrigan took a slip of paper from him. She gulped, looking down to see a space ticket in her hand with passage to an Earth base that would take her home. Swallowing, she glanced up at him, and asked carefully, "What's this?"

"It's a ticket. In your name. One way to Earth. You'll have to make a few stops. Qurilixian transports don't usually travel so far."

"I can see that it is a ticket. But, what are you saying, Ualan? You want me to go? You're sending me away?"

"I know you're here to do a story, Rigan. Your communication with your editor was intercepted. I heard everything. You wish to tell of our lives, of our war with the Var, our marriages." Ualan sighed, too wearied to keep fighting her. "Well, there's your camera. You should have all the information gathered that you need to expose us."

"Expose you?" she gulped, confused. "Why would I want to expose you?"

"You said that you wanted to take your film and expose me," he said. Though, his words held more question than certainty.

"When?" she wondered aloud, never remembering making such a stupid comment. She never intended to hurt anyone with what she wrote. Well, maybe Galaxy Brides Corporation--but she had been mad at the time. She doubted anything would ever come of it.

"When you were sick from poison," he answered. He took a weary seat on the couch across from her.

Morrigan blushed, suddenly remembering what was on the camera. The image of Ualan's naked backside came to mind and she nearly fell over in her embarrassment. Unable to meet his eye, she said, "Expose does mean reveal, but it also means to develop a picture."

Morrigan was mortified. She could barely move. She covered her face with her hands and groaned.

"What picture?" he inquired, intrigued.

"I was going to keep your picture as something to remember you by," she mumbled weakly, not daring to look at him for a long moment.

At that Ualan smiled. His pleasure was short lived. She had picked up the ticket and was eyeing it.

"What are you going to write about?" he asked, cautious. She never said she was staying. But, she also never said she still wanted to leave.

"I was sent undercover to gather information about the brides and your planet. I was supposed to do an article on the four Princes at the Breeding Festival and the lucky women who they took for wife. It would have been a front page exclusive. Earth woman eat that romance stuff up."

"Lucky?" he interjected. She narrowed her eyes at him and his gaze glowed golden in response. She shivered. He won. She looked away first. "And now? What will you write?"

"I could expose you as shapeshifters I guess," she said. "No one knows about you."

"It would hurt us. We need brides and not many women would come to marry a dragon. We would have to go back to kidnapping, which is frowned upon. It could start a war with humanoid planets."

Morrigan nodded in agreement. His features were blank, but she could feel the pain her agreement caused him.

"The story would make my career," she said softly. "I would be able to get any assignment I wanted at any price."

"If your life back home is so important to you, then go. You have all the evidence and the story you need." Ualan stood. He was too tired from battling the Var and his own heart to fight with her. Sighing heavily, he said, "Go home, Morrigan. I will not stand in your way."

"What of us? Our marriage?" she asked, knowing all too well what he was willing to give up to see her happy. He was willing to sacrifice his lifetime of happiness and companionship to give her what he thought she wanted. No one else would ever sacrifice that much for her.

"You came here for me, not a story. The Gods brought you here to me and the crystal helped me to find you. And so it is I who is letting you go. I will not be the cause of your unhappiness."

She knew it was true. The story had always been an excuse. Part of her wanted to get away from her life. Part of her wanted to be protected and happy. She was tired of traveling, but had been unwilling to admit it before now. The dreams that were buried the deepest, were the hardest to get rid of. She had held tight onto her childhood fantasy of space exploration with both hands. The reality was nothing like the fantasy. Adventures were few and far between. The endless days spent alone in a space pod, traveling to a dank slime pit on the outer regions--that was the reality.

"I should call my editor," she whispered softly.

Ualan nodded, sad. He waved to his bedroom. "The communicator is up there. I thought you might wish to contact him with your flight information and have left orders that your communication not be monitored."

Morrigan stood, walking slowly to the stairs. The communicator and weapons were put back on the shelf. Next to them, she saw her crown. It looked different than she had first remembered it. Mede had told her in the hospital that it had been broken when she fell ill. Picking it up, she realized it glistened with the shards of Ualan's broken crystal. It was beautiful.

Setting the crown down, she picked up the communicator and hooked it on. The floating screen popped up and, with a click-click, she dialed Gus.

She didn't have to wait long before she heard the man bellow, "About damned time, Rigan. Where the hell have you been?"

"Hi-yah, Gus," she forced her tone light.

"Hi-yah? Hi-yah, Gus?" he demanded before calming. "I'm opening the lines, Rigan, send your story. It goes to press tomorrow. I've been holding the front page of the intergalactic edition for you."

"I can't do that, Gus. I don't have it."

"What? You still writing? Hum," he pondered. "Well I guess you're calling for your annulment papers. I tell you what. You send me a story and I'll give you everything you need to get out of that marriage--first class ticket and all. How does that sound, Rigan?"

"Sorry, Gus. There is no story here. I was wrong. Oh, and I quit."

"What?!" the man screeched. "You can't quit on me, Rigan! You're the best damned reporter I have. No one could cover that slime planet like you did! Come on, you can't leave this business. It's in your blood. You'll go crazy without it."

"I found a Prince, Gus," she said, a soft smile on her lips. "And I think I am going to keep him."

Morrigan glanced up to see Ualan standing in the doorway of the closet. An affectionate smile was forming on his lips in understanding. Emotion flowed sweetly and openly between them, the one last obstacle having been torn down by her hand.

"Rigan?" Ualan whispered, hope shining brightly in his handsome eyes.

"It would make my career, Ualan," she whispered back. "But you make my life."

"Rigan!" Gus screeched. "I can't hear you, what did you say? Oh, never mind, you're talking crazy anyway. Listen, I'll let you out of your contract no problem, but you got to give me an exclusive."

"Sorry, Gus," she said, staring boldly at Ualan. "Take care of my apartment would you? Sell everything, but mail me my maid units--all of them."

"I got it," Gus said, not listening, "Star reporter falls for story."

Morrigan smiled, not really paying attention to the blustering man. Her eyes shone with love for her husband.

"No, wait," Gus broke in with his harsh voice, "Princess Reporter finds her Prince."

"Nope," she said, her eyes beginning to travel over Ualan's firm body. He lifted a brow, moving to take off his shirt at the come-hither tilt of her head.

"Rigan, come on girl, you got to give me something!" Gus's words were followed by the sound of a slamming fist.

"Sorry, Gus, no can do."

"What about a book deal?" he offered. "I'll give you a huge advance!"

"Nope. I want to live life for awhile. I'm tired of watching it from the sidelines."

"What about the Princes?" he insisted. His words almost sounded like a whine. Morrigan's eyes were busy devouring her stripping husband. She stood to join him, pulling at her own top and throwing it aside. "What can you give me on them?"

"There's not much," she answered with a devilish wink.

Ualan's brow rose high on his head in mock affront. He threw his shirt at her head. She caught it and tossed it away.

"They're completely uninteresting," she persisted, pursing her lips with a mock sigh of boredom.

Ualan's eyes turned to golden fire. Danger and excitement coursed through her at the look. She smiled with a beckoning heat. Ulan slid his pants from his waist, standing proud. Morrigan opened her mouth in mock surprise as she stared naughtily at his erection.

Wickedly, she said, "And they're very, very...," her eyes got rounder with each word as she finished coyly, "... small."

Ualan growled, pouncing forward. He swept her into his arms and pressed his naked body to her.

"Rigan? Rigan?!" came Gus's voice. They ignored him.

Ualan nuzzled her throat before bringing his eyes to bore into her. Morrigan grinned. His hands traveled over her back to press under her pants to her warm buttocks.

Quietly, she drew her finger over the muscles of his chest. "The doctor was here earlier to check on me."

His eyes narrowed. Morrigan bit her lip, hesitantly moving his hand around to touch her stomach.

"What do you think?" she mouthed, almost shy.

"I think, no I know I'm in love with you," he whispered, realizing she told him she was pregnant.

Morrigan's eyes shone brightly. "Really?"

He chuckled, leaning to kiss her deep and tender, his expression saying, Of course, silly woman.

"Oh," she breathed when he let her claim her breath. Weak kneed, her eyes dreamy with desire, she moaned, "I love you, too, Ualan. I could never leave you."

"Rigan," Ualan growled, crushing her with a deeper passion. Gus kept yelling but they ignored him. "I've loved you since that first moment. I've loved you and only you my entire life. I promise to make you happy. You'll never regret choosing to be my Queen."

"You've already made me happy," she whispered, her heart in her eyes. Then, pulling back, she asked with a grimace, "Queen?"

"Didn't you know? I'm the oldest," he said, sighing, leaning to sprinkle kisses over nose and cheeks. "When my parents decide to step aside, you will be my Queen."

He tried to claim her mouth and she let him for a brief second. Then, pushing his arm, she asked, "Wait a minute. How old are you anyway, dragon?"

Ualan merely grinned. He found hold on her back as he lowered her over his arm in an embrace that stole her words and her heart. Their souls were forever joined. No more talk was necessary.

"Rigan, damn it, you got...."

Ualan pulled back, chuckling, intent on having his way with his wife. By the look in her eyes, she was going to have her way too--for a very long time. Pulling her back up, his hand began working on her waistband, pushing her pants down to the floor.

"Rigan!"

Ualan grinned at her, devilishly eyeing her lips as he lifted his foot to the blaring communicator.

"Rig--!!"

Crunch.

THE END

Printed in the United States
56232LVS00001B/292-339